D1245512

CRIME AND PERIODICALS

GREEN VALLEY LIBRARY BOOK #2

NORA EVERLY

WWW.SMARTYPANTSROMANCE.COM

COPYRIGHT

This book is a work of fiction. Names, characters, places, rants, facts, contrivances, and incidents are either the product of the author's questionable imagination or are used factitiously. Any resemblance to actual persons, living or dead or undead, events, locales is entirely coincidental if not somewhat disturbing/concerning.

Made in the United States of America

Print Edition
ISBN: 978-1-949202-07-6

CHAPTER ONE

SABRINA

"You are not a sexy librarian," I said to myself in the mirror.

There would be no hair-shaking, glasses-removing hot babe reveal in this girl's life. I did not have an inner goddess. I had an inner band of nerds and they were all wearing headgear and geeking out to *Reylo* fanfic online. I didn't have to worry about being a cliché because I wasn't even a librarian. I was just an assistant.

I finished touching up my lipstick and put it in my pocket and stuck my tongue out at my reflection. I had spent ten minutes winging my eyeliner this morning only to hide all the effort behind my black cat eyeglasses.

I smoothed my black curls back with my headband, blinked, then rolled my eyes. Who wants to be a stereotype, anyway? What a waste of makeup.

Why do I even keep trying?

"Sabrina! There is a phone call for you, honey. It's Harry's school," Mrs. MacIntyre called from behind the check-out counter.

I glanced at the bathroom door with a sigh. Probably another meltdown.

"Coming," I called back. I turned away from the bathroom mirror and finished drying my hands with a paper towel, and then used it to open the door.

I once had wild ideas, a few friends, hope for the future—stuff like that. Now I was a small-town assistant librarian stuck in Green Valley, Tennessee. I was a twenty-seven-year-old virgin with no prospects in sight. Even if a prospect crossed my path, I wouldn't be brave enough to flirt, or even speak to him, anyway. I hid in the horror section whenever I spotted a man heading to the check-out counter—because, *yikes.*

There was no shortage of male talent in this town; that was a known fact. But I would have to *go into town* for one of them to notice me. I was starting to lose hope and I was pretty sure I would die a lonely old spinster. In this town everybody knew everybody, but nobody knew me. I lived my life in this library and at home. I took care of Harry, Ruby, and Weston and nurtured my Kindle like the baby I would probably never have.

Mrs. MacIntyre held out the ancient cordless phone with a sympathetic smile. "Bring him here if you need to, dear," she offered. I smiled and mouthed 'thank you' to her. She was the head librarian and the sweetest boss in the history of bosses.

"Hi, this is Sabrina." I listened, then I sighed. "I'll be right there."

"Can I…?" I started to say, but Mrs. MacIntyre was already shooing me to the door with my purse and keys held out. Bless her heart—I meant that the nice way.

The brisk fall air ruffled my hair as I trudged through the crunchy leaves littering the parking lot on the way to my Jeep. Harry did not attend Green Valley Grade School; they did not offer the class he needed. I had to drive through the mountains to get to his school. I hated that drive. Even though I grew up here, mountain roads freaked me out. The drop offs, the treetops, the endless plunge into oblivion.

I managed though. I always managed.

I rang the bell and stuck my face in the security camera to get buzzed in. I was right. He had a meltdown and they weren't sure what set him off.

I took in his angry little face and tear-streaked cheeks before he threw himself into my arms. I picked him up, but it was hard. He was growing up so fast and I was lucky he was small for a nine-year-old.

"Sabrina," he said. "Sabrina. Sabrina."

His teacher hooked his backpack over my arm with a sympathetic smile for me. "We're not sure what set him off, but he seemed a little sad this morning during our social circle."

"I'll try to talk to him about it when we get home," I told her.

"Let me know if you figure it out." She patted Harry on the shoulder. "I'll see you on Monday, Harry. I hope you feel better."

"Bye, Teacher Allen. Bye," he answered. At least the crying had stopped.

I thanked her and then we were on our way. Hopefully, he'd be okay to go back to work with me. I didn't like leaving my shift early, even though Mrs. MacIntyre said it was okay. It felt irresponsible. I would always feel like I needed to prove myself, to prove to everyone I was worth hiring. I was sure they only hired me because of who my father was. I didn't want to let anyone down.

I set Harry down and helped him into my Jeep. "Buckle up, Harry," I instructed.

"Buckle up," he repeated. When Harry started repeating everything people said with that monotonous tone of voice, I knew something was wrong.

"What's wrong, Harry?"

"Wrong, Harry," he repeated. "Where is the mountain Hood?" he asked without looking at me.

"It's in Oregon," I answered, hoping my knowledge of random mountain trivia would hold up until we got home. I shut his door and ran around to get in.

"Where is the mountain Rainier?" he said loudly.

"In Washington. Want to talk about it?"

"Where is the mountain Diablo?"

"In California, Harry." I started the car and took off.

"Where is the mountain Le Conte? The mountain Clingmans Dome? The mountain Chilhowee? Oh. Oh. Oh. The mountain Guyot?

Chapman? Old Black? Kephart? Collins?" He was just yelling out the names of the mountains by this point.

"Harry, where are we?" I stopped him. Sometimes giving him an anchor helped him come down from his agitation.

"Where are we? Green Valley, Tennessee. The Great Smoky. Appalachia." He paused for a second. "Where are you? Sabrina?"

"Right here, sweetheart. Right here, like always."

"Right here. Very good, Sabrina. Tickle hugs, please. Tickle hugs, Aunt Riri."

"I'm driving, Harry. When we stop, okay?"

Please...just hold on a few more minutes, Harry.

He rocked into the back of his seat, hard. I could feel the car jerk with his movements and I frantically looked for a place to pull over. He rocked into his seat again and again until his seat belt locked. Then he screamed so loud it rang in my ears. He threw his shoe; it bounced off my shoulder onto the passenger seat.

"Harry, stop. Please, Harry. I'm trying to drive. I'll pull over soon."

We were on a twisty-turny backwoods Tennessee mountain road for crap's sake. There was nowhere to go except over the freaking side.

"I'm looking, Harry. I'll pull over as soon as I can. Shh." I tried to soothe him.

He would not stop screaming. No matter how many times this happened, I had never become used to it. It was hard to concentrate. My knuckles were white on the steering wheel and I was afraid my panting breath would fog up the window. Finally, I found a spot to pull over. Thankfully, it had a guardrail on the side. I parked, turned the engine off, and climbed over the console into the back seat. I unbuckled Harry and pulled him into my arms. His red, sweaty, tear-streaked face burrowed into my chest as I pulled him closer and wrapped him up tight. After that drive, I needed hugs too.

"Tickle hugs, Aunt Riri. Tickle hugs, please."

A hysterical laugh escaped me as I wiggled my fingers along his sides and rocked him. He was almost ten. How would we manage when he got older? I heard the brief sound of a siren, then saw red and blue lights reflected in the rearview mirror.

Just great. Exactly what I need right now.

"Harry, I have to let go for a minute," I whispered.

He gripped my cardigan in his fists, burrowed further into me, and would not let go. I was stuck—pinned in the driver's side corner of the back seat.

There was a tap on my window.

"Everything okay in there?" he said loudly.

I heard him, but I did not see him, on account of my being buried under a melting down nine-year-old boy. I reached around Harry to unlock the door and push it open. I found myself looking up into the concerned face of Deputy Sheriff Jackson James. I let out a sigh of relief. Jackson was handsome and nice—I wasn't afraid to talk to him. He came into the library sometimes. I only talked to him that first time years ago because he surprised me in my horror section hiding place. Jackson is a big Stephen King fan, like me.

Jackson raised his eyebrows expectantly. "Are you okay, Sabrina?"

"This is my nephew, Harry. He is on the autism spectrum," I explained. Harry would soon be my son—after the adoption went through, that was. I was waiting on his dirtbag biological father to sign the papers like he'd promised my father and our attorney. But I was keeping that news to myself until all the ducks were in a row, not wandering around in the street like maniacs.

Jackson nodded his understanding.

"He's having a rough day. I just picked him up from school, and I had to pull over," I continued.

"That's understandable. But this isn't the safest stretch of road to stop on, sweetheart."

I nodded, because it sure as all heck was not. I wouldn't drive it at all if I had my way.

"He threw a shoe. He was rocking my Jeep. I had to stop. I didn't know what else to do," I said. And to my mortification, tears filled my eyes. I tried to blink them back, but one fell anyway.

Jackson nodded decisively. "Stay here," he ordered.

Well, that should be easy enough. I scrubbed the tears away after he walked off.

He returned with another officer following behind him. "This is Wyatt Monroe, one of our deputies. He'll drive you home. Y'all buckle up back here." Jackson tapped the top of my Jeep with a smirk and walked away.

Someone else replaced Jackson in my line of sight. My mouth dropped open as I watched him step toward my door. He was so tall, and broad—I had never seen muscles like that in real life.

Gah, don't be such a creeper.

I snapped my eyes from his body up to his face and my tears dried up. Holy mother of hot guys. Wow. That body had nothing on his handsome face. Deep brown eyes the color of chocolate stared back at me, the best kind of chocolate. The kind where you could only eat one piece because it was so rich. Except, I was sure I would want more than one piece of him.

His eyes crinkled at the corners when he smiled at me.

Smile back, dummy. I did what I said and smiled back.

"Who is there? Who is it, Aunt Riri?" Harry said, then pulled back from my chest to turn his head and look.

"My name is Wyatt. I'm a deputy sheriff." He smiled and held his hand out to Harry.

Harry looked at it for a second, then shook it. "Like Wyatt Derp," he said.

I couldn't help it, I laughed. As did the hot sheriff. He had a sense of humor—bonus. Plus, the laughter made his eyes twinkle adorably, in addition to that spectacular corner crinkle.

"It's Earp, sweetheart," I gently corrected.

Harry twisted back and looked at me. "'Destiny is that which we are drawn towards and fate is that which we run into.' Top ten Wyatt Der—Earp quotes." He had moved on from listing mountains. It was a good sign. Quoting was better than listing when it came to Harry's coping mechanisms.

"Did he say that, honey?" I asked him.

"Yes. I had a bad day, Aunt Riri," he sighed and cuddled into me. I hugged him back and kissed the top of his head.

"Is your name Riri?" Sheriff Hottie McOhMyGod asked with a smile.

A gorgeous smile from delicious looking lips...that were still smiling at me.

Holy Hufflepuffs—he is the most gorgeous man I have ever seen.

"No, my name is Sabrina," I murmured, suddenly even more acutely aware of him and the effect he was having on me.

Quit it. He's probably married. Or gay. Or has an epically awesome girlfriend that would actually know what to do with that body when she was lucky enough to get her hands on it.

I glanced down at his left hand—no ring. *Niiiice.*

"That's a pretty name. It's nice to meet you." He held his hand out for me to shake.

I placed my hand in his and had to fight my instinct to *squee* out loud. His big, warm palm dwarfed mine.

"It's nice to meet you too. Uh, I think we'll be okay though. You don't need to drive us," I stammered.

He grinned at me. "Actually, I do. It seems Jackson left me here."

"Oh, well. Okay then. The keys are still in the ignition. And thank you, but we're not going home. I'm going to the library. I have to work until three." Since Harry seemed to have calmed down, I decided to finish my shift. There wasn't much left of it, but I'd feel better if I finished it out. Harry loved the astronomy section, and he adored Mrs. MacIntyre and Naomi Winters, who was on the schedule to close this evening.

"No problem. Are you a librarian?" he asked.

"No, I'm an assistant librarian. I help shelve the books and sometimes I clean the bathrooms." *Well, gosh, I'm sure he found that fascinating.* I shut my eyes and shook my head.

Harry had fallen asleep on me. I wasn't surprised, as he had been quite worked up and he usually took a short nap after an outburst. I tried to shift him to the side, but my arm was full of tingles from him laying on it and he was getting heavy.

"Do you live in Green Valley?" Deputy Monroe asked.

I nodded yes.

"I just moved back to town a few months ago. That's probably why I've never seen you around before."

Unlikely. He hadn't seen me before because if I was not at the library then I was usually at home. Plus, I went to a private school—all girls—so even if he were near my age, we wouldn't have crossed paths that way either.

"Let me help you with him. I'll pull him over." He crossed in front of the car, opened the door, and leaned in. He gently took Harry in his arms, slid him off me, and effortlessly propped him up in his seat. When Harry was out, he stayed out.

I leaned over to reach for the seat belt and came face-to-face with him.

"Poor little guy wore himself out," he said. His eyes crinkle-smiled at me again. Up close, it was amazing.

I smiled back. "Thank you. My arm was asleep." I inhaled. My God, he smelled good. So good, like clean laundry and all that was sexy in the world. He was so big. His shoulders took up the whole space in the doorway. I sighed.

He leaned over and patted my tingly arm.

My heart stopped. Then it started back up and pounded like a bass drum in my chest and I froze stock still in my seat.

"You're welcome." He smiled softly and winked at me.

Winked.

At me.

There was no one else here. I fought the urge to turn around and see if there was someone behind me. He meant to do it.

Oh my gosh. I blushed furiously.

My eyes blinked at him and my mouth opened to say—*something, freaking anything*—but no words came out.

He chuckled, then stepped back and gently closed the door. I buckled Harry in and scooted to the middle seat to fasten my seat belt. Harry sank to the side with his head resting on my shoulder.

"Ready?" he asked after he finished adjusting the seat and mirrors.

I could see his eyes on mine in the rearview mirror. This would be an interesting ride into town.

"Yes, I'm ready." I was such a liar. I was not ready. No way. Not one bit.

I worked in a library, surrounded by books all day long. And if I'm being honest, I lived my life within the pages of books. But I was not naïve enough to think books could give me all the answers. They couldn't tell me what to say to Deputy Sheriff McOhMyGod. They couldn't tell me how to act. And they sure as all heck could not tell me what was in his head. All I knew was my palms were sweaty, my knees felt weak, and I was sure my cheeks were as red as my MAC Ruby Woo lips. I mentally sorted through the many (many, many, many) romance novels I'd read over the years, because my symptoms were straight out of one of those. Not the *Merck Manual of Diagnosis and Therapy.*

I smiled back at his crinkle-eyed hotness in the rearview mirror. *Be brave, Sabrina. He is just a human. You can talk to a fellow human in your car and not die.*

CHAPTER TWO

SABRINA

I couldn't do it. I could not talk to a human in my car. I wussed out —hard. But at least I didn't die.

The ride back into town was silent. But weirdly, it didn't feel awkward. Harry was asleep; perhaps that was a good enough reason to justify not talking and eliminate the awkwardness silence can bring. I went with that and tried to shake off my embarrassment. He had parked my Jeep in the tiny lot in front of the library, and I swooned even more over him when he got out and turned to open my door for me. I lost my breath when I stood next to him and had to look up to see his face. I'm a tall girl at five feet ten inches. And today, like every other day, I was wearing heels. He was still taller. Plus, there was something about him—aside from his outrageously gorgeous looks—that made me want to be near him. I wanted to know more about him. He seemed kind. He seemed *good.* He was able to interact with Harry and that never happened on anybody's first try. People shied away from Harry, especially when he was upset. Harry had a unique perspective on things and some people found him peculiar. Having Harry around was a good litmus test for determining who had asshole tendencies, or latent jerk face qualities. I quickly glanced through the window. Harry was still asleep.

"So..." Deputy Sheriff Monroe said and grinned down at me.

Ooh, he had a dimple, just one, and it was magical. I wanted to lick it. Wait, no I didn't. Was it inappropriate to think this way about him? I had never wanted to lick a dimple before.

"It was very nice to meet you, Sabrina." That eye crinkle was back and aimed right at me.

By now I was pretty sure that every time I looked directly at him my IQ lowered because I could not think of one stinking word to say to him. I opened my mouth anyway though, just in case the flirt fairy decided to bless me with a witty anecdote or some charming repartee. Nope. That was a big fat nothing coming out of my mouth.

Can I disappear now?

His right eyebrow cocked, and his grin got bigger as he studied my face. "I'd like to get to know you better. Can I take you out to dinner Saturday night?"

My eyes got huge. I felt them bug out behind my glasses.

"Or maybe a movie? Or both?" he added with another wink.

My mouth opened wider, then shut, and I blinked rapidly. *Answer him. Say yes. Say yes, dammit—this is what you've been waiting for.* But I just stood there and stared.

His smile shrank down to just a half grin, and my heart broke a little bit when he lost that irresistible eye crinkle and the dimple disappeared. I inhaled sharply, my eyes burned as they lowered to the ground.

"You're adorable," he said.

Hot guy, say what?

I snapped my eyes back to his. The crinkle was back. "Would it be okay if I come to the library sometime this week and try this again?" He finished talking, then *boom,* the dimple was back too.

Holy effing crap.

Nod your head, Sabrina. You nod it right now.

I nodded my head.

He chuckled again. "I'll see you real soon, darlin'. Tell Harry goodbye for me."

"I will tell him," I said and smiled back. I finally found some words, and a small smile. Better late than never.

Darlin'... I let myself feel the top-to-toe tingle that word gave me. I sighed as I watched him walk away, admiring how each step made his uniform tighten across his glorious bottom and broad shoulders. I watched his hips move, and it made me think...things, thoughts—bad ones. I should really be ashamed of myself. I was objectifying the crap out of him. I sighed when he stepped off the curb and crossed the street toward the sheriff station up the road. I jumped when he turned around to wave and smile at me. At least I managed to wave back before I spun around to open Harry's door. I also realized I was still nodding.

Good gracious, he might ask me out again. What am I going to do?

"Wake up, sleepyhead," I said distractedly. I jumped again when I looked down at Harry to see he was already awake and staring up at me.

"He was nice," Harry said, then yawned.

"He was," I agreed. "Do you feel like going to work with me?"

Harry beamed. "Yes, Riri. Yes, I do feel like going to work with you. Can I read *Harry Potter and the Sorcerer's Stone: The Illustrated Edition,* by J.K. Rowling and illustrated by Jim Kay and sit in the purple bean bag? Is Miss Naomi here today?"

"Yes, yes, and yes. Then, after work we'll stop at Genie's Bar to pick up—"

"Fried chicken! It's family dinner night! Pop will be home. And Ruby and Westie too! And we met a nice sheriff who looks like Superman. The worst day ever just turned into the best day ever. Isn't that funny?"

"It sure is. Are you going to taste the chicken tonight?" Harry's sensory issues became especially pronounced with food. "Maybe one tiny bite?"

His face wrinkled up in disgust and he gagged before he regained his neutral expression. "Maybe. One bite. I will ponder it and then tell you my decision at the table. Maybe it can be my *amuse-bouche*. But I don't think dead chickens are amusing at all, unless they're ground up in a dinosaur shaped nugget. I really will have to think about it." He shook his head as he mumbled the last part. He was about to get lost in his thoughts.

I interrupted his mumbling by holding my hand out to him. "Deal," I said. He looked at my hand and then up at my face for a second before taking my hand with a sideways grin.

I helped him out of the Jeep, and we headed to the library entrance. Harry stopped to admire the big picture window next to the book return slot. Naomi had finished decorating while I was gone. A colorful fall faux-leaf garland wound with twinkling fairy lights festooned the interior of the window, black cat silhouettes peeked out from each corner, and two smiling scarecrows stood on either side of a table she had piled with stacks of fall-themed children's books. Pumpkins filled the area under the table and the tops of the short shelves in the front of the library beneath the side windows. This place was already magical, but the decorations added that extra something special. You could step inside, open a book, and go somewhere else—somewhere beyond the confinements of Green Valley. I loved this library, and thankfully, so did Harry. He was always at peace here.

"Riri, look at that. Look. At. That. It is the fall and the autumn. It is the orange and the black." He turned to look up at me. He was jumping up and down by the time he got to "the orange and the black." The smile that lit up his face was infectious; I grinned back at him and squeezed his hand.

"Naomi did a great job," I observed as we shuffle-skipped through the leaves on the pathway to the double front door and into the library. My heels clicked on the old linoleum as I led Harry to the tiny children's section in the back corner. He ran around the colorful bean bags to his favorite double-sized purple one and plopped into it with a sigh.

I waved to Naomi, who was busy shelving the latest additions to the children's section. My father had donated money for those new books, and I couldn't help but think he had done it so I could keep my job. Rumors of the library's possible closure had been circulating, and I was dreading it. This is the only work I'd ever done. They'd hired me six years ago to replace the beloved Bethany Winston. I wasn't even a real librarian, just an assistant who loved to read and had a vast knowledge of books. When you do nothing but read in your spare time, that could happen.

"Hi, Naomi. I hope you don't mind that Harry is here." Guilt crept over me as I greeted her.

"Of course I don't mind. We're buddies. Aren't we, Harry?"

He nodded up at her with adoration. Naomi was special, beautiful and sweet, and full of light. Sometimes—okay, all the time—I wished I wasn't so shy. I would like to be her friend. But something always held me back from talking to her about anything real. I could only manage 'hi' and 'bye' and library business. She sat down next to Harry and grabbed the illustrated *Harry Potter* book that was waiting on the low round table next to the beanbag.

"I'll finish the shelving," I offered.

She nodded at me with a smile, then chatted about the book with Harry. I smiled when they moved on to talk about the upcoming autumnal equinox. Harry loved astronomy and Naomi was an expert. I sighed and pushed the small book-laden cart further into the stacks. I adjusted my collar, undoing a couple of buttons. It was getting hot in here; I dabbed at my forehead with the sleeve of my cardigan.

I huffed out a breath as I rolled the cart to the self-help section. I had read most of these books and none of them worked on me—I was still as shy as ever. I laughed softly, quickly shelved them, and then continued walking down the aisle. Naomi had already sorted the returned books into order. All I had to do was follow the numbers. I felt terrible for leaving all this work for her to do. She was so sweet. Even if she secretly hated me for having to leave so often, I bet she would never tell me.

Had someone turned the heat up in here? I took off my cardigan and draped it over the handle of the cart. I felt my chest constrict as my heart pounded. I could hear it in my ears. My head throbbed at my temples. I took a deep breath and then a few shallow, panting breaths. I leaned against the cart for balance. The early afternoon sunlight shining through the windows felt like a spotlight aimed right at me. I felt conspicuous. I felt judged. Logically, I knew I was being silly. Naomi was a kind person; so was Mrs. MacIntyre. Jackson pulled over to make sure I wasn't doing anything nefarious, and since I was not, he was nice to me like he always was. Wyatt was nice too.

I couldn't get my mind off Wyatt. He said he would try to ask me out again. He was everything I always fantasized about. Truthfully, he was probably everything most women fantasized about. He should probably take one of them on a date instead.

My therapist had given me deep breathing exercises to do when I felt myself getting nervous. I inhaled deeply. I counted to five, then ten. I released my breath and thought of my bedroom and my bed with its white eyelet comforter and the soft gray blanket my mother had knitted thrown over the bottom. I wanted to crawl into it and not come out. I thought of dinner tonight with my family and going home where I was safe. I exhaled slowly until my heart rate returned to normal and my legs stopped shaking.

I hate this.

I had no business dating when I was such a ridiculous mess of insecurity and irrational fears. Why would anyone want to put up with this drama? I should say no. Or just say nothing, like I did earlier. Better yet, I should quit my job or call in sick until he forgot about me. I mean, I could call in sick tomorrow, and it wouldn't even be a lie. I'd probably throw up tonight anyway from my nerves. Or maybe I should grow a pair and do the opposite of my usual instincts.

What would Sabrina do? Figure that out, then do the opposite. Forget that—*what would Sienna Diaz do?* My therapist said I should have a bravery mantra, something to get my mind out of an anxiety spiral. Sienna Diaz was my favorite movie star, filmmaker, and a total badass—she created the movie version of Smash-Girl for eff's sake—the best comic book character in the history of comics. Sorry, Wonder Woman. So, like the extreme dork that I was, I used my girl crush on Sienna Diaz as part of my bravery mantra. *What would Sienna Diaz do?* I would die if anyone found out about it.

I jumped and let out a squeal when Naomi popped her head

around the corner of the romance section where I was finishing up shelving the last books on the cart.

"I'm sorry I startled you," she said.

I nodded at her and gripped the handle of the cart in my sweaty palms.

"Are you okay, Sabrina? You seemed to be a bit flustered when you came in," Naomi asked.

"Oh, I'm okay. I'm fine, thank you for asking." I returned her smile then quickly looked down at the cart and picked up another book.

"You know where to find me if you ever want to talk. We could all use more friends, right?" She looked disappointed for a second before covering it with a smile.

My eyes got big. She wanted to be my friend? I forced myself to stand there and not push that cart away and escape like I normally would have done. Like I had done almost every other time she tried to talk to me. She probably thought I was just rude. Everyone probably thought that about me, even though I would rather die than be rude to someone. I inhaled sharply and forced myself to look at her. Her smile was understanding. Her eyes shone with compassion.

I blinked back tears and nodded at her. "Yes," I whispered.

Her jaw dropped for a second before she smiled radiantly at me.

I understood why Harry liked her so much. She could see beyond the stuff that makes most people dismiss others. Like Harry's Autism or my stupid shyness. We had been working together for almost six years and she had never dismissed me; she had always kept trying to talk to me.

I smiled back. "Thank you, Naomi."

"For what?" She laughed, like tinkling bells that spread her good nature around the library.

"For being a good friend to Harry. For making him feel special and safe here. There are not many people with that kind of patience. And, um..." Thoughts I usually kept inside had spilled out.

"You don't need to thank me. It's my pleasure," she answered. "And also, it's three o'clock. You're off. Harry informed me it's time to get the chicken, and he's going to take half a bite tonight."

"Wow, he did?" I asked. There was a lot to unwrap here. First, Harry was going to eat chicken. And second, he conversed with someone about something that didn't directly involve what they were doing. Which would have been astronomy, *Harry Potter*, the purple beanbag, or the library itself. Holy progress, Batman.

She nodded. "And guess what else? I had a bag of M&M's to snack on for my break, and he ate the blue ones! He said they tasted like chocolate sky. But he didn't like the red ones. He said they were hot." We both laughed. Then she hugged me. Most kids would inhale a bag of M&M's if given the chance. But not Harry. Harry was very particular when it came to food. Occasionally, things other than taste and texture compelled him to try a bite of something. In this case it seemed to be the colors of the M&M's.

I hugged her back. *I hugged someone not in my family.* Harry was not the only one making changes.

I stepped away from Naomi and smiled at her. A real one. Not the small excuse for a smile I always told myself would suffice.

"Sabrina, you're lovely," she said.

I blushed. I was fairly certain I turned as red as those hot M&M's Harry didn't like.

But, overwhelmed by the hope she inspired in me today I said, "Thank you, Naomi, I've always thought you were beautiful, and not just your face." I felt my face heat with a blush. If I kept blushing like this, would it stay red forever? Gah, I'm so awkward. What if she thought I was talking about her butt or something? I meant her kindness was beautiful.

"You're fine, Sabrina. I know what you meant," she said knowingly. "Thank you."

"You're welcome. Be careful tonight. It's been getting dark earlier and earlier," I said.

"Change *is* in the air." She smiled and headed off toward the checkout counter.

Change indeed. Spirits lifted, I headed back to the children's area to get Harry.

CHAPTER THREE

WYATT

"Hey, Jackson! Thanks for leaving me on the road, man," I called. I crossed the station to sit on his desk and bust his chops before I met my mother and one or more of my three brothers for lunch at Daisy's Nut House. Jackson James had been a couple years ahead of me all through school. I'd known him since we were kids—he was the same age as my older brother, Everett. But Jackson never hung out with my brother or me. He was too busy hanging around with Ashley Winston back then to give anyone else the time of day. I didn't blame him; if Ashley Winston had chosen me to hang out with, I would have ditched everyone else too. She was as sweet as she was pretty. Sometime after high school, Jackson had won the battle against his acne and braces and become a deputy sheriff. Now, all he had to do was win the battle against his father's shadow. Jackson's father, Sheriff Jeffrey James, was a legend in these parts. I was honored when he hired me to work for his department; it was a dream come true.

Jackson looked up at me with a grin and leaned back in his chair. "You *should* be thanking me—sincerely, Monroe—without the sarcasm. I did you a favor. I left you with a cute little librarian. Scared Sabrina Logan pulled to the side of a treacherous mountain road, just waiting for a big hero like you. Sightings of her in town are rare, unless you're into books. But there are only so many times you can go into the library before it gets weird…so, uh, you're welcome."

"She shot you down, huh? Did she break your heart?" I grinned. For some reason I liked the idea that she shot him down and not me—not yet, anyway. I liked Jackson. He was a good guy, and I enjoyed working with him. But I had found myself really liking Sabrina this morning. Something about her shyness drew me in. She was like a mystery and *I* wanted to solve it. The thought of Jackson going after Sabrina—well, it didn't make me happy and I'll leave it at that for now.

Jackson chuckled. "Not quite. I wasn't trying to hit on her, not the first time anyway. I don't think she even realized it was me that first time, even though she knows who I am—if that makes any sense at all. I ran into her at the library a few years back when I was looking for the latest Stephen King. I think she was hiding back there in the horror section. She jumped about a foot in the air when I walked up and said hi to her. She's a shy one. Completely oblivious to flirting of any sort, but sweet. She always holds the new Stephen King books for me when they come out. She's gorgeous, but too much work for me. I gave up on that a long time ago. Don't worry about me, Monroe. I always have more than one iron in the fire." He smirked.

I shook my head at Jackson with a relief that I could not understand. I had no claim on Sabrina. But, unlike him, I liked a challenge—especially the kind that looked like a sexy librarian hiding behind a pair of glasses. What would it take to get her to go out with me?

"Hey, now. I do not want to know where you put your iron, Jackson. TMI." I returned his look. "Wait a minute, back up. Her last name is Logan? Not one of Doc Logan's daughters?"

"Yep. Cora, the older one, passed about nine years back. You were already at UT, remember?" I did remember; it was a car accident of some type, a terrible tragedy. "Sabrina went to that girls' school in Maryville. That's probably why you don't know her. I know her because I know everyone," he answered me with yet another smirk. I was glad to be back in Green Valley. Everybody knew everybody's business in this town. If Sabrina was too shy to talk to me, I could most likely find out everything I needed to know from alternate sources.

"You're a real man about town, Jackson. You know, Doc Logan fixed my knee when I was at UT," I recalled.

"I saw that game." He cringed. "How'd it feel to have your foot face the other way?"

"About as shitty as you'd imagine," I replied and sat in the chair across from his desk. My last football game at the University of Tennessee, Knoxville had ended with a destroyed ACL, MCL, and other assorted injuries—fun times. I was pretty sure my dashed professional football trajectory is what led to the downfall of my marriage. My ex-wife needed a little more out of life. And that *more* looked a lot like money and mansions and a bigger diamond ring than the one I had given her after she got pregnant with our oldest daughter, Makenna. After our second daughter, Melissa, was born, Isabelle had started working as an assistant to Jefferson Hickson, a big-shot, jackass country music singer in Nashville. Which led to a lot of lying, cheating, and the eventual divorce. These days, if I ever wanted to see her, I could turn on the TV during any country music award show and watch the dollar signs flash in her eyes whenever the camera panned to her. I never admitted to anyone that it wasn't a great loss. I didn't love her like I wanted to love the woman I married. If she hadn't gotten pregnant, I would have never asked. It was a relief when she left me.

"You feel like hitting Genie's after work?" Jackson's voice jolted me out of my thoughts.

"I can't tonight. I'm supposed to have dinner with my folks. My mother is still trying to get my father to quit harping on me about joining the business. I'll probably hear all about it at lunch, too." My father ran Monroe & Sons, the family construction business that had been passed from father to son for over seventy years. The office sat in a huge old Victorian mansion smack dab in the middle of Green Valley. Old Papaw Monroe had built it to show off and it worked. Everyone went to my dad when they needed any kind of construction work done. All three of my brothers worked for my father. It pissed him off when I moved to Nashville after college with my ex and my oldest daughter and joined the police force.

"He started that up again? You've been a cop for over seven years."

"Yeah, he thought when I moved back to Green Valley, I'd work for him. After dinner with the parents tonight, I'll need a few beers. How about tomorrow?" I offered.

"Good deal. I'll be your wingman. Trying to date Sabrina Logan will be an exercise in frustration."

"I'll catch you after lunch. Later, Jackson."

He lifted his chin in response.

I got up and headed out of the station to meet my family at Daisy's.

I was glad to be back in Green Valley. I'd missed my brothers. I'd missed my parents. I had always been close to my mother, and I wished my father would let the whole Monroe & Sons thing go and let me be.

I pulled into the lot and headed into the diner. Daisy's Nut House was a Green Valley staple that had turned into a franchise. Miss Daisy was a friend of my mother's and a sweet lady. But I needed to stay away from Daisy's doughnuts. The fat kid that still lived inside me could eat a dozen of those suckers without blinking. I liked having abs and the ability to touch my toes. Plus, foot pursuits and manhandling drugged-up junkies into the back of my cruiser were sometimes parts of my job and I couldn't do either with a big doughnut gut dragging me down.

I jogged across the parking lot and spotted my brother Everett near the door. Of all my brothers, I was closest to Everett. We were stuck in the middle of our group of four and closest in age.

He waved as I approached. "Dad is here. I've been instructed to not let you leave," he informed me. Then he reached for my arm to pull me back when I turned around to leave. "Come on. Mom will have my ass if I let you go."

"Fine, I'll come inside."

We entered the restaurant. I followed Everett as he led me to the table. They had already been seated and ordered for me. I only had an hour for lunch.

My mother waved at me from a table in the corner with a huge smile lighting up her face. "Wyatt, honey. I heard!" she cried.

I sat down and glanced at my father. He was already eating dessert. He had a piece of pie half-finished on his plate and was staring out the window. He turned and deigned to give me a small smile and nod. I returned his nod. When he was ready to talk to me instead of pout like my daughters do, then I would give him the courtesy of a proper hello. My mother elbowed him and shot him a glare.

"What did you hear?" I asked her and reached for my glass of water.

"About you and that darling assistant librarian, Sabrina Logan. The girls just love her story hour." My eyes shot to hers and I choked on my water. She placed her phone on the table and gave me her full attention.

Everett laughed in his seat next to me. "It's all she's been talking about, bro."

"How could you have possibly heard about that? It just happened." I sank the lemon slice into my glass of water and took another sip.

"Is she okay? Was it an accident that made her stop on the side of the road?" She peered at me over the rim of her glass of iced tea. Her eyebrows were raised in expectation of a juicy story, I was sure.

I looked at her in amazement. "It wasn't an accident—how? What?"

"I listen to the police scanner while I do my gardening. When I heard about you driving Sabrina Logan's Jeep to the library, well, I called Julianne MacIntyre right away to see what happened after that. Those scanners only give you part of the story, you know."

I just blinked at her until she continued explaining. Everett snickered and sipped his coffee. My father continued to stare out the window, studiously ignoring the conversation.

"Julianne was already at her office window, watching. She saw you two chatting and smiling at each other. So, did you ask her out? You should. Julianne told me she's a good girl—shy and sweet and smart as a whip. She'd be much better suited to you than that disappointment you married, and the girls already adore her. They talk about her all the time. We never miss a story hour."

My mouth opened, but no words came out.

"Just eat your lunch," Everett advised. "She'll do all the talking."

"Hush, you," my mother admonished him with an indignant huff. "I love all my boys and I want what's best for you."

"Speaking of that—" my father started to say.

My mother shushed him. "I finally have my grandbabies in the same town as me. I have my boy back, too. You will not ruin this for me, Bill Monroe. You will keep quiet and get over this."

"I can't help how I feel, Becky Lee. He should join the company with his brothers. All Monroe boys join Monroe & Sons. We're a family company and this is what we have always done," he argued.

"No, no. You have three of our boys working for you—that's enough. So, yes. You can get over it and you will." She stared him down.

He got up with a huff, said goodbye, and left.

My mother took my hand and held it. "He'll get over it. You'll see. I'll be working on him. You can bet your bippy on that." She turned away from me and shot one last glare at my father's retreating back. I didn't envy him. My mother was tough.

But despite my mother's obvious determination, I was still not sure she could change his mind. I had three brothers. My oldest brother Barrett was an architect, and Everett was next—he was a carpenter. Then came me, and then Garrett, who was a foreman on one of Dad's crews. They all worked at Monroe & Sons, for my father. They didn't mind that I didn't join them and neither did my mother. Why did my father hate my choices so much?

I picked up my turkey sandwich and took a bite. My mother was something else. I'd never be brave enough to cross her. I wondered how long she would freeze my dad out.

Becky Lee Monroe had managed to whip four obnoxious boys into shape. She could raise one eyebrow and we'd be shaking in our sneakers—her 'mom look' had always bent us to her will. I had considered getting my own 'dad look' to use on my girls, but they'd just laugh at me if I raised an eyebrow at them and told them what to do. Girls were too smart for that kind of thing; they always required explanations and logic, not just threats of time-out.

"So, did you ask her out?" Everett asked, breaking the tension left over from my father's grumpy exit.

I laughed. "I did. She didn't say yes, but she did say I could swing by the library and ask her again. You're right, she's pretty shy."

My mother sighed. "Oh, that is so sweet. I raised you boys right. Such gentlemen, all of you." She picked up her phone.

"Who are you texting?" Everett asked her.

"Julianne, of course," she answered without looking up.

That's just great. Would the whole town find out I'd attempted to ask Sabrina Logan on a date? I already knew enough about her to know that this would freak her out.

CHAPTER FOUR

SABRINA

I was lost in thought, and only half concentrating on the drive toward Genie's Bar to order the chicken for tonight's dinner. Harry was quiet in the back seat. He was probably lost in his thoughts, too.

I didn't want to skip work and hide. I wanted to go out with Wyatt. I wanted to say yes to him if he came back and asked me again. I wanted to go out with him more than I wanted to hide from him. Something like this had never happened to me before. I finally wanted something more than I feared it.

I was jolted out of my thoughts by Harry's voice from the back seat. "Can we stop at the park? I want to look at the leaves. I was counting, and I think there are four different colors, maybe even more."

"Sure, we have time. It's on the way."

I pulled into the parking lot. It was a gorgeous day. Harry was right; there were definitely at least four different colors of leaves decorating the trees and floating in the air on the gentle breeze. Green Valley was always a colorful wonderland during the fall season. I helped him out of the back seat, and he took off.

"Riri, I found a yellow one! Now there are five colors!" he shouted as he ran ahead toward the small playground.

"Wait for me, Harry! I'm wearing high heels," I called out. I was pleased that he listened. He slowed to a stop, and bent to pick up another leaf.

"Orange!" he shouted excitedly with a laugh, then took off again. I wasn't too worried—he had never run away from me before. But I still preferred him to be within my sight.

"Harry, slow down!" I shouted as I left the cement trail and tried to run on my tiptoes onto the grass for a shortcut to the playground. But the pointy heel of my boot dug into the wet ground and I yelped as I stumbled in my quest for balance and landed on my butt on the grass.

Harry stopped and ran back in my direction when he heard me yelp.

"Hey, it's you!" Harry shouted and waved. A huge smile lit up his face.

I turned my head and looked up to see Deputy Sheriff Hottie McOhMyGod standing behind me with his hand held out, and that delicious grin-dimple-eye-crinkle combo lighting up his face. He was out of uniform now, I observed, as my eyes traveled up his denim-clad legs, trim waist, and broad chest covered by a dark gray Henley. The shirt was tight around his biceps and half tucked in behind his belt buckle. My mouth dropped open when I realized I could see his abs through his shirt. Amazing. He must do a lot of crunches.

"Hey, Harry," he said and waved back with a big smile on his face.

I was beginning to develop suspicions that he was as nice as he was hot. And that made him just like a unicorn. A total keeper.

"Hello," I breathed. I had to force myself to look up at him—like when looking at the sun, I did it with a half-lidded gaze.

"Let me help you up." He stepped in front of me, bent forward, took my hands, and pulled me up. He steadied me with his hands on my upper arms. "Are you okay?"

I nodded. "Mm hmm." It kind of sounded more like a moan rather than an answer. "I mean, yes, thank you for helping me up." I lifted to my tiptoes when my heels started to sink in the grass again. My word, he was still taller than me. I brushed away the leaves that clung to the back of my long cardigan and tried not to sigh too loudly.

"You're welcome. Feeling better, little man?" he said to Harry.

"Yes. I had a bad day at school. But then it got so much better. I was at the library, which is pretty much my favorite place in the world. And I have leaves! I want all the colors." He held out his leaves: red, yellow, and orange.

"There are a lot of colors to choose from today, that's for sure," Wyatt answered.

"I know!" he shouted. He then turned around to set them on one of the benches next to the playground. I watched as he ran to the copse of tall yellow poplar trees near the picnic tables to collect a few more of the colorful leaves that had fallen beneath it.

"I'm glad he's okay," Wyatt said.

"I—thank you for your help today. I forgot to say it earlier."

"You're welcome." His eyes drifted from mine; they quickly moved down my body and back up. "Those heels are dangerous in the wet grass. Be careful," he said as I tottered on my toes.

"I will. Thanks." I shivered. I could feel his eyes on me like a touch.

"I guess I'm unlucky. I take my girls to this park all the time, but I've never seen you here before."

"Oh, we don't come here that often. It's usually too crowded, so we do other things…" I trailed off and looked at his boots. They were nice —black—and they looked sturdy and warm.

Look at his face.

I looked up; he was grinning at me. I smiled nervously back and adjusted my glasses with the tip of my finger. We both looked to the parking lot at the sound of a car pulling up and stopping.

"That's my girls," he said. "My mother picks them up from school and keeps them until I get off. It's such a great day, I told her to drop them here instead of my house."

"It is beautiful out today," I agreed. I jolted when I saw two adorable little red-headed girls alight from the car, then quickly looked up at Wyatt when his mother started waving wildly from the front seat. "It's Makenna and Melissa. They're yours? They are little angels! I do a story hour at the library—they always come to it." I beamed up at him. I waved to the girls as they ran up to where we were standing.

"Yep, it's been just the three of us since the divorce," he replied.

I had figured he was single—yay! He's divorced! Was I a horrible person for being happy about that?

They waved at their grandmother from the pathway as she drove off. No offense to Wyatt's mother, but I was glad she left. Meeting her would have probably given me a heart attack. I could talk to kids. It was adults that got me all tongue-tied and stupid.

"Miss Sabrina!" Melissa cried. "You're here at the park! Hi." She held out her tiny fist.

"Hi, honey." I bumped her fist with my own and laughed when she blew it up.

"Hi, Miss Sabrina," Makenna added with a smile. No fist-bump though.

Makenna had always been more reserved. Though I knew we shared a love of old *Nancy Drew Mysteries* and Judy Blume books. She was in the fourth grade, which made her near the same age as Harry. Makenna was a quiet girl and seemed mature beyond her years. She reminded me of myself at that age.

Melissa, on the other hand, was a little firecracker. I already knew she was in kindergarten, loved the color pink, *Fancy Nancy* books, and wanted a puppy more than anything in the world. She was a talker, and she was a sweetheart; she was how I had always wished I could be.

"We're going to collect leaves for our grandma. She wants to make an arrangement for her table," Makenna continued. "Come on, Mel."

They took off, but Wyatt stopped them. "I haven't seen y'all all day. You have no 'hi' for your dad? I want my hugs," he said with a mock frown.

Melissa burst out in giggles and ran at him with a jump. He caught her and gave her a twirl. Makenna hugged him around the waist, and he bent and kissed the top of her head.

And while all of this was going on, I swear I fell in love.

Was that the hottest thing I had ever seen? Why yes, yes it was. My ovaries blew up—that *is* a thing. I believed in it now. Plus, he was making me feel hot all over. I was sure I was blushing as red as the leaf Harry was waving at me from the bench. But worse, I not only felt hot, I felt *other things.* Things I usually only felt when I was alone. In fact, I was sure I would feel those things when I took a bubble bath tonight.

For the love of Dumbledore, stop thinking like that.

"That's better. Now go get Grandma some leaves," he said with a wink.

Wyatt's wink was irresistible even when he directed it at someone else. The only words going through my brain right now were *blargh, guh,* and *blurg*. I needed some real words, and soon.

He watched the girls run over to the picnic area for a second before he turned that dimple my way and I sighed. Sweet, sweet mercy, this was impossible. I could feel him in my heart, my brain was full of mush, and my stomach was doing freaking flips inside my body.

Melissa's little voice snapped me out of my perusal of her father. My eyes shot to the bench where Harry sat with his leaves. "Hi. What's your name?" she said to him.

He had two handfuls of colorful leaves and was studying them with the utmost concentration. I fought the instinct to answer for him or to explain how he was. His therapist and teachers said he should have the opportunity to speak for himself. I could admit that it was not always easy for me to let him. Fighting my overprotective tendencies was always a challenge.

"What's your name?" he repeated without looking up from the leaves.

She giggled. "My name is Melissa. What's your name?"

"Name," he repeated softly.

She giggled harder, then bent forward and put her face in front of his. "You're funny. I'm Mel. Who are you?"

Finally, he looked at her. "Harry James Adams," he said as his eyes wandered over her face and then over her bright, bouncy red curls.

His mouth dropped open. "Red," he whispered reverently, then leaned his face to the side of her head to softly rub his cheek against her hair.

I stepped toward them to make him stop. Harry always did that to Weston after a fresh haircut when his hair felt spiky and soft. But Weston was his big brother and understood Harry. Mel was just a little girl, and still a stranger to him.

"It's okay," Wyatt said, softly putting a hand on my shoulder to stop me. "He's fine. See?"

I watched as Melissa sat down next to him with a bemused expression on her cherubic little face. She shook her head gently against his cheek, making the curls bounce, and Harry sighed. She glanced up at Wyatt with a smile. I watched him smile back at her.

And no, it did not escape my notice that his hand was *on my shoulder.* I was about to join Harry on sensory overload thank you very much.

"Does he have sensory sensitivities?" Makenna asked me.

I jumped, and a nervous laugh escaped me as she popped out from behind a sweetgum tree with a handful of stacked colorful leaves.

"A kid in my class is like that. He sits at my table. I'm his buddy during social studies. Except he likes to rub erasers on his face, not people's hair. I always make sure he gets a clean one," she explained. She crossed to the bench to sit on the other side of Harry. He glanced up at her then laughed with delight when she leaned her head—with equally beautiful, bouncy red curls to match her little sister—onto his other cheek.

"Red," he whispered. "Who are you?"

"Makenna," she answered, "Mak."

"MakandMel," Harry said, running the names all together as if they were one word. They continued to sit on either side of Harry and chatted about the leaves with him.

I gulped back the sob and the laugh that were threatening to come out at the same time. Tears filled my eyes, and I blinked a few times to make them stop. My heart was about to burst wide open.

Wyatt noticed. He squeezed my shoulder gently and stepped closer to my side.

Of course, Harry had friends—the same kids he'd been attending school with since kindergarten. They understood each other because most of them shared the same issues. This was different. This whole entire day had been unusual. I would probably freak out about it later, but for now I was okay. I looked up at Wyatt, who was smiling softly down at me. I reminded myself to look him in the eye like a normal person.

"They're good girls," he simply said.

"Yes. They are wonderful. You must be a good dad to have such sweet daughters."

"I try my best. That's part of why I moved back to Green Valley. It's quiet here. I can spend more time with them, and less time working."

"Riri! Look at me, Riri," Harry called.

I looked back in his direction. They were all three side by side, heads pressed together, jeans-clad legs all in a row, sorting the leaves.

"Red is soft," he informed me. "Red is nice."

"Red is beautiful," I agreed and smiled at him and the girls.

Wyatt's cell rang in his pocket. He frowned. "I have to take this. Could be work."

I nodded and stepped away. "Who wants to swing?" I asked the kids.

"I do, I do. But, only five times," Harry answered. "Then I want to slide."

Mel giggled. "Harry, you're so silly."

He looked at her. "How many times do you want to swing?" he asked.

"Until I can feel the sky," she said and ran for the swings.

He tilted his head. "I would like to feel the sky."

"Y'all are both silly." Mak rolled her eyes, yet she still followed them to the swings.

I hobbled through the grass on my toes, then onto the bark chips that filled the playground on the other side of the picket fence. I pushed the kids on their respective swings for a few minutes until Wyatt turned back to us and headed our way.

"Girls, I have to take you back to Grandma's house. There was a bad car accident on the highway, and I need to go help."

"Okay, Daddy," Mak said.

"Did you feel it, Harry?" Mel yelled as she ran the few feet separating us from the fence and took Wyatt's hand.

"I felt it!" he shouted back from the top of the slide. "And you can really feel it up here."

Mel jumped up and down and waved at Harry and me as she stood next to Wyatt clutching his hand. When she had finished waving, and was seemingly satisfied with our waves back, she twirled around and around, passing under his arm after each twirl, giggling like a demented ballerina.

Wyatt chuckled at Mel's antics before turning to me. "Sabrina." His voice was low and rough. It tickled over my skin like a caress; goose bumps rose in its path.

I couldn't have prevented the shiver that moved through my body even if I tried. My name, spoken from those lips. I would do anything to hear it again. He was different from anyone I had ever met. I wanted to know more about him. But I also started to feel like I wanted *him* to know *me* and I couldn't understand why—I never felt that way before. I looked up at him. "Yes?"

"I'll see you soon, darlin'—at the library. Don't forget." He grinned and gave me the standard hot guy two-fingered salute/wave as he turned, and hand in hand walked with his daughters to his car parked near mine in the lot.

"Okay," I whispered to his retreating back. "I won't forget." As if I *could* forget. I would think of nothing but the possibility of him asking me out again until he *actually* asked me out. Then I would freak the heckerooni out until I had turned into a drooling pile of dead brain cells on the floor.

"Bye, Miss Sabrina," Mak called out, arms full of the gathered leaves for their grandmother.

"Bye, girls," I called back. I glanced back and forth between Harry and Wyatt's car until he drove away. Then I stood there, lost in thought once more, and watched Harry go down the slide. He usually only slid fifteen times, but today he did seventeen before he ran over to me. He had forgotten to count. Naomi was right; change *is* in the air.

"I like Mak and Mel," Harry said from the bench where he was gathering his leaves, one of each color he could find.

"I like them too. Maybe you can go to the next story hour. What do you think?"

"I would like to try. I wish my other friends could go too."

Realization dawned on me. "Is that what upset you today? Did Ms. Allen talk to you about going to Green Valley Grade School?"

He nodded.

His teacher believed that he was ready to enter a mainstream classroom, and we had agreed she could broach the subject with him today. Of all the things to forget about. I sighed.

"It won't be until January, after Christmas break. You have plenty of time to think about it and decide if you are ready," I assured him.

"I will miss them." His eyes filled with tears and my heart lurched.

Why couldn't I protect him from everything?

"I know, baby. But they will always be your friends. No matter where they are."

Oh, how I wished that were true. Life had told me otherwise though. People always drifted away, no matter how hard you tried to hold on to them.

He smiled up at me. "Okay, Riri."

"Time to go get the chicken," I said and held my hand out to him.

CHAPTER FIVE

SABRINA

I pulled into Genie's parking lot with a deep breath and a scowl. It was my turn to get the chicken for our weekly family dinner tonight. A few months ago, my father added me to the family rotation for dinner pickups. He thought it would be good for me to "Get out of the house," "Go into town and have some fun," "Meet people your own age," and my favorite—"Quit hiding your sunshine, sweet pea." I had no sunshine and I enjoyed hiding. My favorite hiding spot was on my bed with a good book. Or the pasture behind our house at the ranch, with a good book. My father had been saying stuff like that to me for years, and I'd managed to avoid doing any of it. When my therapist started to parrot the same stuff my father had been telling me, I knew I was in trouble. I also knew—way deep down—that they were right, and I had to make a change. But knowing I had to do it and doing it were not the same. I was a shy hermit prone to fits of anxiety. I was a hot mess of insecurity and doubt, wrapped up in a cozy blanket of fear.

What all that digressive, meandering brain dump meant was that it was my turn to go inside, order, and wait for the food. That's it. No big deal, right?

I didn't have much to worry about from a realistic standpoint.

Genie was a nice lady. She knew my father—everyone in town knew my father, and everybody loved him. No one would dare be mean to Dr. Roy Logan's daughter. But from the standpoint of my brain, AKA Crazytown, I would go in there and be struck with some kind of humiliating disaster, and possibly die from embarrassment. It could happen.

All I needed to do was ask for "number two," the fried chicken dinner. I took a deep, shaky breath.

Number two, number two. What would Sienna Diaz do?

Not have a panic attack over fried chicken like a dummy, that's for sure.

"Are you okay, Riri?" Harry asked.

His voice startled me out of my thoughts, and I jumped in my seat. "What? Yes. Are you ready?" This was good for both of us. Harry and I —we shared some issues. I got nervous around people and Harry got overstimulated by the noise.

Lucky for us, four o'clock in the afternoon on a weekday was not a busy time at Genie's. In fact, it was dead right now—only one other car in the lot. Saturday night was the time folks liked to come see and be seen at Genie's. I would never come here on a Saturday night. I shuddered at the mere thought of it.

Genie's was a country western bar. Genie just happened to serve the best fried chicken in the world, and my family was addicted to it. Almost as much as we were addicted to our Daisy's Nut House doughnut Saturday mornings. Lucky for me I hadn't been penciled in to the rotation for Daisy's pick-ups—not yet anyway. Everyone in town knew that the Winston brothers were regulars at Daisy's Nut House, and they were all just too fine for words. Especially Roscoe. He used to push me on the swings in kindergarten. He was sweet. But after my mother died, my father put me in private school starting in the first grade, and that was the end of that. My father told me Roscoe was with Miss Daisy's daughter now. I used to play with Simone too. I wonder if they'd remember me.

Enough dillydallying. I grabbed my purse and got out of my Jeep. I leaned against the side for a second to gather what remained of my wits. I spun around to let Harry out and had to laugh at his little face pressed up against the glass smiling at me. His hazel eyes, just like mine and his momma's, twinkled with laughter.

"Let's go, let's go," he said. I remembered his goal to eat half a bite of chicken tonight and opened the door. If Harry wanted to eat half a bite of chicken, then by Godric Gryffindor I could dang well order it for him.

Number two, fried chicken dinner, number two.

"Let's do this," I said and took his hand. We walked up the mound of gravel that led up to the front door. Both of us froze in our tracks right in front of it. My heart started pounding hard. I glanced down at Harry; he looked nervous too. I had to be the grown up, I had to pretend to be okay. "Come on, it's fine. It doesn't sound too loud in there. I can't even hear any music this time."

He nodded and clutched my hand.

My father was right. This was good for us. It was. "The more you do, the easier it will be to do more, sweet pea." He always said that to me. Reluctantly, I had to admit he was right.

I smiled down at Harry and pushed the door open. We stepped into the old-timey wood paneled entryway with coat hooks along the sides. There were no coats on the hooks, which should mean few people inside the bar. I took a deep breath and looked around for Genie. I had talked to her before, I could do it again. I tried to swallow, but my mouth had gone dry.

"It's not loud," Harry said, pleased. His grip eased up on my hand.

I looked down and answered his smile with a small one of my own. "We're okay," I whispered. I closed my eyes briefly, trying to convince myself. I inhaled a huge breath. My heart felt like it was in my throat. I exhaled slowly through my mouth.

Fried chicken dinner, number two. Easy.

We stepped around a table next to the empty dance floor, so we could cross to the bar on the right. I didn't see Genie behind the bar. I might have to talk to someone new. I stopped and took a glance at the booths that lined the perimeter; maybe she was over there.

Mistake!

Oh my God!

There were Winstons at the table in the corner, two of them. Plus Drew Runous, Ashley Winston's husband. Drew looked like a Viking, straight off the cover of a romance novel. I used to have a tiny (massive) crush on him. Sometimes he attended poetry night at the library. If I was at work during the readings, I would lurk in the horror section and listen (watch him like a creeper).

Don't look at Drew—concentrate. Fried chicken dinner, number two.

Harry pointed to their table. "He has red hair," he stated.

"Shh, I know. It's okay," I shushed gently.

Cletus Winston and one of the redheaded Winston twins were over there. The redhead had to be Beau; Duane was hardly ever in town anymore. Beau always did the tune-ups on my Jeep. I'd spoken to him a few times. He was very nice, and not at all scary. He had a friendly smile. Cletus was nice too. He made lots of requests for books at the library—always about weird and varied subjects—if I weren't such a big scaredy-cat I'd ask him just what in the Sam Hill tarnation he needed with all those strange books. But I just wrote them down and ordered them. I suspected he requested the books from me because he knew I wouldn't say anything about it and gosh darn it, if didn't that make me even more curious.

Bottom line—I did not need more hot guy attention today. Wyatt had already done my head in. I was operating on brain fumes. I needed to get home so I could lie down. I needed to ponder and ruminate. I needed to figure out how I had talked to Wyatt at the park so I could do it again if he came into the library to ask me out for a date.

I tugged gently on Harry's hand and turned to step in the direction of the bar, but instead I stepped right into Roscoe Winston. Gah! Where had he come from? The bathroom? I stumbled back and he held my arms so I wouldn't fall.

Great bearded Hagrid, what was going on? What kind of twisted, messed up luck was putting so many people in my path today?

"Sabrina Logan!" he said. He remembered me. Aw, how nice.

"Number two," I blurted.

Number two...that's poop.

I immediately shut my eyes.

As if that could really make you disappear, dummy.

I opened one eye, just to peek.

I opened my mouth and my trademark nothing came out. I bit my lip. I just knew my face had turned as red as Beau Winston's hair.

"Wow, you're just the same," he said with a huge smile.

"Hi," Harry said.

"Hey there." Roscoe smiled down at him.

"Sabrina! Sugar, your daddy called. I have your order ready and it's all paid for," Genie called to me from behind the bar. I spun in her direction to see her waving and smiling.

"Bye," I said to Roscoe and started walking to the bar.

"Bye, Sabrina." He smiled and laughed. Not mean. He wasn't being mean, I knew that. But he laughed. At me. Because I was funny. I was *weird.*

I made it to the bar to get my order. I think I said thank you. I took the food. One bag full of fried chicken and one low-sided box holding the mashed potatoes, gravy, corn, and a paper bag full of biscuits and honey butter. One foot in front of the other. I could do this. I just needed to get the heck out of here so I could go home and lie down.

I whirled around. "Come on, Harry," I said and glanced down at him.

He nodded and started to follow me toward the door.

But I was not watching where I was going. Just as I thought I would be able to make it to the exit without further embarrassment, I crashed right into a hard chest attached to a tall body and the box went flying. Biscuits rolled across the floor and the potatoes and gravy landed with a *splat* and a *sploosh.* I gasped in horror. This was a nightmare. This was terrible. This was like all my greatest fears just took a number freaking two right on top of my head.

"Oh, Riri," Harry said and looked at the floor. "Oh, no. It is a big mess. No, I mean it is a super huge mess." He got on his hands and knees and started crawling after the biscuits.

I clutched the bag of chicken to my chest and stood there gaping like a fish. My brain cells had ceased to function.

"Whoa, I'm sorry. Are you okay?" I looked up at the sound of the voice and all those rolling biscuits got buttered, because *holy crap* how much more could I take before my head exploded?

I had crashed right into Jethro Winston. Of course I did. I had inadvertently interrupted a Winston brother bonding session at Genie's Country Western Bar. But the embarrassment from crashing into him was not enough. Dreams also had to die. Jethro had married Sienna Diaz a few years ago. I love Sienna Diaz. My secret bravery mantra was born because of Sienna Diaz's inspirational badassery. Now, she was going to find out what a klutzy, bumbling idiot I am. My dreams of someday running into her around town, getting over my ridiculous shyness and becoming her new BFF were ruined. I mean, I crashed into her husband. I may have injured him, perhaps even grievously. What if I left permanent damage on his chest from the hot biscuits?

"What would Sienna Diaz do?" I couldn't help but think it. That mantra got me through a lot of crap in my life.

"She'd probably make a joke, like—what do you call a teacher who never farts in the library?" Jethro said to me with a huge smile.

I stared up at him with big eyes. Holy crap, I had said my secret bravery mantra out loud instead of in my brain. I inhaled a huge breath. Now she would know I'm a klutzy, bumbling idiot who almost killed her husband with biscuits *and* add me to her potential stalker list. I shut my eyes. I was a hopeless mess. I should go home and take up permanent residence under my bed, like a freaking troll, and never come out.

"What?" Harry shouted from the floor, his hands full of the murderous biscuits. "What do you call the teacher who never farts in the library, mister?" Harry loved jokes, and if the joke involved farting or butts, he'd be your best friend forever.

"A private tutor," Jethro answered him with a big beautiful grin.

Harry burst out laughing. "Hey, hey, hey, mister, hey—how do you make a witch itch?" he said through his giggles.

"How?" Jethro asked Harry.

"Take away the W." Harry let the biscuits fall out of his hands, clutched his stomach, and cracked up.

"Good one, little man." Jethro chuckled.

I made myself laugh at the jokes, but it came out nervous and I probably sounded insane. I took a step back and braced myself. There were probably Winston brothers hiding in every crevice of this bar. I shoved my glasses up the bridge of my nose and looked around. I tried to do it surreptitiously. But I was sure I had crazy eyes.

"Take a deep breath." I turned my head to the sound of the voice. Sweet merciful McGonagall, it was Drew Runous talking to me. Did people really swoon? Because I felt like I was gonna do it right now. Drew was married—my hopeless crush had long since died—but he was still so pretty to look at. Instead of swooning, I did what he said and took a deep breath. It helped, a tiny bit.

I looked around the bar—Winston brothers were everywhere—helping Harry collect the killer biscuits and throw them in the trash. Scooping mashed potatoes and gravy up into napkins and cleaning up my mess.

Beau led me to a chair and handed me a glass of water. He seemed oddly understanding, and as nice as he always was whenever I dropped my Jeep off at his shop. "Sit down, Sabrina. You'll be fine," he said.

"Thanks," I murmured.

He smiled and waded into the mess to help. My father always said those Winston brothers were good folk. And everyone in the library missed their momma like crazy.

"Willa!" Genie shouted. "Bring another number two out front, darlin'. Minus the chicken. And grab the mop."

Willa?

Could it be?

My Willa?

I caught a glimpse of wild blond hair and a familiar profile before she placed a bag on the bar and disappeared back through the swinging door to the kitchen.

"Here you go. Bless your heart, honey. You're just a mess, ain't you?" Genie said as she headed my way and placed the bag with the new number two on the table next to me.

I shut my eyes. God, I *was*. I was such a mess. And why couldn't the food have been in a bag the first dang time? "I'm so sorry, Miss Genie. Please let me pay you for the replacements."

"No need, darlin'. Accidents happen. Plus, your daddy replaced my momma's hip! I'm gonna replace your side dishes. It's the least I could do. You make sure to say hello to your daddy for me."

I nodded at her. "I will." I looked around for Harry.

He was just fine, busy high-fiving multiple Winston brothers and one smiling Viking named Drew and thankfully not bothered at all by my distress about the mess I had made.

"Thank you, Miss Genie." I hesitated before I blurted, "Is that Willa Hill working in the kitchen?"

Genie gave me a sly look. "It sure is, honey. But I'm not supposed to say anything about that yet."

"Oh." I was torn between just getting the heck out of here and waiting around to see Willa when she came back out front with a mop. I'd met Willa when we were kids. She was my very best friend in the world until she ran away from home. She knew my secrets and dreams; she knew my heart and I knew hers. She'd been gone for almost ten years and this was the first glimpse I'd had of her in all this time.

"She's on nights the rest of the week, sugar. If you want to come back later."

I decided to come back without Harry. "Thanks."

"Harry. Ready to go?" I said weakly and stood up. Then, because I had been raised to have good manners—I thanked them all—every last Winston in the bar, plus Drew Runous. I didn't look at them when I did it, but I did it all the same. It still totally counted.

Harry ran to my side, and we were finally ready to go home.

Finally.

CHAPTER SIX

SABRINA

I reached up and clicked the gate opener on my sun visor. The black iron "Logan Ranch" gate slowly slid to the sides. I drove through and onto the long meandering gravel path that led to the house. Logans didn't raise horses anymore, but we still had the land—and the money. My family had always been wealthy and my father kept that wealth prospering through his stock market hobby and career as a renowned orthopedic surgeon.

I drove over a small hill and smiled with relief when I saw my father's car parked in front of the house. He had been working out of town all week. He held an advisory position at the University of Tennessee Medical Center, consulted with various sports teams in Nashville, and had an office here in Green Valley. He was semi-retired and I doubted he would ever fully stop working.

"Pop is home. There's his car. It's home time, homey, homey home time." Harry sang and laughed from the back seat. "Can I get out and run?" he asked.

"Sure, you can. But wait for me on the swing while I park in the garage," I instructed.

"Okay, Riri. I'll swing ten times. I bet you can't park before I'm done swinging."

"You're on." I watched as Harry made a dash for the tire swing hanging from the big red maple in the center of the front yard. I sighed happily and felt the tension leave my body as I got closer to the grand old farmhouse. With its red brick wraparound porch, white siding, and tall columns, the house stood out like a beacon against the rolling green of the grass that surrounded it. Just beyond the house you could see the colorful trees that dotted the mountains of the Great Smoky Mountains National Park that bordered our property.

My family believed in intergenerational living. This house had always been full of Logans. When I was a child my grandparents from both sides lived with us until they died. But now it was just my father, my late sister Cora's kids—Weston, Ruby, and Harry—and me.

I stopped my Jeep as Harry jumped from the swing and ran toward the porch. I continued around the half-circle driveway to the detached six-car garage that sat perpendicular to the house. Weston's car wasn't in there yet. But Ruby's was, just waiting for her to pass the test and get her driver's license. I got out and grabbed the food and Harry's backpack. I slammed the door shut and headed for the house.

"I swung ten times!" Harry yelled, "I beat you, Riri!"

"Oh, well," I said with pretend disappointment and laughed as he made the 'nanny nanny boo boo' face at me.

"Come on, Riri, I want to see Pop."

I unlocked the door, and we went inside. "Don't forget to take off your shoes!" I yelled.

My mother hated germs. She refused to allow anyone into the house with their shoes on. She passed away when I was five, yet my father still enforced most of her rules. Harry kicked his red Chucks off and threw them into the giant pile of shoes at the side of the entryway. He took off in search of my father. I sat on the tiny bench by the door and removed my boots, stretching my feet in the process. I almost always wore heels, and every pair I owned made me over six feet tall. I could look over the heads of most people. It made it harder for them to notice my lack of eye contact. People got weird when you didn't look them in the eye. But looking people in the eye made *me* get weird, so I always employed various life hacks to hide it.

I headed for the dining room. A housekeeper came once a week for deep cleaning, and she always set the big table in the dining room with my mother's fancy dishes for our weekly family dinners. It was nice to eat on them. It made me feel close to her in a weird way. I wished I could remember her better, other than the random feelings of longing that arose from time to time.

Those vague memories of my mother were nothing like how I missed Cora. I missed my big sister with an excruciating ache whenever I allowed myself to remember her. I was five when our mother died, and Cora was seventeen. Cora took care of me like our mother had. She was more than just a big sister—she was always everything I ever needed. I was seventeen when Cora died, and I vowed to always take care of her kids like she took care of me. I glanced at the big framed picture hanging above the fireplace at the end of the dining room. Cora was sitting under the red maple tree out front, hugging little Weston and Ruby to her chest with that sweet smile that used to light up our lives. There were no pictures of her with Harry. She was hit by a car in front of her doctor's office and it put her into early labor. It was a hit-and-run, and they never caught the driver. She died in the hospital while giving birth to Harry. I had held Cora's hand and tried to make her hold on, but she slipped away just as we heard Harry cry for the first time.

We all looked alike, with wavy black hair, big hazel eyes, and freckles on our noses. I quickly looked away from her smiling face. I'd had a strange day. I didn't need to add sad memories to it. I could walk by pictures of my mother and Cora every day without seeing them. But something about that picture caught my eye today and wouldn't let it go. Deciding sometimes it was necessary to feel a little sadness to remember the happy, I walked over to the fireplace and studied their smiling faces.

You'd be proud of Harry today, Cora.

I sighed and turned back to the table, filling the platters and covered bowls with my contributions from Genie's. I lifted a lid and saw that my father had already added the fancy mac and cheese from the Front Porch to the table. The Front Porch was a ritzy steak house in town—a great date night place, or so I'd heard. But what I really wanted was dessert. I was hoping for banana cake from the Donner Bakery. With fingers crossed, I turned to the buffet to sneak a peek under the covered cake stand. Yes! Cake! My father's voice stopped me before I could swipe my finger through the frosting.

"I should hide it next time." I whirled around from the buffet at the sound of his laughing voice—busted.

"Dad!" I beamed.

My father was standing in the doorway with Harry clinging to his back like a little spider monkey. "Hey, sweet pea." His tall frame and smiling face filled the room and his hazel eyes twinkled underneath white eyebrows. "Where are Weston and Ruby? Dinner will get cold."

"I don't know," I answered.

We jumped when we heard the front door slam, followed by shoes hitting the floor, and the sound of rapidly running feet.

"Pop." Ruby darted into the room and skidded on her socks to crash into me. I grabbed onto her arms to steady her. "Weston is so pissed—I mean, angry. We saw Dad at the Piggly Wiggly and now Weston is outside punching the heavy bag in the garage. I mean, it's better than punching Dad's face, which he almost did. I could barely make him stop. We didn't get your Dr. Pepper. I'm sorry."

"Whoa, whoa, whoa, it's okay. Don't worry about the Dr. Pepper —" Dad said, but I was already running outside to the garage.

Poor Weston. The kids' father was the worst. Why my sister put up with him for so long, I did not know. Well, I could guess. He was very good looking, and he didn't start off being an a-hole, he eased into it and tricked us all. Cora had a soft spot for that jerk for years. They were always on and off. They had been childhood sweethearts. He used to be good to her, to all of us. He kept getting her hopes up he would change—then he would cheat on her, run up gambling debts, get back into drinking and drugs, and smash those hopes right back down again. She wanted her kids to have a father like we had. Hope sprung eternal for Cora, I guess. Luckily, after she died, my father gained custody of the kids so they could continue living here at the ranch with us, and not have to move in with a father they barely knew.

"Weston!" I called as I entered the garage and flipped on the lights. Weston had set up a gym on one side of the garage and was busy pounding the crap out of the heavy bag hanging in the corner.

"I don't want to talk!" he shouted between punches. "I hate him. I wish he was dead."

"What happened?"

"Come on inside, Weston," my father said from the open door. "Let's not allow him to ruin our dinner. A tradition maintained is good for the soul."

Weston stopped and stood there, jaw tense and rage radiating from him like a storm cloud. I rushed over and took his hand in both of mine. He'd gotten so handsome in the last few years. He looked like a man now. He was a senior at Green Valley High School and the quarterback on the football team.

"Come on. Let's have dinner and talk," I said.

Weston nodded, pulled away from me, and jogged toward the house. I exchanged a look with my father before he turned and followed Weston inside. I stood there for a second wondering just what in the heck was going on with this crazy day. I stepped outside the garage to find Ruby opening the back of Weston's Jeep.

"Hey, Aunt Sabrina. You look extra stressy tonight. What happened?" Unlike Weston, Ruby seemed to be fine after their run-in with their father.

"Ugh," I answered and looked at the sky.

"That bad, huh?" she said sympathetically.

"I ran into some of the Winston brothers at Genie's when I was picking up the chicken."

"Which ones?" she asked.

I leaned against the side of the Jeep. "I don't know. All of them, I think. And I mean that literally. I crashed into two of them. Gravy—it was everywhere, like a brown nightmare," I grumbled.

She laughed and patted my shoulder before standing straight with a start. "Oh! Winstons! That reminds me. I need to talk to Cletus.

Don't let me forget to text him after dinner. I got the interview he wanted for the podcast. But it has to happen tomorrow." She reached in the Jeep's cargo area, grabbed her huge backpack, and slipped it over her shoulder. Ruby was basically the sixteen-year-old girl version of Chandler Bing. She was beautiful, but disgruntled. She had a genius IQ, was the first chair clarinet in the Green Valley High School band, president of the debate team and the audio-visual club, and she'd recently started producing podcasts in her spare time. The biggest one being *Green Valley Views and News,* hosted by Cletus Winston—one of the illustrious and ever-present Winston brothers. She was very active at school and in the community. I envied her gregarious nature, especially because she tempered it with her quick-witted sarcasm.

Thanks to Ruby, Cletus Winston's podcast, plus my father's senior center gossip sources, I was able to keep up on the news around town without having to spend any actual time in town.

"I'll try to remember," I answered her and reached for one of the Piggly Wiggly bags. "Even though the mere mention of a Winston will probably scar me for life after I embarrassed myself in front of them today. Whatever you do, don't mention Cletus at the table—it'll get Dad started on the whole shuffleboard thing." Cletus was a regular at the senior center and my father's shuffleboard nemesis.

"Lord, have mercy, Sabrina. Cletus doesn't cheat at shuffleboard. If anything, he lets Pop win sometimes." Ruby rolled her eyes. "We stopped at Grandma Essie's before we saw Dad. They couldn't come tonight, but she made a batch of her soup for Harry."

I took one of the bags from her. She grinned and passed me another. "Tell me what happened at the Piggly Wiggly?" I prodded.

"Dad said he wants to visit us. He also wants us to talk with Pop about us eventually moving in with him. He thinks we can convince Pop to pay him child support. You know how he is, Sabrina. It was his usual bull crap—money, money, money. Ever since Weston and I started high school...every few months, it's something with him. I ignored him, like usual. But Weston blew his top—like usual." She took the last bag from the back then slammed the rear door shut with a gusto that betrayed her nonchalant attitude. "Weston told Dad he would make his life a living hell if he refused to sign Harry's adoption papers. Heads up though, I'm pretty sure Dad was high again." I watched her eyebrows raise and her lips purse in disgust.

"Crap. I'll tell Dad to call the attorney after dinner. And, drugs? I'm sorry you had to deal with him. I'll do what I can."

She shrugged. "It is what it is," she said and started stalking toward the house. I watched her walk away. She was more upset about the run-in with her father than she was letting on.

I inhaled a huge breath and tried to let some bravery get in along with the air. I promised my sister I would be there for her kids, and that included running interference between them and their loser father.

Luckily, while the kids had a miserable excuse for a father, that did not extend to his parents. Joe and Essie Adams were the best grand-parents any kid could ask for. Joe was an attorney and Essie was the secretary to Bill Monroe, the owner of Monroe & Sons, a big construction company in town. I gasped as realization dawned on me like a tragedy.

Monroe.

Wyatt.

Wyatt Monroe.

Oh. My. God. I have got to get my head out of the clouds like Ruby keeps telling me.

A few months ago, I had heard from my father that one of the Monroe & Sons boys had come back to town. Wyatt must be the one —the son that just came home. Didn't he say he had just moved back to Green Valley? Oh, my freaking gosh, he did say that. That meant he was... No, I can't think about that right now. I shook my head and continued staring off into space.

"Earth to Sabrina." Ruby laughed from the porch. "Let's go in. I'm starving."

"Uh-huh. Coming." I unstuck myself from my spot on the pathway and headed to join her.

I had gotten lost in my humiliating thoughts. It wouldn't be a problem. No one ever had to know anything. I'd just avoid him, and therefore avoid embarrassing both of us.

I followed her inside. We took our usual seats at the table. I noticed the seat Lizzy usually sat in was empty again. Weston's girlfriend hadn't been coming around as much. Gah! Lizzy *Monroe*—she must be Wyatt's niece. Weston was crazy about her. I could kick myself for not realizing who Wyatt was when we met him earlier. His roots in Green Valley ran so deep I should have known. I must have been struck stupid by his man beauty. I'd suffered from a case of temporary hot-guy induced amnesia. I blame his dimple! That dimple sucked the intelligence right out of my head like a black hole sucks stuff out of the universe or whatever. See?

I sighed and passed the bag filled with tiny jars of soup to Ruby, so she could help Harry dish it up.

"Ruby. What is it, Ruby?" Harry was so excited he was bouncing up and down in his seat.

"Grandma Essie's rainbow soup," Ruby answered. Essie invented rainbow soup for Harry to accommodate his need for his foods not to touch and his compulsion to sort and organize things. It was vegetables of all different colors cooked in her homemade chicken broth, then separated and put into individual jars. I decided not to remind Harry of his promise to taste the fried chicken this week. We'd shoot for next week instead.

"Best day ever. Best soup ever. Best Grandma Essie ever," Harry said in a singsong voice. His mood was so contagious, even Weston smiled.

"I'm glad someone had a good day," Ruby said and held her fist out for Harry to bump.

"Oh, Ruby. Bump it. Bump the fist. Just like Mel did. Just like at the park today with Sheriff Wyatt." Harry bumped his fist to hers then blew it up. "Blow it up, Ruby."

Ruby sat there, fist held out, in shock that Harry had finally bumped it. Time after time, Harry left her hanging.; he had never once bumped it. He usually just looked at it and smiled or waved and ran off.

"*Psssht*," Ruby provided the sound effect as she blew it up and took her hand back. "He bumped my fist. Did y'all see it? He finally bumped it." She let out a whoop. "All right, Harry." The residual tension created from Weston's bad mood had been broken, and we all let out a collective sigh.

Ruby sat back down, then turned to me with her eyebrows up. "So, Aunt Sabrina. What did Harry mean? Just like Mel? Sheriff Wyatt? The park? Anyone else want to know what's up with that?" Ruby asked the room as she passed me the iced tea.

I sank down in my seat.

"Sheriff Wyatt? Monroe?" my father asked.

I sank lower and reached for the chicken.

"Sheriff Wyatt is very nice. He is the dad of Mak and Mel. He looks like Superman. Riri is going to go on a date with him," Harry said through a mouthful of orange carrots.

"I thought you were asleep!" I cried, before I could think of a way to avoid the topic entirely.

"Asleep?" Ruby prodded. "Now I'm really curious. Start at the beginning, Aunt Sabrina." She leaned back in her chair with an expectant look.

I rolled my eyes and shook my head.

"There is no way you aren't spilling," Weston added. "No offense, but you never have news. I can't wait to hear this."

"I never have news because I'm invisible. No one in this town knows who I am," I huffed.

Ruby laughed. "Oh, Aunt Sabrina... You do realize that when you're out and about with your head in a book or the clouds or wherever you keep it when we're in public that other people *can* see you? You're not invisible because you refuse to pay attention. You're not really hiding. You look like a hot Snow White. Believe me, everyone notices you."

"They do not," I protested. She was right. I was not invisible, no matter how hard I tried to be. And sometimes that terrified me.

"They do too," Weston argued. "Not to be gross, but I've heard 'your aunt is hot' way more times than I'm comfortable with. I might be scarred for life." He shook his head at his plate, then shoveled a forkful of mashed potatoes into his mouth.

Ruby laughed at Weston, then turned to me. "Sabrina—you have a date with *Wyatt Monroe?"*

My face was now as red as the bell pepper Harry was currently spearing onto a fork. I shook my head and shut my eyes, willing her not to say anything more. I opened one.

Ruby looked intrigued. Her mouth opened—

Don't say it, don't say it.

My eyes shot to my father as he interrupted, "The Monroes are good folk. Their sons are nice, responsible boys. Any of them would be good for you, Sabrina. But Wyatt—I like that boy. I operated on him after he injured his knee during a football game when he was at UT. He couldn't play anymore after that. It killed his chances to go pro. He didn't let it ruin his life; he carried on. He's upstanding. Good for you, sweet pea." He nodded his approval.

Great.

"I haven't said yes yet," I protested.

"But you will," Ruby said, eyebrows up and eyeballs glaring at me. "You are going to say yes. You had better say yes."

"He's going to ask her again at the library. She didn't answer him at the car," Harry informed everyone.

"I thought you were asleep!" I cried again.

Harry just tilted his head, ate a bite of yellow squash, and shrugged.

"You say yes to him if he asks again. Or I'll find him and say yes for you," Ruby threatened.

I looked to my father for help, but he was just chuckling and spooning another helping of Front Porch fancy mac and cheese onto his plate.

I looked over at Weston. He had already quit paying attention. He was busy stuffing his face with chicken and staring at his cell phone.

And Harry—he was a tiny little traitor.

"You wouldn't," I countered.

She raised an eyebrow.

She would.

"Fine. I'll say yes—*if* he asks again," I huffed.

"Good. Pass the biscuits please," she said with a cat-eating-the-canary smile.

I twisted my lips and handed her the biscuits.

The rest of dinner was quiet. They were probably all shocked that I had news for a change. I could hardly blame them. I mean—I shocked the heck out of myself today.

CHAPTER SEVEN

SABRINA

Since he was home, my father took over with Harry for the rest of the night. They had already gone upstairs to play Minecraft before bedtime. I was free. I did not need to be free. I needed distractions. Weston had left right after dinner to go hang at a friend's house and I didn't know where Ruby had disappeared to. Which left me alone. Being alone when I was in this kind of mood was awful. I already knew what my night would be like. I'd relive every embarrassing thing I did today while cringing, hating myself, and wondering where I went wrong.

I headed into the kitchen and stood on tiptoes to reach up to the wine rack, up high in the walk-in pantry. I grabbed a bottle, uncorked it, and poured a big glass. I rummaged around in the snack basket and found some dark chocolate to go with it. If I was going to dwell on my crazy day and torture myself, I would need reinforcements. I snagged a bag of potato chips off the counter as I passed. Extra stress called for extra snacks.

I headed out of the kitchen through the family room to the short bookshelf-lined hallway that led to my little one-bedroom apartment —also called a mother-in-law unit—attached to the side of the house. I had my own entrances. One on the outside of the house and one inside. I also had a bathroom, a kitchen, a living room, and everything else you would expect from an apartment. I loved it in here. It was my own comfy little lair. I always felt safe and comfortable while surrounded by my things, especially my books—otherwise known as my escape from reality. I liked that I could be so close to my family but have privacy whenever I wanted.

I entered my tiny living room and found Ruby sprawled on my overstuffed white couch. She had pushed all my books aside and placed her laptop on the coffee table. So much for privacy. I should have known she wasn't going to let it go.

"Sabrina. Oh. My. God!" she squealed.

Which was weird. Ruby was usually not the squealing type. Something must be up with her. She'd been squealy since dinner. Eye-rolling, sarcasm, and observations laced with a lot of snark—that was more Ruby's type.

"Ruby, I am trying not to think about it." I held my glass of wine aloft as evidence.

She laughed. "Too bad. I can't believe you might go out with him. We must have watched that video ten times."

I had watched it *with her* ten times. And another one hundred times on my own—*at least*.

About a year ago, when he still lived in Nashville, Wyatt had gone viral. He was the inadvertent star of one of those 'hot cop' videos on the internet. Wyatt had been the first officer on the scene of a robbery in progress at a Stop and Go convenience store. During his tussle with the robber, the spinny hotdog cooker-thing had crashed to the floor, caught fire, and caused a big panic. A group of little old ladies had been in the gas station at the time and Wyatt had carried them out—one-by-one—of the burning convenience store. The women screamed and swooned, and the smiles on their faces when he set them down outside were a testament to his bravery. A woman in the parking lot filmed the whole thing on her cell phone. Later, someone combined her video with the surveillance video footage from inside the store and put it online. The building didn't burn down, and eventually the news anchors agreed that the incident contained more smoke than actual fire. But even so, they still hailed Wyatt a hero. He became famous locally, with pictures of him popping up everywhere online. #StopandGoSuperman.

The sight of his gorgeous body carrying those sweet, tiny old ladies out of the smoky Stop and Go had permanently embedded itself on my brain. Except, in the video, his face was obscured by the smoke. His bulging biceps and strong thighs, tall frame and thick dark hair were all on magnificent display. Then he turned around and —*that ass.* It was the most glorious badonka-booty I had ever seen in my life. I had thoroughly enjoyed the sight—multiple times—by myself. It was my favorite thing to watch when I felt the feelings.

I flopped down on the couch. The wine sloshed a bit in my glass. I tossed the chips and chocolate to the coffee table and sighed loudly for good measure. All of this time spent with my head in the clouds had come back to bite me on my own badonka-booty. I was in such a swirly brain fog when I met Wyatt today that I didn't recognize him. But I might have if he had been surrounded by smoke and carrying an old lady. I sighed again.

Unfortunately, I could never face him. His hotness had blinded me from reality—twice! In the video, and in person today. How had I not recognized him? Now that I knew what I should have known this whole time: Wyatt was the Stop and Go Superman, he was one of the Sons from Monroe & Sons construction. And as if those two things were not enough—he was also the unwitting star of my nightly bubble bath fantasies. Gah! I could never look him in the eye again.

He would know. Somehow, he would figure out what I did when I watched his video and did the things, and then I would die. I would drop dead of embarrassment. I would be the first documented case. People would study it, and then I would come back to life and drop dead again.

I managed to get out of my head enough to glance at Ruby. She was laughing at my dramatics while she scrolled through her cell phone.

Um, rude.

"Are you done obsessing? Can we watch it now?" she asked me

with a smile. She placed her phone on my end table and fluffed the pillows behind her.

"I doubt I'll ever be fully done obsessing. But for now, I guess so," I groused and took a huge gulp of my wine.

"This is the best, most awesome thing that has ever happened to you, Aunt Sabrina. I'm happy for you. For real. I feel like—I think it's joy? My heart has grown or something. It feels weird."

I laughed. "Ruby, I don't think I can say yes to him. How can I go out with him after the things we said about him when we watched that video?" We had both expressed our avid appreciation of his *ass*ets. And that doesn't even get into the thoughts inappropriate for sixteen-year-old girls I had not shared with Ruby.

"I'm not gonna tell him!" she exclaimed. "No one knows but us. Let's take a sacred vow. Right now. We can take it on your wine. Can I have a sip?"

I laughed. "No, you cannot."

"Fine," she huffed. "I pinky swear that I will never tell a living soul that we perved on your future husband's viral video together." She held out her pinky.

I linked my pinky with hers.

"And so, it is done," she said solemnly. "Let's seal it by watching the video together one last time." She eyed the chocolate bar on the coffee table. "Can I have the chocolate?"

I handed it to her. "Yes, you may."

She smiled at me and clicked play.

One last time won't hurt, and Ruby was right, no one ever has to know. I settled back into the couch and sipped my wine. Ruby socked me on the arm at the first glimpse of Wyatt with old lady number one. She waggled her eyebrows and made a kissy face at me once he turned around to head back into the Stop and Go and we got a glimpse of that fine ass. I felt better about not recognizing him earlier today. You really couldn't get a good view of his face. Plus, I'll be honest—this video was all about that butt in those police uniform pants.

"Hubba hubba." Ruby snickered and took a bite of chocolate.

"Oh, give me a break, Ruby." I laughed. Then I let out a breath and just watched the rest of the video. *Damn.*

"Are you nervous?" she asked, after the video ended.

I let out a laugh. "Of course I am. I might actually end up getting a date. With him!" I pointed to the laptop. Is this my life?

"You got that right. You might get a date with the hottest guy in town. I mean—it's like Henry Cavill, Joe Manganiello, and Shawn Mendes got together and made a baby. It makes no sense, but it's hot AF. You're going from zero to *whoa* in one day."

Yep. I sure was.

Yikes.

I might see Wyatt. He might ask me out again. I would have to talk to him. I would have to use words that made sense, appropriate facial expressions, normal human body language, and everything else that people did. And I would have to do it all at the same time. I sighed and leaned back against the cushions.

She smiled sympathetically at me. "You can do it. Oh! You should wear your red sweater, just in case you see him tomorrow. It's tight around your boobs. You can substitute boobs for at least forty percent of your personality until you get comfortable around him." She looked me up and down. "With your boobs I would say you could get away with only using, like, twenty-five percent of your personality. Maybe only ten." She sat up straight in her seat. "Oh! I know! You could just smile and nod—men love that." She grinned at me and flopped back against the cushions.

I stared at her open mouthed. "Where do you come up with this stuff?"

"*Cosmo.* Also, Marianne." Marianne had been best friends with Ruby since they were toddlers.

I made a mental note to pick up a copy of *Cosmopolitan* the next time I was at the Piggly Wiggly.

"Wear your hair down too. No headband," Ruby instructed.

"Anything else?"

"No more of your nerd-wear. Ditch the cardigans and skirts,

Sabrina. Wear some of the stuff we bought when we went back to school shopping for me."

"You mean the stuff you forced me to buy?" I smirked.

"Yep. You already wear heels and makeup all the time—that's good. Just replace the skirts with the jeans we picked out and you'll be fine. Oh, start wearing your contact lenses and put your sweaters in the dryer next time you do laundry." Her broad grin and smiling eyes showed how happy she was for me. Her joy was infectious; I couldn't help but feel it too.

I shook my head with a grin. "Anything else, Yoda?"

"Yourself you should be. Funny and smart you are." She laughed, then turned serious. "I mean it, Sabrina. Don't get all hung up on stuff that doesn't matter. If he asks you out—awesome. If he doesn't, that's okay too. What matters is you put yourself out there, right? Carpe diem. Seize the dude, get a life, be yourself, and all that."

"Yeah, but who should I be? Who am I? I feel like I'm two people—the me I am at home, with you guys, and the shy bookworm librarian I am everywhere else. I've never been myself outside of this house. At least not since..."

"Since Willa left and then Mom died and you started helping Pop take care of us?" she finished for me with a knowing look.

I nodded.

"But you already know who you are. You just said it. You are *you* when you are here with us. Just do that everywhere. You're Sabrina Louise Logan. You're hilarious and smart. You are kind to everybody. You love to read—and yeah, you are kind of a nerd—but in a good way. You're also shy. But being shy doesn't mean you can't have friends or get a boyfriend if you want one. Quit being afraid to *be you*."

"You're pretty wise, Ruby. I like how you combined superficial fashion advice with high-quality life advice."

"It's one of my special gifts. I'm a complicated individual." She shrugged with a grin. Then with her eyes narrowed, she pointed a finger at me. "Just don't make me hunt him down and say yes for you. That offer still stands," she added. Offer? It felt more like a threat to me.

"Oh, I know it still stands. Don't worry. I want to do this. I think I'm ready for a change. Or at least, I want to be ready for a change."

"You deserve more out of your life," she declared. "You're the best aunt in the world. You're always there when I need you. I'm going to be there for you, Sabrina. I promise. I'm going to be just like Rupert Everett in *My Best Friend's Wedding.*"

"Oh, freaking great, Ruby. So, we're going to dance together at Wyatt's eventual wedding to some blonde bimbo? Typical for my life," I teased. I grinned at her and sipped my wine.

She threw a pillow at me. "Crap, no. I'll be like—like a fairy godmother. Bibbidi bobbidi boo." She reached out, booped my nose with her finger, and burst out laughing.

"Thank you, Ruby. You're always there for me too." I smiled at her.

Her face softened. "Well, I love you. I want you to be happy." She stood up. "I'm going to bed. But, wish me luck. You're not the only one who might end up with a date. Homecoming is coming up. And I have my eye on Trent Buckley."

"Weston's friend? Good luck, sweetheart. I love you too."

She nodded and beamed at me before turning to leave.

I finished my wine and stood up to search my closet for the red sweater Ruby mentioned. I found it and held it in front of myself as I stood in front of the mirror. I imagined what it would be like if Wyatt asked me out. What would he say to me? Would I be able to say yes to him? Or would I struggle for words and say nothing like I did this morning?

I had managed to talk to him at the park though. I couldn't believe that words had actually come out of my mouth. How had I done it? It must have been a fluke borne of this insane day. Maybe Mercury was in the seventh house of the rising sun, or something else astrological or possibly even scientific, like high tides or a full moon or chem trails seeping into my pores and changing my brain waves around…

I couldn't think straight anymore.

I inhaled a huge sigh. I couldn't even remember what we'd talked about. The kids! We had talked about the kids. I probably said something dumb. Maybe he didn't want to ask me out anymore. What would be worse—if he forgot about me, or still wanted to go out with me?

This was my constant struggle. Did I want people to know me and maybe not like me? Or did I want people to be completely indifferent toward me and not know me at all? If I could figure that out, then I could change my life. If I could figure out why I was such a freak, it would be a miracle.

My stomach lurched as I stood there and contemplated what I wanted from my life. Then I thought of all the possible ways in which I would eventually humiliate myself in front of Wyatt and it lurched with intent. I tossed the sweater on my chaise in the corner and ran for the bathroom.

After I finished throwing up, I sent a text to Mrs. MacIntyre and told her I had the stomach flu. I crawled into bed. Dread filled my heart as I thought of waking up to see my cowardly face in the mirror. I pulled the covers over my head and fell into a fitful sleep.

CHAPTER EIGHT

WYATT

It was early morning. I was in bed, something tickled my chin, and I felt purring against my chest. No, I did not have a hot date last night. Mel had stretched out on her stomach perpendicular to me on my bed to breathe down my neck. Her cat, Princess Buttercup, was the one purring. That's right, I was spooning a cat and being poked in the face by a five-year-old girl.

"Daddy, are you awake?" She poked my cheek more insistently, then tapped me on the forehead.

No, five more minutes.

All I wanted to do was stay asleep and continue my dream. Maybe wake up alone and rub one off. Was that too much to ask? I was sporting some serious wood under these covers—didn't I deserve to get rid of it the fun way? Plus, my dream was still playing like a movie in my brain, starring one hot assistant librarian named Sabrina.

"Daddy, I want waffles for breakfast. But I want the kind Grandma makes—out of a bowl. Not out of the freezer like you make." She used a finger to pry open one of my eyelids and at the same time, my alarm went off on my phone. I checked the time. *Shit.* I must have pressed snooze a few times in my sleep.

"Okay, okay. I'm awake," I yawned.

She hopped up and ran out of the room, shutting the door behind her.

I lifted the covers and tried to will my erection away by glaring at it. When willing it away didn't work, I tried bargaining: "Get lost. You can come back later." I sat there for a minute and thought of stuff I hated—doing my taxes, scrubbing the toilet, cleaning up after Princess Buttercup's toxic hairballs—until I could get up and get the girls ready for school.

I tapped on Mak's door as I passed it. Mak had just turned nine and she was a hater of mornings just like me. "Mak, wake up, honey. Mel, are you dressed?" I hollered as I lumbered down the short hallway, rolling my shoulders as I headed to the kitchen. My body was always stiff in the morning from my football days. I needed coffee—a lot of it. And a good workout.

Mel answered first, "Not yet. I have to feed Princess Buttercup."

"Okay, but give him his own food this time, only one scoop!" I shouted. "No more Froot Loops." That was not a pretty mess to clean up, no matter how colorful it was.

I made it to the kitchen and froze.

"Look, Daddy," Mel said.

I looked and immediately wished I hadn't. Mel was at the kitchen island dumping waffle mix into a plastic cereal bowl. I almost laughed when the powder puffed out of the attached straw—almost.

"I'm making waffles like Grandma." Mel had located the Bisquick. There were only so many places to hide shit in this kitchen and I was beginning to fear that I would have to hide *everything* from her.

"Dad." Mak crashed into my side and wrapped her arms around my waist. "It's so cold. I want to go back to bed."

I returned her hug, and she sagged against me.

"Come on, ladybug, get dressed. Mel is cooking us breakfast."

Mak looked at Mel and cringed. "You're a mess, Mel."

Mel stuck her tongue out in response.

I opened the freezer, grabbed a box, and put some waffles into the toaster with a pointed look at Mel. She crinkled her nose and ran toward her room.

"Girls, get a move on. We overslept today. Ten minutes left! You can't miss the bus again; it makes me late for work."

The waffles popped up. I spread peanut butter on them, and then folded them in half like tacos. Breakfast was served.

I turned back to the automatic coffee maker and reached for my cup to fill it.

"Daddy! I can't find my shoes!" Mel yelled.

"They are right by the clothes you picked out last night!" I yelled back.

"I don't want those shoes anymore!" she shouted. "They are making my socks get all bunchy." Said shoe went flying into the hallway.

I sighed, set my still empty coffee cup down, and started down the hall. "Mel, no throwing things."

"Yeah, you could kill somebody!" Mak shouted from her room. "What if you hit Princess Buttercup? Do you want him to die?"

Mel burst into tears. "I don't want Princess Buttercup to die. I love him," she sobbed.

"He won't die from a shoe." I entered her room and tried to soothe her.

She cried harder. "These leggings are itchy." She pulled them down her legs and tripped over them as she threw herself at me.

I caught her and picked her up. "How about some sweatpants?"

"Okay," she sniffed. "But only pink ones."

"Are you ready, Mak?" I shouted.

"Yeah, Dad!" she shouted back. "Yay! Waffle tacos." I heard her say from the kitchen.

One down.

"How about these?" I bent over and grabbed a pair of pink sweatpants.

"And the hoodie too." She was hanging on my neck. She laughed when I bent over again to reach the hoodie.

"You like that?"

She giggled some more.

I bent again—up and down—while I reached for a pink sock, then a T-shirt, then the other sock. She laughed the whole time. This should be a workout—maybe I could bench press her later.

"I want to touch the ceiling," she said.

I lifted her over my head.

She placed her palms on the ceiling and beamed down at me.

Worth it. Every bit.

I put her down. "Hurry and get dressed, sugar. We can't be late."

"Okay, Daddy."

"I can't find my backpack," Mak announced when I'd made it back to the kitchen.

"On the hook by the front door."

"Oh, yeah." She laughed.

I couldn't blame her; in this house it was odd whenever something was where it belonged.

"Is Mommy going to call us tonight?" Mel asked when she came out of her room.

"No. She forgot she has kids," Mak answered before I could. She stomped through the house to the front door.

I sighed. "I don't know, ladybug. I hope so."

"Will you remind her to call us?" Mel's big green eyes shone with hope.

I sighed. I'd texted and called Isabelle every time she missed her calls with the girls, but she had not answered me—not once. We'd been back in Green Valley close to three months and they'd had only one brief call with their mother.

"I don't think she'll be calling tonight," I admitted. Something had to give. I couldn't keep making excuses for her. I couldn't keep stringing the girls along with no real answers. I knew what feeling like you weren't good enough could do to a person and I didn't want that for my girls.

Mel's face fell.

"But I'll still try to remind her," I promised. What else could I do?

"Thank you, Daddy."

That smile, that hope in her eyes—it was going to kill me to see it gone later this evening.

I could shield the girls from a lot. Give me a homework problem to solve, a bug to squash, or someone to knock out. But there was no way to protect them from the hurt of losing their mother. There was no way to protect them from this pain. All I could do was be here to pick up the pieces, and it pissed me right off.

"Come on, ladybugs, it's time to catch the bus," I announced. "Backpack," I reminded Mel when she ran for the door without it. She spun around with a laugh and ran back to get it. I slipped on my shoes and met Mak at the front door.

"She forgets everything," Mak complained.

"Maybe she has a lot on her mind," I suggested.

"I don't think she has anything on her mind," she shot back.

"Mak, not everyone deals with their feelings the same way. If you want to talk about your mom, just say something. Promise?"

She looked at me with sad eyes before hardening her expression and rolling her eyes. "I don't want to talk about *her*."

I knelt in front of her. "I love you. I'm lucky I get to be your dad."

She blinked rapidly and looked away. "I love you too," she whispered.

Mel entered the room, dropped her backpack on the floor, and ran at Mak and me with open arms. "I love y'all," she said while trying to wrap us both up in her tiny arms. I gave her a squeeze then stood up.

"I love you too, Mel." Mak sighed and returned her hug.

"And I love you both—the most." I smiled at them and then snagged Mel's backpack from the floor. I threw it over my shoulder and opened the front door. "After you, my ladies." I swept my arm out as I held the door for them.

"Daddy, you are so silly." Mel giggled and skipped down the front walk.

Thankfully, we made it to the bus stop on time.

When I finally made it back inside, I decided to skip coffee at home and go straight to the shower. I could grab a coffee with Jackson at Daisy's Nut House on the way to the station. I shot him a text and we arranged to meet there.

I stepped under the hot spray. I let it beat down on my shoulders while I tried to stop thinking, worrying, driving myself crazy.

It was barely seven thirty in the morning and I already wanted to go back to bed. These sleepless nights were doing me in. I didn't cope well when I couldn't fix a problem.

I adjusted the water, closed my eyes, and let my mind drift. I smiled involuntarily when it drifted back to sweet Sabrina with the gorgeous red lips, long black curls, and intriguing wiggle in her walk. I had been thinking of her more than I would like to admit. That woman was a knockout, but she didn't act like it. She had no game. Her game was so bad it *became* game. It was clear when I spoke with her that her shyness embarrassed her. It shouldn't. It was hot. It attracted me like a damn magnet. It made me want to do something cheesy, like slay a dragon for her, or protect her from something, anything—*everything*.

She was shy, and I barely knew her, which probably made the thoughts running through my head inappropriate.

I hadn't had a woman since Isabelle and that was over two years ago. I was due—more like *over*due. It had been a long time since I'd had someone warm and soft in my bed. Princess Buttercup didn't count. Plus, Sabrina also seemed to be sweet and sincere, and I'd never had someone like that.

I sighed and turned the water to cold.

I had to focus on my girls and that was okay. I needed to learn how to date *and* be a father. My girls came first, and they always would. I needed to find a woman who could understand that.

A woman like Sabrina.

The way her eyes lit up when she saw Mak and Mel at the park the other day made me believe that she might understand where I was coming from. The way she seemed to love her nephew like he was her own child told me she would be worth the effort to find out for sure.

I shut the water off, quickly dressed, and headed out to meet Jackson at Daisy's. Thoughts of Sabrina swirled through my brain as I drove. I couldn't get her out of my head. Every day this week I had stopped by the library with no sign of her. Yet, I couldn't make myself give up. Part of me wondered if my attraction to challenging women would always be my downfall.

"Hey, Monroe!" Jackson shouted when I pulled into the parking lot.

I got out and met him at the door to Daisy's Nut House.

"So, is today the day?" He grinned at me as I approached. And I have to say that his grin was the shit-eating kind. I got the sense that Jackson liked to know about everything going on in Green Valley.

"The day for what?" I pretended like I didn't know what he was talking about.

"The day to go to the library—again." Maybe he wanted me to be shot down by Sabrina for the sake of commiseration. Or maybe he was just nosy.

We turned to head inside.

"Officer! Deputy Sheriff! Wyatt Monroe! Hey!" I looked over my shoulder to see a girl who looked almost exactly like Sabrina wave her arms wildly while walking toward us from the parking lot, followed by another familiar kid. "Weston, stop walking," she said and grabbed his arm to stop him. His face was stuck in his phone.

I smiled. "Hey, Weston," I greeted my niece Lizzy's boyfriend. I'd met him a few times over the summer. He was a good kid.

"Hi," he greeted me. "Wait—Wyatt?" He turned to the girl. "He's the one?"

"God, you need to spend less time on your phone. The world—it spins all the time—not just when you're looking, Weston. Or maybe, you should just be less slow," she berated him. "I'm Ruby." She held her hand out, and I shook it. "Sabrina is my aunt—"

"Ruby, stop. She'll kill you," Weston interrupted her. I couldn't picture timid Sabrina killing anyone, much less losing her temper. But there was always more to people than met the eye. Weston's statement only added to my intriguement—it should be a word—of Sabrina.

"Weston, shush. This whole thing is taking too long. And no, she won't kill me because this never happened. Right?" She raised her eyebrows at me.

I raised mine back with amusement. "I won't say anything."

Jackson chuckled then narrowed his eyes in thought. "Ruby, your voice sounds familiar. Are you the producer of Cletus' podcast? A teenage girl?" He scoffed.

She stepped back and looked down at herself with her jaw dropped in feigned amazement. "Holy crap, a teenage girl. That's me, Ruby Adams." She held her hand out and Jackson shook it.

"Is your middle name really Tuesday?" Jackson asked, oblivious to her sarcastic jibe. "And what about the dog catchers, are they going to be back on the podcast?"

Ruby turned red. "Cletus has a big mouth, dang it. And I'm not sure about the dog catchers. They aren't speaking to Cletus or to each other at the moment—it's so ugly, y'all. I'm trying to smooth it over—"

"Her middle name really is Tuesday," Weston interrupted without looking up. He was scrolling through his phone again.

"Yeah, and that frickin' song is all I hear in the halls at school now, thanks to Cletus and his big ol' mouth," she huffed.

"This is interesting. I feel like I'm back in high school. I'll meet you at your locker later, Monroe." Jackson slapped my shoulder and stood back to watch the scene unfold.

"I'll be sure not to interrupt your kissing-Ashley's-ass schedule, James," I shot back at him.

Jackson grinned and rolled his eyes.

Ruby sighed impatiently. "Whatever, y'all. He needs a hint." She looked at me. "Find a way to get Sabrina's number and call her. She's shy but she'll be better on the phone. Her mind scrambles when she has to look people in the eye. I don't know if it's physical. Maybe her olfactory nerves affect her brain waves when it comes to talking to people. I'm doing my science project on it. Synesthesia and communication or being visually overstimulated when you are shy and get nervous. I haven't narrowed it down yet and I doubt that Sabrina would let me study her anyway—I digressed! Shoot!" She pointed at me and continued, "And, no. I'm not going to give you her number. That would be cheating. That's it. That's the hint."

"Maybe I'll see if she's around today," I said. I couldn't help it. Sabrina had me interested. I wanted to ask Ruby more questions, but I was unwilling to endure the heaps of shit Jackson would shovel my way if I participated any further in this conversation.

"She's supposed to close the library tonight," Weston added then looked to Ruby for approval.

"Good job, Weston." She patted his arm. "We're done here. Carry on, officers. Let's go." She and Weston headed into Daisy's Nut House.

Jackson and I exchanged a look, then followed behind them to get breakfast.

CHAPTER NINE

SABRINA

I'd forced myself to come back to work today, freaking Tuesday—five days after I'd called in sick. It was my day to do the afternoon story hour, which was always my favorite day of the week. I loved kids. And I liked to think they loved me back. Naomi always stood at the edge of the small children's section and greeted each parent and chatted—about whatever humans chat about—before beginning her story hour. I always hid in the horror section and peeked around the shelves until all the kiddos were seated in the story circle before I began mine. Some kids would sit on the colorful beanbags and some would sit crisscross-applesauce on the solar system rug that covered the floor. Whenever they were ready for me, I would make my way to join them. I never looked beyond the circle, *ever*. I couldn't match a kid to a parent if I tried and I liked it that way. I wouldn't be able to read to the kids if I saw that their parents were watching me.

Kids never judged. Kids accepted differences and found them interesting instead of weird. A kid would hold your hand and try to help if you were scared or didn't know what to say. In fact, sometimes our story circle became a circle of tiny held hands. Some of the smaller kids cried when they were separated from their parent, even if it was only by a matter of feet. I understood exactly what that felt like.

When I was five, I was separated from my mother. Unfortunately for me, it was for more than a few feet. I had always felt like the kids knew that I got where they were coming from. They knew that I understood their fears. If a child started to cry, I would sit on the floor and hold their hand to read the story from within the circle instead of on the squat, red rocking chair at the side of it. I'd never had a child leave my circle.

I peeked around the shelf to see if they were ready for me. I clutched my copy of *Alexander and the Terrible, Horrible, No Good, Very Bad Day*—a book I could relate to on a soul-deep level—to my chest, hurried over to join them, and sat in the little red rocking chair.

"Knock knock, Miss Sabrina," a tiny voice said once I'd settled in.

I grinned and answered, "Who's there?"

"Duane."

"Duane, who?" I said and grinned at Benjamin—my favorite little charmer with the gorgeous brown eyes. I loved it when he attended story time. This kid cracked me up.

"Duane the pool, I'm dwowning."

"Good one, honey," I said with a laugh.

"Ooh, I'm gonna tell Uncle Duane," his tiny little brother threatened.

"It's just a joke, Andy. You're so dramatic." Benjamin rolled his eyes then looked to me with one eyebrow up for some commiseration.

I winked at him. He winked back at me, the adorable little flirt.

Uncle Duane. Winston? They were probably talking about him. Green Valley might as well change its name to Winstonville there were so many of them. It occurred to me that I may well have been trading knock-knock jokes off and on for the last couple years with Sienna Diaz and Jethro Winston's child. I immediately shoved that thought right out of my head. My eyes got big, but I avoided lifting them beyond the circle. It was better that way. Better if I didn't know for sure.

But, was it?

My therapist had always told me I needed to expand my circle. Since my sister died, my circle consisted of my family and no one else.

Sure, I had people like Naomi and Mrs. MacIntyre with whom I would exchange the occasional pleasantry or talk about work, but I didn't have friends to confide in. I could admit that I was afraid to let anyone new into my heart. After losing my mother, my grandparents, then my sister, I feared the eventual loss of anyone else. I found it highly ironic and insane that people literally surrounded me right now while I was having these thoughts. But, like with everything else in my life, I would never make a change unless something hit me over the head. I needed more than an Oprah-style 'aha' moment. I required brute force or pummeling by the complete and utter obvious to get me out of my head and into the world around me.

What would Sienna Diaz do?

Sienna Diaz would definitely look up.

I took a huge breath and raised my head.

I saw parents chatting together quietly in the corner. And I saw Winstons. Of course I did— they were everywhere. I saw Jethro Winston holding a baby in his arms. I gulped when I recalled the chicken incident at Genie's, but I managed to shake that embarrassment off and sallied forth. I saw Drew's wife, Ashley Winston-Runous, with a darling toddler on her hip.

I smiled shakily at Ashley and Jethro. "Would you like to sit with your little ones in the story circle?" I offered. Kids should not miss out on stories just because they were too little to sit still. I kicked myself at the thought that I had neglected to be inclusive while dwelling in my shyness and not *looking up*—not looking outside of the circle.

Ashley returned my smile. "Yes, that would be wonderful." Ashley and Jethro joined us.

I was ready to begin when an older woman rushed up, waving at me with a huge smile on her face. I recognized her as Wyatt's mother. She had dropped the girls off at the park the other day. "We're late—I'm so sorry. Go on, girls."

My eyes bugged out behind my glasses for a moment as Wyatt's girls darted around the shelves and sat down. Yeah, my glasses were still on my face like a shield and nerd wear still covered my body from head to toe. I was not ready to take Ruby's advice from last week and change my look. I placed the book in my lap, smoothed my long skirt over my legs then gripped the arms of the rocking chair as the girls approached.

"We're so sorry we're late, Miss Sabrina," Makenna said softly.

"It's okay, sweetheart. No trouble at all. Hi, Melissa," I greeted Wyatt's youngest daughter.

She grinned at me; she had lost a front tooth. Adorable.

"Ready?" I asked and a chorus of enthusiastic "yesses" answered me.

After I finished with the story, I made myself stay and say goodbye instead of running off to hide while everyone left. #progress

The rest of the day moved slowly. I couldn't concentrate. I had one thing on my mind—and it was not my job. *Spoiler alert!* My mind was on Wyatt. Lucky for me the library was slow. Naomi had already left for the day, and Mrs. MacIntyre was taking a break at Daisy's Nut House, leaving me alone in the library. I organized the front counter and occupied myself with meaningless busy work until there was none left to do. Then I stood there and brooded. Brooding sucked if you didn't have wine, or chocolate. Unfortunately, it was the end of the day. I was closing the library tonight, and I had eaten all of my purse Kit Kats yesterday.

Despite my earlier success with my story hour I found myself growing nervous again. Wyatt's girls had been here, but there was no sign of Wyatt. He hadn't said exactly when he would stop by. It might not even be tonight. What if he had stopped by last week when I had taken to my bed like a swooning Victorian? What if he had changed his mind about me and found someone else to pursue? Or worse, what if he had died? Poor Makenna and Melissa…

Stop it. Just because someone doesn't show up when you want them to, doesn't mean they hate you or died. Get a grip, Sabrina.

My cell phone vibrated then binged in my pocket. I jumped out of my skin and let out a quiet scream followed by a startled laugh. I took it out and opened the text, from my father. He wanted me to stop at the Piggly Wiggly and pick up the Dr. Pepper that Ruby and Weston didn't get the other day. I returned the text and added that to my list of things to do. I set my phone on the counter and did some of the deep breathing exercises my therapist had recommended for me to use when I felt nervous. It didn't help. I ran down the short hall to the bathroom to check my face again and possibly throw up.

Nope, I had not turned into a self-assured, confident woman in the half hour it had been since the last time I checked my face. And nope, I was not going to throw up, but my stomach felt like it was in a nervous knot. I shook my head at myself in the mirror. I let out a huge breath and flipped my hair. I pursed my lips at myself in the mirror—MAC Lady Danger red was still in place. At least I didn't look like dog doodoo, even if I felt like a big fat pile of it.

I stared at my eyes that had seen too much.—and yet so little at the same time. I'd had a front row seat for death and birth, and both had left me afraid to live. Now, here I stood, stuck in the mirror, wanting to live so badly and not knowing how. Could someone be bad at life? Was living a skill?

Alas, I was not being paid to hide in the bathroom and stare at my face. I had to get back out front. I opened the door and walked down the hall. Halfway to the checkout counter, I stopped short, took a huge step backward flattening myself against the wall when I saw that I was no longer alone in the library.

Wyatt was leaning one hip against the counter and looking around the library—*for me?*

I'd never had a man look for me before, which was probably good because this was the first time in my life I had ever wanted to be found.

He was in uniform—a short-sleeved khaki brown shirt this time. I almost drooled when I noticed how tight it was around his biceps and chest, just like in the Stop and Go video. Except in the video his shirt was navy blue, from when he worked for Nashville PD.

Quit thinking about that video. Just stop it before you get all tingly and stupid.

Too late—I got the tingles when I peeked around the corner and saw him turn around. The darker khaki green pants did wonderful things for what had to be my number one favorite part of his body.

And the belt didn't hurt either. It was full of badass stuff like his gun and radio, and probably handcuffs. That booty was going to get me into trouble. I wanted to smack it or pat it, or maybe even bite it. I had never wanted to bite a butt before, and it was freaking me out.

My heart raced wildly in my chest, my stomach dropped, and my mind had left the library. Wyatt gave me all the feelings. Every single one. In all the best places. I felt my knees tremble and get weak as I walked toward him, with the counter between us.

"Hi," I said, barely making a sound.

He heard me though, his head jerked around to where I stood. His eyes caressed my face as a slow smile crossed his. "Hey, darlin'. I missed you last week. Mrs. MacIntyre said you were sick. I hope you're feeling better."

I smiled at him. I opened my mouth to speak but nothing came out. He made me nervous. But not the nervous that made me want to vomit. This was a new nervous—this nervous made me want to be close to him, maybe even kiss him, while at the same time wanting to run and hide from him. I didn't understand it. Plus, he tried to find me last week. Oh. My. God.

His eyes drifted over me, then lingered on my sweater. He reached out a fingertip and touched the pin on the lapel of the shawl collar of my cozy gray cardigan. "I still believe in 398.2," he read aloud. "What does that mean?"

"Huh?" I murmured. I was lost—like, through the freaking door to Narnia, out of my mind lost. Who was I trying to be, standing in front of this gorgeous man hoping for a date? This was a normal occurrence for most people, but I felt like a freak. "Oh, my pin." I let out a nervous laugh. "398.2 is a Dewey Decimal number. It's where fairy tales are located in the library."

"You believe in fairy tales?" A slow smile crossed his face as his eyes met and held mine captive.

I blushed; good thing I wasn't wearing that red sweater Ruby told me I should wear. My face would have matched it right now. "Uh, I'd like to think good things can happen, um, happy endings and stuff—I don't know." I stammered.

"You're adorable," he said to me. He must like red-faced, stammering nerds. Lucky me?

I smiled softly. "Thank you." I had no idea what to say to him. I remembered Ruby's advice from the other night, *smile and nod.* I could do that. And according to Ruby and *Cosmo,* he would probably like it.

His smile got bigger, and that scrumptious dimple appeared. "Is this your phone?" He gestured to my cell that I had left on the counter.

I nodded.

"May I?" His head tilted to the phone.

I nodded again. Then I added a smile to change it up.

He picked it up, swiped to the keypad, and entered a phone number.

I jumped and giggled softly when I heard his phone ring.

"Got your number." He chuckled. "And you definitely have mine." His eyes burned into mine.

I couldn't look away—not that I wanted to.

He handed the phone back to me, brushing my hand gently with his. I clutched the phone to my chest.

"About that date..."

My eyes got big.

"Do you like the Front Porch?"

I nodded. Gah! I needed some words.

His mouth quirked up at the corner. "Would you like to have dinner there with me next Saturday?"

I smiled again, then started nodding.

His sideways smile turned to a full one. "The Logan Ranch, right? Can I pick you up at six?"

I kept nodding like a simpleton.

His smile changed to one that was sweet and understanding, my heart melted. "Can I hear the words, darlin'?"

"Yes," I whispered. Then raised my voice to what I hoped was a normal volume. "I would love to go out to dinner with you, Wyatt. I will text you the gate code. You can drive right in."

"Perfect. I have to get back to work. I'll call you soon, and hopefully I'll see you around town."

"Okay. Goodbye, Wyatt," I murmured.

"Bye, Sabrina," he said and walked out of the library.

Holy crap. I have a date.

I scrolled to my recent calls and there it was. I had his number. I saved it, then added the heart eyes emoji next to his name. I looked at it for a few minutes while more tingles distributed themselves throughout my body. How would I ever sit across from him at dinner? Or maybe even kiss him someday? Just thinking about him was making me melt into a puddle of Sabrina goo.

CHAPTER TEN

SABRINA

The rest of my shift at the library had gone by in a blur. After Wyatt left, I lost all track of reality. It felt like I was stuck in a delicious daydream I couldn't get out of. Who knew how long I'd been sitting in my Jeep staring mindlessly at the pig in the middle of the Piggly Wiggly sign like a ninny? I sure didn't. I had come here straight after work to pick up the Dr. Pepper and I was afraid even such a small thing like grocery shopping would be too much for me to focus on.

I sighed and got out, put my purse in a buggy, and headed inside the store. I was wandering slowly toward the produce aisle on the edge of the store, still lost in my daydreams, when I felt someone grab my arm.

"You can't take Harry from me, Sabrina. I'm not signing the fucking papers. Tell your father to drop this whole adoption idea," he said, then jerked me around to face him. I hit my hip hard on the edge of the refrigerated bin that held the bagged salad. I lost hold of my buggy, it rolled away to stop against the banana display.

Ouch. I stumbled into him, then lunged back with clumsy steps before righting myself and standing firm.

Michael. That rat-bastard, mother-effing, son of a Slytherin.

Weston was not the only one that lost his temper whenever his father was around. I had spent most of my young life watching my sister cry over this a-hole. Then I had the misfortune of watching Weston and Ruby cry over him too. Luckily, Harry didn't know him at all, and that was why I was going to adopt Harry. Weston and Ruby were almost adults, but Harry was only nine. My father was afraid he would die before Harry turned eighteen and wanted to make sure that I got to keep him.

After Cora died, my father had threatened Michael with lawyers and custody battles and probably even violence to get custody of the kids. Michael's parents took my father's side. They disowned him after the despicable stunts he pulled right after Cora's death. Trying to take the kids when they hadn't seen him in years. Trying to make my father give him money and Cora's car, even though they were divorced. Trying to visit Harry while he was still in the neonatal unit in the hospital. I couldn't even remember all of it.

Michael used to be a nice guy. He was once a good husband and father. Then he got into gambling—drag races, horse races, poker games—anything he could bet on. I used to hear him and Cora fighting about all the money he had lost. He'd even been to jail a few times—Cora had a fit about that. He hung around at the Dragon Biker Bar and cheated on my sister with girls from the Pink Pony and the G-Spot, a couple of local strip clubs. He used to be an accountant with an office in town. We would sometimes see odd, criminal looking people going in and out of it. He had probably helped them cheat on their taxes or laundered dirty drug money or something. I don't know what he does now for a living, and I don't care. I just know he is bad news and I don't want him anywhere near the kids. I saw the hurt he caused my sister and the kids, and I hated him more than anything. I glared at him.

He lurched forward and grabbed my upper arms to shake me, so hard I felt like a bobblehead doll. "Who do you think you are, huh? You dumb fucking bitch. Harry is mine. They're all mine." He stared daggers at me. I would probably have bruises later from the way his fingers dug into my arms.

I steadied my head. "Let go of me," I hissed and tried to wiggle out of his grasp.

He'd never put his hands on me or Cora or any of us before. He'd also never talked to me like this, ever. It shocked me, but I was not too shocked to remember the self-defense training my father suggested I take at the community center last year. I raised my arms straight up and brought them down hard, loosening his grip on me. I stepped back.

"Leave me alone," I managed to say. I couldn't seem to catch my breath.

I was shy. I could get nervous and freak out, but that didn't mean I was a pushover. And if it involved my family—watch out. I would do anything for my family, especially Harry. He needed me the most.

He lunged forward to—I didn't know what he would do, but I was not about to take any crap from him.

I pushed him in the chest, hard. "Go away, Michael."

He stumbled back a few steps, looking first shocked, then pissed.

I was not kidding myself. If Michael really wanted to hurt me, he could. I got in a lucky shot and surprised him.

"What the hell has gotten into you, Sabrina?" he yelled and shoved me back. My bottom hit the salad bin. I almost fell in, but I managed to throw my hands out and catch the edge in time.

"Stay away from me!" I shouted and pushed myself up. I sidestepped the salad bin and backed up.

Michael followed me until I was up against the shelves with nowhere to go. He stood there looming over me, the anger in his eyes scaring me. He didn't look right; he was shaky. His eyes were red-rimmed and glassy, the darkness beneath them stood out against his pale face.

Michael whirled at the sound of rapidly approaching footsteps.

"Sabrina!" It was Wyatt with Jackson. Both in uniform, rushing up the aisle. "Are you okay?" Wyatt asked, inserting himself between Michael and me.

"Yes, I'm okay," my voice trembled. I hated how weak it sounded.

Michael turned and started to walk away.

"Don't make me chase you," Wyatt growled. My eyes darted to Wyatt. He was so tall and broad as he stood there; he looked like an immovable force. Like he could just glare Michael into submission. It calmed me down. He wouldn't let Michael hurt me.

Jackson moved to block Michael's path from behind and prevent him from leaving.

I stood there and tried to catch my breath and calm my racing heart.

Michael froze then turned back to face Wyatt. "We're family, Sabrina and me. I used to be her brother-in-law," he explained with a phony smile. "We had a disagreement about the kids is all."

"Is that true? Was it just a disagreement?" Wyatt asked me.

I shook my head—too freaked out to speak.

"Did he hurt you, touch you, threaten you?" Jackson asked me as he stepped closer to Michael. Jackson was scary too. I'd never noticed what a badass he was. I guess all the Stephen King talk at the library made me see him as a book buddy, not a hot sheriff. Which was good. Because if I had seen him as a hot sheriff, I would have never been able to talk to him at all.

I nodded. "He shook me. I almost fell into the salad," I whispered.

"Adams, you're under arrest," Jackson said and pulled out a pair of handcuffs.

"She pushed me—arrest her too!" Michael shouted.

"Sabrina pushed you?" Jackson laughed. "Yeah, okay. We'll talk about that at the station. Would you like your regular holding cell, Adams?" Jackson said as he led Michael away. He turned back to Wyatt. "Finish dinner, and take care of her. I got this."

I heard Jackson read Michael his rights as they headed to the exit. I stood frozen in place and watched them go.

"Hey, it's okay now," Wyatt said and took my hand.

I held on and took a deep breath. "Thank you."

"You're shaking." He pulled me into a hug and held me. I clutched at his shirt and leaned against him for a second. He felt safe, warm, and strong.

"Better?" he whispered in my ear.

I nodded. I was all out of words and out of my mind with worry for the kids.

"Come on, I'll walk with you while you get what you need."

"Thank you," I murmured.

"You're welcome, darlin'. Is that yours?" He gestured to my buggy with my purse still in it.

"Yes. I only need a couple of things. Thank you for staying with me."

"My pleasure." He reached up and brushed a strand of hair out of my face.

Oh my...

Heat flooded my body, shoving a bit of the fear out. I blindly reached for a bag of salad from the bin and tossed it into my buggy.

"I heard him yell at you. Does he bother you often?"

"No, he's never acted like that before. And it's been months since I've even seen him in town."

"You let us know if he does it again later, okay?" We passed the bakery and headed toward the snack aisle.

"I will." I grabbed a box of Goldfish crackers and tossed it into the buggy.

"My daughters love those," he remarked.

"A few years ago, Harry would eat nothing but these crackers. He's come a long way."

"He's a cute kid. Is Michael his father?"

"Unfortunately. But my father has custody for now. My father also has custody of Weston and Ruby, my other nephew and niece." I reached for a box of Twinkies off the display. I might need those later. They paired well with rosé, and this would definitely be a wine night.

"Twinkies, huh? My favorite." His sideways smile was adorable and sexy at the same time. The odd combination drew me in—as well as scared the crap out of me.

"I can't quit them, even if they are completely artificial," I confessed.

"Same." He grinned and reached out to tug lightly on a curl that had swooped over my shoulder. "You take care of him, don't you?"

"Harry? Yeah, since he was born."

"I never knew your sister. And I didn't realize you were one of Doc Logan's daughters until after I went back to the station, the day I met you."

"I'm easy to overlook," I murmured.

He raised an eyebrow. "No, Sabrina, you are not. You had to be hiding out somewhere. And once I found you, I asked you out. It didn't take me long now, did it?"

I blushed. "Oh, yeah. Um, are you on duty?"

"I'm on my break. We stopped here to get dinner and I'm glad we did. Because here you are." He reached over and touched my nose with his index finger.

"Boop," I said. I felt my cheeks heat as a massive blush rose up my neck to cover my face.

"Boop?" He chuckled.

"You booped my nose," I explained.

"I couldn't help myself. You have a cute nose. I love your little freckles." His gorgeous brown eyes were in full twinkle.

My eyes widened as I took in his smiling face. "Thank you," I said. I was in imminent danger of a deep swoon. I gripped the handle of my buggy for support. "And I love your dimple. I want to climb inside of it and have a tea party." *What the heck did I just say?*

"What?" His chuckle had disappeared. It had turned into a full-blown, glorious, belly laugh. "I've never heard that one before. But I'll have a tea party with you any day, darlin'."

"Well, okay. Then I'll shop for tiny cups."

"You do that. Then let me know when, and I'll bring the tiny sandwiches."

I was laughing with him and not dying of an incendiary blush. This was awesome and unexpected. *I like him.*

"I like you," I said. *What is wrong with me? I need some freaking guile.*

"I like you too, Sabrina," he said and rested his hand next to mine on the buggy. *Then again, maybe guileless is the way to go.*

I grinned at him.

He grinned back.

We had already stopped walking, but now we were just standing there, staring into each other's eyes—grinning together next to the huge tower of stacked Dr. Pepper, next to the deli.

"Hey, Wyatt."

We both jumped and laughed.

The deli clerk who broke our moment was standing behind the counter waving Wyatt's sandwich in the air. "I have your call-in order ready," he said.

"Thanks, I'll pay up front." Wyatt turned and grabbed his sandwich.

"You're welcome. Hey, Sabrina, are you okay? I heard Michael yellin' at you. I was about to run over and help, then I heard Wyatt and Jackson putting the smack down on him and just stayed put."

I looked at his concerned face. "I'm fine. Thank you for asking."

He grinned at Wyatt. "Good thing y'all showed up. I haven't kicked any ass since way back in high school."

Wyatt laughed. "I'll see you tomorrow, man. Take it easy."

He waved to us as we walked away.

"Do you need anything else?" Wyatt asked me as we walked.

"No, I have everything."

We headed to the front of the store to pay. As we approached, Sara Stokes waved us over to her lane. From what I had heard, her husband was almost as big a jerk as Michael. "Sabrina! Are you okay? I heard the scuffle with Michael—I had the nine and the one already dialed on the telephone, but Wyatt and Jackson showed up before I finished callin'. Hey, Wyatt—or should I call you Piggly Wiggly Superman." She laughed.

Wyatt shot a quick glance at me then shook his head. "No way, Sara. Please don't get that started." He laughed it off, but I could tell he was embarrassed.

I placed my items on the counter, and Sara grinned at me as she rang me up. I had not realized she knew who I was. But I probably should have. This was Green Valley; if I knew about her a-hole husband, she was sure to know about my a-hole ex-brother-in-law. Small towns and all that… "Uh, thank you," I said with a small smile.

"You're welcome, Sabrina," she answered. Ruby was right—I was not as invisible as I had thought. Deep down I knew it was true already. But acknowledging it was another story. I found the idea of being known around town both oddly pleasant as well as terrifying. I shoved it out of my mind to ponder later. Or not.

After my stuff was all bagged up and we were ready to leave I made sure to look at her as I thanked her instead of just mumbling it to my purse. And I smiled and said goodbye just to show myself I could.

Wyatt took my bag and carried it for me as he walked me to my Jeep.

"Feeling better?" he asked.

"Yes. Thank you." I smiled up at his gorgeous face and felt the urge to kiss him. Instead I opened my back door so he could put my bags inside.

"Can you tell me what happened between you and Michael?"

I explained what had happened before he showed up with Jackson.

"I'll put it in the report. We'll call you if there are any further questions."

"Okay."

He opened my door and gestured for me to climb inside. "I want you to lock up your Jeep and go straight home. Is your father going to be there?"

"Yes."

"Good, tell him what happened."

"I will, Wyatt."

"I'll call you tonight. Would that be okay?"

Yay! Yes!

"Okay, I'd like that," I murmured.

"Good. Until tonight, darlin'." He booped my nose, shut my door for me with a big grin, and turned away.

I watched him walk to his patrol car and get inside. He waved to me before he drove off.

I backed out of my space and turned on to the road to home.

It wasn't until I pulled up to the garage that I realized I forgot the dang Dr. Pepper again.

CHAPTER ELEVEN

WYATT

"We're home," I said softly as I pulled into the garage. We'd had dinner at my parents' house. My father was hard at work, trying to land a big project in town, or so my mother said—he hadn't joined us like he was supposed to, much to her consternation.

"Daddy, is Mommy going to call us tonight?" Mel yawned from her booster seat in the back.

Shit.

I had tried calling Isabelle several times today, like I did every day. Her phone number no longer worked. That was a big, fat clue to the status of my ex-wife's relationship with my girls if I ever had one.

Mak got out of the car and slammed her door. She stomped to the door that led inside the house and stood there with her foot tapping and an angry look on her face.

"She's not going to call us, Mel. She doesn't want us anymore!" Mak shouted before I could answer.

"She doesn't want us anymore?" Fat tears filled Mel's eyes and spilled down her cheeks.

"I'm so sorry. I couldn't call her today. Her phone number wouldn't work. I don't think she'll be calling anymore. It will be just you girls and me from now on." It was better to get this done—like ripping off a Band-Aid—then we could heal.

Mak gasped and turned around to stare at me. She was angry with Isabelle before. But I was afraid that I'd just broken her heart.

I pulled Mel out of her booster seat and held her against my chest. She wrapped her tiny arms around my neck and sobbed. I headed for the door and unlocked it to go inside.

"Come on, ladybug," I said to Mak and took her hand.

I expected her to pull away, but she didn't.

"I want my mommy," Mel cried into my shoulder. Her body shook as her arms tightened around my neck.

"I know, honey. I know. We'll be okay, shh..."

I glanced down at Mak. She was looking away from me, but I saw her wiping her cheeks with her free hand.

Damn you, Isabelle.

We crossed through the entryway to the hall. Princess Buttercup stretched in the window then hopped down to follow us.

I flipped on the hall light and headed for my bedroom. I sat on the edge of the bed. Mel curled up against my chest like she used to do when she was a baby. I scooted to the middle of the mattress, my back against the headboard. I stretched out my legs, shifted Mel to one side, and held my other arm open for Mak. "Come on, sweetheart," I said.

Her face fell as she crawled over to me. The tears that had been hiding behind the wall of anger she had built up over the last few months finally spilled over. I pulled her onto my lap. Her little body shuddered against mine as she finally let go and cried for the loss of her mother.

"It's okay, just let it out," I whispered.

She clutched at my shirt and buried her face in my chest.

I had no clue what to do. There was nothing I *could* do. I couldn't force Isabelle to be their mother. I couldn't *make* her call them. I'd tried that before. I had left message after message. I texted and I called her every single goddamn day with no answer. Now, with her cell phone number no longer working, I had no way to contact her. And Jefferson Hickson's maid or secretary or whoever the fuck answered the phones at their house threatened to call the police on me if I called there ever again.

Rage filled my body. Rage that had nowhere to go.

I looked down at Mel. She had fallen asleep, her face still wet with tears. Mak gasped and hiccupped out the rest of her tears, then closed her eyes. They had cried themselves to sleep. It was only seven o'clock. Normally, they would argue to stay up later.

I wanted to hit something. Punch a hole straight through the fucking wall.

Frustrated tears filled my eyes, but I forced them back before they could fall.

I looked down at their sleeping faces. I had never felt so powerless in my life. I did not understand how Isabelle could do this. I had *everything*, the entire world, right here in my arms and it hadn't been good enough for her.

How could that be?

How had she fooled me so well? All those wasted years...I should have packed up the girls and come back to Green Valley as soon as Mel was born instead of trying to hold on to a worthless woman like Isabelle.

I settled Mak down at my side. She tucked her hands under her cheek and sank into my pillow. I shifted Mel over and settled her next to Mak. She didn't wake either. I took off their shoes and covered them with my quilt. Princess Buttercup curled up at their feet and went to sleep.

My heart twisted into a knot at the sight of them snuggled together on my pillow. I was no longer tense with anger; I felt useless, worthless, stuck in place, with nothing I could do for them and no idea how to make it better.

Their mother was gone. It was obvious now. She didn't care, and she wasn't going to visit them.

Anger flooded through my veins again when I studied their sleeping faces. I stood up and left the room.

On my way to the living room, I saw the pile of mail from this afternoon sitting under the mail slot and stopped to pick it up. Cold anticipation filled my heart when I saw a large manila envelope in the middle of the pile.

I inhaled a slow, shaky breath and sat on the couch. I unsealed the tape that held the silver tab down and pulled out a sheaf of papers. One small sheet fluttered to the floor, and I bent to retrieve it.

It was a check. For one million dollars. Signed by Jefferson Hickson.

A bitter laugh escaped me as I rifled through the papers and saw Isabelle's handwriting. She wanted to relinquish her parental rights to the girls. She had written them goodbye letters. She was trying to buy her way out of their lives with a million dollars of guilt money. The rest of it was just legal documents. Sign on the dotted line, take the money, and the girls were all mine.

I finally had my answers.

I tossed the papers to the table. I was tempted to tear that check apart––fuck her guilty conscience. But that wasn't my choice. That money belonged to the girls. I opened the drawer to the coffee table and slipped the check and the papers inside. I would ask my mother what I should do with it.

I stared at the walls, the stone fireplace, and the toys that littered the corner in front of the pink toy box. The silence of the sleeping house enveloped me; it pulsed inside my ears. My mind raced as I took in the walls that suddenly felt too small to contain me.

I stood up, paced to the kitchen, and opened the refrigerator. My throat felt tight, and my eyes felt hot. I grabbed a bottle of water, removed the cap, and drank a few sips before capping it to hold against my forehead as my breaths grew shallow. The cold did nothing to counter the anger that simmered in my heart.

I walked back to the living room and stood at the tall uncovered window next to the front door to stare out at the dark night. The wind scraped the tree branches against the house and set the dead leaves to flying. It crept inside me—that dark breeze outside filled me up with its cold empty air. I turned and threw the water bottle against the fireplace; it hit near the ceiling with an explosive pop. Water drenched the stones and spilled over the mantel. Drops landed on the picture of me and the girls to spill down the glass frame like tears.

I collapsed backward to the couch. My phone sat on the coffee table—like a life preserver there to save me from drowning. I was swirling in a confusing riptide of anger and hopelessness. God, I needed someone to pull me out.

Sabrina.

We were supposed to talk on the phone tonight. I shouldn't let her down right out of the gate...*should I?*

Putting my feet up on the coffee table, I swiped through my contact list. I tapped my foot against the coffee table while it rang. Was it a mistake to call her when I was this upset? I shook my head; it was too late for second thoughts now.

"Hello." Her voice was breathy and sweet. The sound covered me like fresh air.

"Sabrina, how are you tonight?" I asked. I sank back against the cushions and took in a deep breath.

"I'm great. So...how are you and the girls? Are they up?" she asked.

"No, they fell asleep." Should I tell her what happened? I sighed into the phone.

"Wow, it's early. Harry is still up playing Minecraft with my dad," she said.

"They usually stay up later. They had a rough night. I can't believe I miss the sound of their arguing."

"Aw, I never argued with my sister. She was so much older than me." Her voice was sweet, but wistful. The sweet drew me in, but the wistful made me want to stay right here and keep talking to her until I found out exactly what made her tick.

I cleared my throat and tried to get a handle on my rapidly racing thoughts. "I fought with my brothers constantly. I spent most of my childhood sitting next to them, all in a row, in time out." I laughed, but my heart wasn't in it.

"What can I do?" she asked.

"What?" Clearly, I wasn't doing a good job of hiding my feelings.

"You sound kind of sad. Can I help?"

"Just—keep talking to me?" Twisting my body, I stretched out across the couch. I shoved a toss pillow under my head and tried to relax.

"I can do that. Do you want to tell me what happened? You can if you want to, or not. It's up to you."

I decided to tell her. If I was determined to date her, keeping this a secret would end up being pointless. "I'm going to have sole custody of my girls. Their mother gave me papers—asking to relinquish her rights to them. I got them in the mail today."

"Oh, no, Wyatt. I had just assumed they were sick or something like that. Those poor babies..."

"They were already hurting because of their mother. It's been happening since we moved here. Even before—she never was an attentive mother. She was hardly ever around." Was I unconsciously testing her by telling her this?

"It will be hard, of course it will. But eventually they will be okay. And it will be because they have you. I believe that and you should too. You don't need both parents to be a happy kid. Kids just need love. Just keep loving them, Wyatt. Everything will get better as time goes by."

I took that in. Her words moved through me, soothing me. "I hope so."

"How old are you?" Her voice, changing the subject, jolted me out of my melancholy.

"I just turned thirty. You?"

"I'm twenty-seven. Did you always want to be a sheriff?"

I chuckled. "Yeah, I did. I always wanted to help people. Plus, I was a fat kid—I got bullied a lot—I can't stand bullies and abusers. I liked the idea of throwing them in jail. That, and I wanted to drive fast with the sirens blaring."

She laughed. "You're cute."

"Sabrina, there's nothing cute about being a sheriff. It's a badass job," I corrected with a chuckle.

She laughed even harder. The sound of it reminded me of Tinkerbell in the movies my girls were obsessed with. It made me smile.

"You're right," she said. "I'm so sorry. Only badasses can do your work —busting up robberies and rescuing old ladies from convenience stores." She was teasing me; it was adorable.

"Oh, God, no. You've seen the video too..." I groaned. That video was the bane of my existence. I wouldn't wish that kind of attention on my worst enemy.

"I saw it. It was everywhere. Even on the news," she confessed.

"I'm just glad Green Valley doesn't have a Stop and Go." I couldn't go near a Stop and Go anymore. Whenever I did, it made me either a walking punchline or a heartthrob, depending on who noticed me.

"Is that why you left Nashville? To get away from 'the Stop and Go's Superman'?"

"Ha ha ha, you're quite the little smarty pants. I didn't realize you had that in you—I like it."

"It's always easier for me to talk when I'm not face-to-face with someone." She sounded embarrassed. She shouldn't be; her shyness was one of the things that first drew me to her. Aside from her knockout good looks, of course.

"I'll admit I was making a mental list of ways to get you to talk to me. And all I needed was your phone number." Ruby was right. I made a mental note to thank her for the advice.

She laughed. "I'm glad you came back to the library. It's easy to forget about someone like me—lots of people do."

"Then they're missing out," I declared.

"You say sweet things," she whispered.

"It's the truth," I whispered back. "So, what's your favorite color?"

"Pink. Yours?"

"Green. Favorite food?"

"Pizza. Yours?"

"Also pizza. What kind?" I asked.

"I don't want to say," she groaned into the phone. That groan was sexy. I wanted to hear it again, in person.

"Uh oh. You like pineapple, don't you?" Teasing her was fun. She was blushing, I knew it.

"Yeah, I do—with pepperoni and jalapeños. Please don't judge me."

I laughed. "Never. Unless you tell me you're a flat-earther or something equally ridiculous."

"Ugh, I have a brain. I mean—gravity, Sir Isaac Newton, basic logic—hello, science? What food do you hate?" she asked.

"Now *I* don't want to say."

"Oooh, except, now you must. Come on, Wyatt," she cajoled.

"Potatoes..." I had to force myself to hate them. Potatoes in all their forms were one of the major contributors to my chubby childhood. Now I was fully convinced that potatoes disgusted me.

"You're crazy! What's to hate about potatoes?" Her outburst was hilarious. "They're multifunctional. They're creamy, fluffy, and potato-y. You can boil them, mash them, and stick them in a stew. Think of the French fries, Wyatt! I'm judging you now."

"Well, what do you hate?" I managed to ask through my laughter. "This better be controversial or I'll judge you right back, so hard."

"I like everything. Except food that looks like other food," she said with an adorable giggle. I wished she were here right now so I could see her smile, hear that laughter, and maybe steal a kiss or two.

"What?" I could barely form words through my laughter. She might just be the cutest woman I'd ever met.

"I may or may not cut you if you ever give me a birthday cake that looks like an avocado," she informed me.

"Ahh, I'll make note of that. What about food that looks like something else? Like a unicorn or a Chihuahua."

"Gray area."

"God, Sabrina, it's official. I'm cheered up. Thank you."

"Woo-hoo. Mission accomplished."

"So, Miss Librarian. What's your favorite book?"

"That is a complicated question. Tell me what yours is first."

"*The Hobbit*," I immediately answered, then sat up. Talking to her made me feel good. The gloom of my earlier mood was gone.

"I love *The Hobbit*," she burst out.

"Maybe it was meant to be. Now you." I caught a glimpse of myself in the mirror hanging above the chair in the corner. I had the goofiest smile on my face. I quickly looked away. Seeing that much hope reflected back at me made me nervous.

"Okay, okay. I don't really have a favorite. It depends on my mood, or even what time of year it is. I guess that I could say *Dr. Seuss's Sleep Book* is always a favorite because I remember my mother reading it to me before bed every night when I was a little girl. It's one of the few real memories I have of her. I read the *Harry Potter* books with Cora, and then again with her kids. Or I could say the *Twilight* series and the Smash-Girl comic books because of the way I devoured them with my best friend when we were in school together. I love Jane Austen and the Brontë sisters. So does Mrs. MacIntyre—she's fun to talk about books with. And I love Stephen King. Jackson does too. Oh, *A Midsummer Night's Dream* is a favorite, which technically isn't a book, but it's the first piece of Shakespeare I'd ever read and I fell in love with it..." she trailed off.

"Don't stop now, Sabrina. I want to know more. I want to know everything about you. You talk about books like..."

"Books are just like life. Books used to *be* my whole life," she whispered.

"You attach your memories to books. I want to read all of them—every one of your favorites. Then you can tell me all the reasons why you love them."

"Wyatt," she softly murmured.

"Sabrina, I mean it. Everything I find out about you, I like. I'm lucky I met you that day. It will always be my favorite traffic stop."

"I feel the same about you," she said.

We ended up talking for hours after that. We talked about everything and about nothing at all. And all the things that lived between. I felt like I knew *her* better now. And I liked everything I found out. We talked until we were both exhausted and our phones were dying.

Sabrina had attracted me from the moment I first saw her. She was a beautiful woman. But I knew for sure I wanted to get to know her better when Mak and Mel had sat with Harry and shared his leaves at the park and she'd almost cried. She had leaned against me and shared that moment. Light had radiated out of her like a bright beacon and I had wanted some of that light for myself. Now, after this phone call, I found myself wanting it for my girls too.

She had sensed I was down tonight and did something about it—she cheered me up without letting her shyness stop her. She cared enough to try, and that was all I needed to let me know that I shouldn't give up on her.

I stumbled down the hall to crash on the edge of my king-sized bed next to Mak and Mel. Staring at the ceiling, I felt the weight of my responsibility to my daughters. I glanced across the bed—I had to be careful with their hearts. I had to protect them, no matter what.

Nothing and no one will hurt you like this ever again, I promise.

I had jumped in headfirst when I got Isabelle pregnant. All I wanted was to be a good father to our baby, to do everything possible to make them happy.

Could I trust myself to make the right decisions when I had made so many mistakes in my past?

CHAPTER TWELVE

SABRINA

I was still in a dither from my phone call with Wyatt last night. We had talked for three hours and thirty-seven minutes. I checked the call time when we finished. I knew him a lot better now, and I liked him a lot. But even if I didn't end up with him, I would still make changes in my life. I still needed more. I still needed to *get a life*. I stepped onto the front porch and squinted against the bright glow of the early evening sunlight glinting off the windows.

We had just finished dinner and I had decided to confide in my father. He always encouraged me to talk to him. But I rarely ever talked in-depth about myself with anyone, unless you counted my therapist. I usually only talked to my father about the kids or my job or random things like what was for dinner and books we had both read—things that were light and easy.

He was inside fixing a cup of coffee. I sat on the swing to wait for him. Then I stood up and started pacing. I wasn't afraid to talk to him, that wasn't it. But talking about the changes I was making made it feel real. Openly acknowledging that I was trying to change my life would mean everyone would know if I failed.

I jumped when the door opened, and I spotted his smiling face. "Hey, Dad."

"What is it, sweet pea?" he said as we took our seats, him in his favorite rocking chair and me on the porch swing across from him. He took a sip of coffee and I wrinkled my nose in disgust. He always added blackstrap molasses and apple cider vinegar to it—it was a hideous concoction that he swore was good for his digestion. I would rather be constipated than drink that. I'd take cream and sugar until the day I died, thank you very much.

I took my time getting comfortable in the porch swing, fluffing the outdoor pillows and arranging them just so before I finally just bit the bullet and started talking. "Well…um…can you watch Harry on Saturday night for me? Because I have a date with Wyatt Monroe. He stopped by the library and asked me again and I said yes." I watched his eyes widen as he froze with his coffee cup halfway to his mouth. "Secondly, I'm going to Genie's tonight. Will you watch Harry for me tonight too?" I took a huge breath in and held it. There was no way to tell what his reaction would be—I hadn't had a date since I was sixteen.

His head drew back, and his eyes widened. He looked like he didn't know where to start. "Genie's?" he finally asked. His incredulity was deserved. I mean, the thought of me hanging out in a bar *was* crazy.

"I saw Willa there when I picked up the chicken last week. I want to go back and see her. Genie acted like no one was supposed to know she's home yet." I let this information burst out of me to distract him from the date announcement.

"Willa's back?" Ruby cried as she barged into our conversation. I jumped and almost swung my butt right out of the swing at the sound of the front door slamming behind her. She must have been listening in at the window again. Ruby had always adored Willa. Willa used to come over here every day after school let out.

"Yeah, I saw her at Genie's Bar last week," I explained as I resituated myself in the swing and tried to pretend that I had not just almost fallen out of it.

"Oh, I've missed her so much. Get her back, Aunt Sabrina." She sat next to me and bumped her shoulder against mine.

I wrapped my arm around her and smiled. "That's the plan." My voice was too bright. Trying to hide my nerves always made me sound crazy. I took another deep breath and tried to force my shoulders to relax.

My father was smiling at us over the rim of his coffee cup. "Okay, that makes more sense. I'm glad Willa is back," he said. "It's about dang time. I'll call Genie after we talk about your date with Wyatt Monroe."

"What? Why? Don't call Genie. And we don't need to talk about that," I protested.

He looked away from me. "I'll make no such promise. Michael is out there refusing to sign the papers and acting the fool. Genie will keep an eye on you. She'll be discreet. You drive straight there, stay inside the bar, and then come straight home when you're done. I know you're an adult and I want you to get out there and live your life. I'm glad you want to do that. But I'm worried about you."

I sighed. He had a point. Ruby smirked at me—she usually had to endure the dating lectures, not me.

He continued, "I'm glad you said yes to Wyatt. But even though he's a good man from a good family I'm still going to worry about you. Wyatt is a deputy sheriff, which means I don't have to worry so much about your safety where Michael is concerned when you're out on the town. But you haven't been on a date in a long time, sweet pea. I don't want you to get carried away and end up getting hurt. I want you to be careful; guard your heart before you let him inside of it. Be really sure you can trust him. And of course, I'll take Harry tonight or whenever else you need me to. You know that."

"Thank you, Dad. And don't call Genie. Please." I was twenty-seven. How humiliating would it be to have my father call the bar I was going to hang out in? Gah!

Ruby stood up in an indignant huff. "Wait. That's it? Pop! That's all you're going to say to her? When I went out with Mason Drake you lectured me for like, almost an hour." I chuckled; she had her hands on her hips. It was about to get serious.

"Ruby, you're a sixteen-year-old girl. Sabrina is an adult. There is a huge difference there." My father rarely ever lost his cool. He merely looked at her and sipped his gross coffee, waiting for her to calm down.

She twisted her lips and sat back down. "Fine. I guess you're right. But tell me you got at least one lecture from him, Sabrina. I mean, come on."

I exchanged a grin with my dad. "I got at least one, maybe two."

He stood up with a laugh, leaving his coffee cup on the side table along with the others he seemed to be collecting there. "I'm going to head to the senior center for a spell. I'll see you girls later."

"Okay, Dad. Don't call Genie, okay?"

He avoided my eyes when he answered me. "See you later, sweet pea. I'll pick Harry up at Essie's and put him to bed tonight. Don't worry about a thing." He headed to his car in the garage with a wave.

"Okay," I said and exchanged a look with Ruby.

"You know he's going to call Genie," she informed me with a huge smile on her face. She was enjoying this, the little turd.

"Yeah, I know," I said with a huge sigh then poked her in the side, right where she was ticklish.

She squirmed then got up to dart across the porch with a squeal. "Well, I'm glad you said yes to Wyatt too. He's hot. It'll be nice to have some good eye candy to look at during holiday dinners and stuff like that."

"You're a nut, Ruby."

"What are you going to wear? You should wear Mom's red cowgirl boots. They'd be perfect for Genie's Bar. I wish I could go with you. Curse my youth." She shook her fist in the air then plopped into dad's rocking chair.

"I wish you could too. I could use a wing-woman. Or whatever it's called. Basically, I wish you could come and do the talking for me. What in the heck am I going to say to people?"

"Just try to get out of your head and not worry so much. You can talk to me and the rest of the family just fine. That proves you are capable of it. Right?"

"I guess so." She'd made a good point. "No, you're right, it does prove it. I can do this."

Weston joined us on the porch. "Ready to go, Ruby?"

"He's going to drop me off at Marianne's house. Will you tell me everything in the morning? Wait, let me rephrase—you're gonna spill your guts in the morning." She laughed and flounced down the porch steps to the garage.

"Later, Aunt Sabrina," Weston said.

I waved goodbye as they took off, living their best teenage lives.

Tonight, I would go live my best twenty-seven-year old life. I had missed most of my teenage life. Between my shyness—which was not as crippling as it was now—Willa running away from home, and my sister's death, I hadn't experienced much.

Back then, I was shell-shocked and had holed myself up at home. I took care of Harry like he was my own baby. I held him and rocked him, and we cried for Cora together—sure, he was a newborn and I was seventeen, but we'd both needed her.

Can a person get a second chance to come of age? I stood up as a sudden surge of bravery filled my heart.

I was about to find out.

Tonight would be a test of my newly gained bravery as well as my social skills.

I would go to Genie's Bar.

I would find Willa and get my best friend back.

But first I would find appropriate country-western bar attire. Blending in would help with my state of mind.

I pulled open the door to the entry hall closet and searched the floor. Cora's cowgirl boots were there, just where she had left them. I had always coveted these boots. They were fierce, just like Cora. They were fire engine red and had a wing motif flowing softly over the gently worn leather. The embroidered pattern made me think of Fawkes, Dumbledore's phoenix, rising from the ashes. I used to try them on when I was a little girl and go clomping through the house pretending to be Wonder Woman, or a wizard, or whatever else had made me feel brave. Cora would laugh and encourage all of it. She would tell me I could do anything, be anything I wanted to be. She always used to say to me, "Go farther than I did, sugar pie. You deserve the world."

I picked up her boots and shut the closet door.

I had gone nowhere.

I had done nothing.

But that was about to change.

I crossed through the big archway into the living room and sat on the edge of the couch. The bright colors of the evening sunset shone through the wide picture windows that took up the front of the house. For the first time in forever I wanted to be out in it. I looked over to the bookshelf-lined hallway that led to my rooms and for the first time in a long time, I didn't feel the immediate urge to retreat. I did not want to hide in there and bury my life in yet another book. I didn't want to read about people doing things. *I* wanted to do the things. I wanted—I didn't know exactly what I wanted. All I knew was that I wanted something for myself. Something *mine.*

I stood up. I had to change…everything.

But I would start with my clothes. I walked to my room in a daze, all shallow breaths and pounding heart. I opened my closet and pulled a lacy white tank top from its hanger and tossed it to my bed. I rummaged around until I found my cropped brown leather bomber jacket and tossed that too. I gently placed the boots on the chaise in the corner of my room and headed for the bathroom.

I took a deep breath before letting it out in one big whoosh, then absentmindedly grabbed a lipstick from the tray on the counter—MAC Dare You. It made me laugh. I accept your dare, MAC lipstick. All my lipsticks were red. Red was a power color—at least that's what Cora had always told me. She wore MAC reds too, and I had always wanted to be just like her. God, how I missed her. She would know just what to say so I wouldn't be afraid. Or maybe she would just wrap me up in one of her hugs and make me feel better that way.

I glanced into my eyes as I deepened the black liner from this morning and then added a smoky smudge of eyeshadow. The black and gray of my makeup made my normally hazel eyes look like sparkling steel. After a quick internal debate, I left my glasses on the counter and put in my contact lenses.

I always wore makeup. Cora and I would spend hours in Sephora picking out pretty pallets and trying different shades. She had taught me how to create the perfect winged eye. After she died, I kept wearing it. Only it became a mask to hide behind, a barrier people wouldn't look beyond. Bright red lips and a dark smoky eye could hide a lot of sorrow. Funny how I was wearing it now for the opposite reason. I wanted to be seen. I finally *wanted* to be myself, whoever that was.

I fluffed my hair and put the lipstick in my pocket for bravery. The way I applied it, I wouldn't need a touch up. Slipping on the tank top, I sat on the edge of my chaise, staring at Cora's red boots with a wavering heart. She would want me to do this, to go for it. Finally, I gained enough nerve to put my feet in her shoes and leave the house.

I pulled into one of the last open spaces in Genie's lot. It had grown dark, but I found a space underneath a light pole. My father always said to find a well-lit parking space if it was dark outside.

I hopped out of my Jeep, already able to hear the music from inside—it was *loud*. I could hear Brooks and Dunn singing about a "Neon Moon." I could hear laughter, and fun, and *people*. This was nothing like the afternoon I had picked up the fried chicken. This was a different world.

I had thought Genie's would be slow on a weeknight. Boy, was I wrong.

I slammed the door of the Jeep and took a small step through the gravel parking lot toward the lights of the bar. I could do this. I talked to people at the library, and Harry's school, and sometimes at the Piggly Wiggly. I had survived the Great Winston Chicken Incident in this very bar and then invited them into my story circle for goodness sake!

What would Sienna Diaz do?

Sienna Diaz would go party her ass off at Genie's Bar, dang it.

Plus, I was wearing Cora's badass red cowgirl boots. I *was* going to do this. I picked up my pace and walked straight through the front door. The volume of the music almost blew me right back outside. Moonlight from the high windows and fat-bulbed strands of lights woven through the wooden beams of the ceiling were the only illumination across the massive dance floor. The dim light along with the deafening sound from the music made me nervous. Needing a moment to collect myself, I darted off to the side by the already almost-full coat racks. I took mine off and found one of the few empty hooks left. I had my wallet, phone, and keys in my pockets, along with my lipstick. *Dare You.*

I looked at my feet and inhaled a huge breath. After a mental pep talk, I carefully wove through dancers and chatty groupings and little by little made my way toward the bar.

I came to an abrupt stop when a tall man in a black cowboy hat stepped in front me to block my path. "Baby, let's dance," he slurred. I looked up. It was one of the King brothers. I couldn't remember which one was which. Was this Timothy or WhatsHisFace, the other one? Their a-hole qualities made them indistinguishable in my mind. Luckily, they most likely couldn't read that well because I'd only seen them at the library a handful of times. But that handful of times consisted of creepy leering at my boobs and crude comments—about my boobs—which resulted in me running off to hide while Naomi told them off and kicked them out of the library.

I gagged as the smell of cigarettes and whiskey breath assaulted me. His beefy hands wrapped around my upper arms, his fingers grazing the sides of my breasts. I tried to step away with a grimace, shaking my head, but he thwarted me with his grabby hands.

"No, thank you," I said.

He ignored me and pulled me closer. "I've always wanted to get my hands on you, sexy Sabrina," he groaned into my ear.

I considered using the shove I employed on Michael at the Piggly Wiggly. One good push should get him off me. But I didn't want to make a scene. Unlike the other day at the Piggly Wiggly with Michael, this place was full of people. I didn't want anyone to know I couldn't take care of myself in a bar. Maybe I should 'accidentally' step on his toes. I rejected that idea and swayed hard to one side then tried to turn away. He responded by pulling me into his chest and grabbing two handfuls of my ass.

"Okay, dang it." There was going to be a scene, because NOPE. "That's enough," I said firmly.

"Don't be like that, baby doll. It's just dancing." He grinned down at me right before he leaned his face into my neck and ground himself against me.

I pushed at his chest. He held me so tight I was afraid I would fall if I pulled away too hard.

"Please let me go. I don't want to dance with you!" I shouted. He either didn't hear me, or he did and just didn't give a crap.

I hadn't planned this evening very well. I was so worried about freaking out over the crowd that I hadn't even considered what to do about overly aggressive male attention or date rape. Or flunitrazepam or gamma-hydroxybutyric acid—freaking roofies for Filch's sake!

Timothy King had his hands all over my ass. This was my ass, dang it. And I had not given him permission to touch it. My breath grew shallow, and I saw white spots in my vision. I pushed on his shoulders harder, but he pulled me even closer. I could feel his...*parts*...against my stomach. He had a freaking boner. I was going to get date raped, and I'd never even been on a date.

Enough. I've had enough of this smelly, hillbilly, motheryokel, with his grabby hands and pokey pecker. He can just eff right off.

I stomped on his foot with the heel of my boot.

"Now what did you go and do that for?" he hollered, drawing back.

My angry glare turned quickly to surprise as I watched Jackson rush up behind him and yank him away from me. He shouted, "The lady doesn't want to dance with you, Timothy! Time to go."

Timothy King was no longer indistinguishable. He outranked his brother now on the a-hole scale. I glared at him. I wanted to punch his stupid face off.

Timothy King immediately grew contrite when faced with an angry Jackson James, standing there like a handsome blond hero. Wow, Jackson was hot. I can't believe after all that time talking about Stephen King books in the library I never noticed. I guess the library was too safe; he'd never needed to step in and rescue me like a distressed damsel.

"I'm sorry, Sabrina," Timothy addressed me. "I'm a little drunk. I'm going to go..."

Jackson let him go and he wandered off.

"Are you okay, sweetheart?" Jackson addressed me.

"I'm fine. Thank you, I—"

Words caught in my throat as I caught sight of my long-lost best friend rushing onto the dance floor. "Miss Sabrina Louise Logan," she drawled as she got closer.

"So, it is you, Miss Willa Faye Hill," I countered with a smile, the drama with Timothy almost forgotten.

She beamed at me then grabbed my hand and pulled me after her. "Come with me."

"Just great..." I heard Jackson say as I followed Willa.

I turned back. "Thank you, Jackson." I smiled at him.

He shook his head with a smile. "You're welcome."

Willa led me to a booth in the corner, near the bar. It had 'reserved' printed on a card in the middle. She swiped the card and gestured for me to get in. I slid onto the smooth wooden bench and she slid in across from me. We were quiet as we looked at each other with goofy smiles on our faces.

"Did Genie send you over there to help me?" I questioned.

She looked at the ceiling and a sideways grin crossed her face. "Maybe she did. But, Sabrina! I can't believe you're here. What are you doing here by yourself? You need to know how to handle yourself in a place like this. Genie's is usually pretty tame, but you never can tell what will happen when men get drunk, no matter what kind of place it is." She swept her hair behind her shoulder and I saw it—a tattoo wrapped around the entire length of her arm. A mermaid with flaming red hair, her body colored in shades of blue, violet, and aqua, swimming defiantly toward the surface leaving rippling black waves in her wake. The mermaid and swirling waves did a good job hiding the wicked pink ribbon scar running jaggedly up her arm, but it would take more than ink—no matter how beautiful—for me to forget about it.

She noticed my study of her arm. "I call her Ceto," she said with a smirk. Of course, she did. Willa would never name her mermaid something like Ariel or Madison.

"So..." I began but stopped when I saw the wall go up behind her eyes. I twisted my lips and tilted my head, deciding to let it go. I'd follow her lead, for now anyway.

"So..." She tilted her head to match mine and smiled expectantly at me. "What are you doing here? Have you made drastic personality changes in the last ten years?"

"No. I made them in the last ten days. And I don't know if they will stick."

Her smile softened. "They'll stick if you want 'em to stick."

I had missed her so much. She used to know me so well. I missed being known, having someone my age to confide in, having a friend.

I shrugged. "So, what are *you* doing here?"

"Workin'. And I've got to get back to it." She grinned.

"That's all you can say? It has been ten years. Are you still with Tommy? Did y'all ever get married?" I watched that wall slam down again and I knew whatever had happened was bad. She ran away with her boyfriend during our junior year of high school and hadn't even left me or her family a way to contact her when she left.

"We're not talking about that. Not yet anyway." She reached for my hand with a tentative smile. I let her take it. "Can we maybe talk later? Please?"

"Okay. We can talk about something else now." I leaned forward, elbows on the table. She tugged my hand until we were hugging across the small rectangular table of the booth. I pulled back and smiled at her. She looked almost the same, but I could see a new depth in her eyes. She'd grown up. Could she see the difference in me too?

"I can't talk right now. I really do have to get back to work. But I have a break soon. Will you stay? You can stay right here in this booth and I'll come sit with you whenever I get a break. I'll bring you a Dr. Pepper and some fried dill pickles. You still like those?"

I nodded, appeased by her sort-of promise to talk later. "I'll stay. And bring lots of ranch. And a real drink. Not a Dr. Pepper."

"Ooh wee, I'll be right back with something real for ya." She slid out of the booth and headed back through the door behind the bar.

I watched her walk away, and I wasn't the only one. Willa was something else—six feet tall and covered with freckles. She had the body of a supermodel and a face that seemed sculpted out of marble. Her eyes looked like the sky, and that light blond mermaid hair I was always jealous of flowed in a wild, wavy ponytail down her back. And my gosh, I *so* hoped she was back in Green Valley to stay.

I looked around the bar from the safe vantage point of my booth. There had to be some 'normal' people that preferred to sit in the corner. I wasn't hiding. I was *here,* and that would have been unheard of for me last week. I smiled to myself.

You did it. No going back now.

I had a date with Wyatt Saturday night. I was sitting in a bar and I might have my best friend back.

Who *was* this girl?

Willa came sashaying back to our table with a tray held aloft. She set the tray down with a flourish, placed the fried pickles and ranch down in front of me, followed by a filled pint glass and a shot, then she proceeded to light the contents of the shot glass on fire.

"What is that?" Startled, I drew back into the booth.

"A flamin' Dr. Pepper," she retorted.

I saw no Dr. Pepper, just a pint glass full of something and a shot that was now burning like a big ol' candle.

I laughed. "Do I blow it out like a birthday cake?"

"Nope, just drop the shot in the beer, the fire goes out, then chug it. Hurry."

My eyebrows hit my hairline. "Really?"

She nodded with a grin.

I returned her grin, gingerly dropped the shot into the beer, waited a beat for the flame to drown out, and then chugged it. It tasted almost exactly like a Dr. Pepper.

I inhaled a deep breath through my mouth. "You're still a smart-ass, Willa," I choked. My stomach felt warm and my knees were loosening up. Nothing like a little bit of liquid courage—it couldn't hurt.

She passed me a glass of water. "If you get drunk, I'll drive you home," she promised then stuck out her pinky. I linked mine with hers. The familiar gesture made it feel like the ten years between us had disappeared. "I have to get back to work," she said.

I nodded and ate a pickle. My heart felt light, and it was not because of the alcohol. I looked up as Genie approached the booth. She slid me an icy drink in a tall glass.

"Got a Dr. Pepper for you, honey. A real one." She chuckled. "I'm glad you're here. 'Bout time you had some fun, girl."

I smiled at her. "Thank you, Miss Genie."

She nodded then headed back to the bar.

I munched on the pickles, sipped my drink, and people-watched. People sure liked to dance close, even if the song wasn't slow. Unless they were line dancing. But even then, I saw some ass grabbing and a few grindy debauchees.

Humans are weird—or was I the weird one?

I swirled the straw around in my glass and waited for Willa to come back. I contemplated the nature of weird. And the nature of hands and where one should put them whilst dancing in public. Where would I put them if I were dancing with Wyatt? It was a good thing he wasn't here. I knew exactly where I'd want to put them—right on that epic booty.

"I'm on break, Sabrina. Let's dance." I looked up at Willa, then out at the dance floor again. Garth Brooks was playing, and everyone was dancing in a line.

"I can't do that. Willa, I can't line dance." I tugged on my hand in hers, but she pulled me out of the booth to stand at the edge of the dance floor. Plus, the song was "Ain't Goin' Down" and it was just way too fast. I would fall down and die from an inadvertent boot stomp to the head.

She examined me, up and down. "You're wearing Cora's boots," she said. Her smile grew sad for a brief second. *She understood.* "You got this, come on. Do it for Cora and the power of those red boots." She nudged me with her arm.

"I'm not good at organized sports, Willa. You know that," I argued half-heartedly, because I knew—I *was* going to do it. I had to do it. Sienna Diaz would definitely do it.

"Hush, it's just like P.E. class. Like the electric slide, remember that? Hold my hand, we're going." I looked out to the crowded dance floor. Dim light and pulsating music, people in lines and in pairs having fun. Could I do that?

The song changed. Luke Bryan this time—"Country Girl." Oh, God, I would have to "shake it."

Holding our hands above our heads, Willa tugged us into the crowd. I watched her hips sway side to side to the beat. She moved so fluidly. It was sexy. I wished I could be like her—at ease with myself. Dancers stood aside to let us in the line. Of course they did. Who could resist Willa in all her glory? Ripped black jeans, black cowboy boots, and a tight black 'Genie's' tank top tied at the side of her tiny waist. She must make so much money in tips.

She picked a spot, dead center and stopped. "Come on now," she cajoled.

I smiled sideways and joined her. It *was* like the electric slide, but with the addition of boot stomps, hip slapping, and the obligatory booty shake in deference to the song.

"You're doin' great!" she yelled. "You look hot!"

"It is getting warm in here!" I yelled back.

Her head went back as she cracked up. "God, I missed you."

"I missed you too," I mouthed the words. It felt wrong to yell them.

She grinned back. Her eyes got big as she looked over my shoulder. "Wyatt," she said.

I spun around to look and crashed right into him. He steadied me with his hands on my shoulders.

I was too shocked to freak out or say anything, so I just stood there like a ninny. *Holy crap,* just look at him. Blue plaid shirt half tucked into jeans that should be illegal. I took a quick glance down—cowboy boots. I gulped. I was in trouble. If he turned around and I caught a glimpse of that booty? I was sure it would be fatal. Or at the very least, completely humiliating.

"You okay, Sabrina?" he asked.

Pssht, no, I was not okay. I was about to dissolve into a pile of lust-addled body parts right here on the floor of this bar. I nodded at him though, just to keep up the pretense that I was sane.

He glanced at Willa. "Hey, Willa."

"Hey," she answered.

Jealousy surged shamefully through me. I shouldn't feel that way—he wasn't mine. *But he was totally mine, dammit.*

Wyatt grinned at me. "I keep running into you. I can't believe you're here. You look stunning. It must be my lucky night, darlin'."

"Maybe." I grinned back. *Did I just say that?*

Out of the corner of my eye I caught Willa looking expectantly past Wyatt. I hauled my eyes from Wyatt's to see what had caught her attention.

Holy Hufflepuffs. The jealousy I had previously—shamefully—felt disappeared once I saw the way Willa was checking this guy out. Eye effing would be putting it mildly.

This had to be one of Wyatt's brothers. They looked so much alike, except this guy's hair was long. It curled down to touch the collar of his shirt and he had a beard. Wyatt was usually clean shaved but he had some intriguing dark stubble right now though.

"This is my brother Everett. Ev, this is Sabrina and Willa."

"Nice to meet you," I said.

I knew that Wyatt had three brothers. Everyone in Green Valley knew that. Were the other two Monroe brothers as hot as Wyatt and Everett? Because God bless America if they were.

Everett held his hand out. Willa shook it because I was stuck in place staring at the two gorgeous Monroe brothers like a big ol' dummy. I couldn't believe I had just met Wyatt's brother. We hadn't even gone on our date yet, and I had already met a brother. Was that even allowed?

"Care to dance?" Everett asked her.

I whirled to face Willa who shook her head. "I've had nothing but

Diet Coke all day. I'm hangry and highly caffeinated—could be dangerous."

He burst out laughing. "I'll take my chances, sweetheart. I have a feeling you're worth the risk."

She shrugged and placed her hand in his. He pulled her to the edge of the dance floor with a smile.

A slow song played and the energy in the place calmed down but crackled with more emotion as people coupled up and swayed together.

Wyatt smiled down at me expectantly. "May I have this dance?"

I shook my head. "I can't. I don't know how to slow dance. Or do any of that twirly, two-step stuff." *I am a twenty-seven-year-old dork, who has never slow-danced with a guy before.*

He grinned. "Don't worry, darlin'. It's a slow song. Only one of us needs to know how. I got you."

Compelled by the power of his dimple, his smiley eye-crinkle, and absolutely every other thing about him, I took his hand and followed him to the center of the dance floor near Willa and Everett.

He held my waist with one hand while his other hand kept mine tucked up tight to his broad chest as we moved side to side. I slid my free hand up his arm to his shoulder, feeling all the bulges and contours on the way. I vowed right then that one day I would categorize and examine each and every muscle on his body up close, personal, and *naked*.

Everyone needs goals, right?

I glanced over at Willa and Everett. He had just finished twirling her out and back, then dipped her low across his bent knee. Her delighted laughter floated across the floor.

"Wow, he can dance," I observed.

I gasped when Wyatt's hand on my waist slid up my side then up the underside of my arm to take my hand from his shoulder and link our fingers together. It was just like in *Dirty Dancing,* except I was facing him instead of away like in the movie. His grin grew a little bit wicked right before he used both of my hands to turn me. His front was now at my back with our arms crossed in front of us.

I felt his warm, hard body behind mine and I felt...way too much. Tingles covered every square inch of me. The air felt different against my skin; I was burning up.

His chin dipped low to rest on my shoulder. "Are you okay?" he whispered into my ear. His breath ruffled the hair against my neck, and I shivered.

"Yes," I whispered. Then I nodded in case he didn't hear me. I felt his stubbled jaw graze the side of my face.

Every inch of his body pressed up against every inch of mine. I began to experience heretofore unknown feelings. Feelings that differed vastly from when I was just by myself. My perception of what was possible for my life shifted. My brain had disengaged, and I floated along on pure sensation.

We rocked side to side like that—closer than I'd ever been to anyone in my life. I felt him sigh against my hair. His chest rose and fell against my back as his arms tightened around me. The last of my conscious thoughts dissolved and I succumbed to pure feeling. His body moving against mine became my world. His hands in mine kept me tethered, lest I float away on this cloud of sensation that was gradually becoming overwhelming.

I had never felt anything like this. I never even thought feelings like this were possible in real life. In romance novels, sure. But to feel such contentment laced with giddiness right now was something I had not expected. Before I could succumb to the spreading tingles and dwindling brain power and embarrass myself, he raised our arms up high and twirled me around and around underneath them. I giggled and squealed. Apparently, I was *that girl*—a squealy, laughing, girly girl. But maybe we were *all* that girl in the right circumstance.

He was right. I did not need to know how to slow dance when I was with him. We danced close—so close his knee was between my legs. I delighted at the feel of his soft, warm skin when he placed one of my hands on the back of his neck. He moved his free hand low on my waist, hooking his thumb in my belt loop to guide me in slow, small circles over our spot on the dance floor, then back and forth using his hands to push me out and pull me back into his body. He coaxed me where I needed to go. I felt weightless and graceful.

The whole bar and everyone in it disappeared until it was just us dancing together, bathed in the moonlight filtering in through the high windows, and the little lights—so much like stars—illuminating the dance floor with their tiny rays. As the song ended, he spun me out—just like Everett did to Willa—then back up against his body to dip me low with his arm wrapped tight around my waist. He grinned down at me with those gorgeous lips and beautiful chocolate brown eyes and I—

I would never forget this moment. Not ever.

I beamed at him as he pulled me up without letting go. He held me close and we continued to slowly sway, even though the song had switched to a fast one. His eyes held mine captive.

"I don't want to let you go yet." His words were soft, like a whispered caress.

"Then don't," I murmured.

He smiled, but it wasn't the big dimple-icious smile that drove me crazy. It was better. It was sweet and simple—a small smile that was meant just for me to see. At least the way his eyes burned made it feel like *mine*. I exhaled slowly.

Quit imagining things.

The fast song cut off, right in the middle. The Dixie Chicks replaced it. "Cowboy Take Me Away." I wrenched my eyes from Wyatt's and looked around. Genie and Willa were behind the bar, each giving me a thumbs-up with goofy smiles on their faces. Everett was sitting on a barstool next to Jackson, both holding a beer. Everett winked at me. *Sexy winking must be a Monroe brother thing.* Jackson waved at me with a grin and a shake of his head.

Wyatt was not a cowboy, but he had taken me away. I wasn't on earth anymore. I wasn't in Genie's Bar and I was no longer in my right mind. I was flying; I was falling.

I felt my face heat. He pulled me closer and twirled me out of their sight. He moved us to a dark corner of the dance floor and turned so his back was to the room, keeping me hidden from view.

We weren't alone by any stretch of the imagination, but it felt like we were.

I wondered if he felt like I did. I would be brokenhearted if I never saw him again. I couldn't help but think of tonight as a *beginning*. But I had no frame of reference for whatever was happening between us, so I let those thoughts drift out of my mind.

I tilted my head back to see if I could get a hint about what he was thinking. His eyes were already on me—like he had been waiting for me to look up and see him. I smiled softly. His face dropped low as he leaned into me. His arm tightened around my waist and his hand splayed low to grip my hip as his other hand sifted into my hair. I tightened my arms around his neck and pressed as close as I could get. He felt big and strong against me and I didn't want him to let me go.

My eyes drifted closed. My lips parted and my tongue darted out to wet them.

Kiss me.

I felt his breath against my mouth right before he brushed his lips over mine. Gentle at first, then more firmly as I melted against his body and parted my lips beneath his.

His hand in my hair softly tightened as he tilted my face to the side and deepened our kiss. His tongue slid against mine and I gingerly met it with my own. This wasn't my first kiss, but I couldn't help but wish it was.

I felt his kiss from my lips to my toes. My knees grew weak. I leaned further into him and gave him my weight. I had to; I was about to melt to the floor.

His hand drifted out of my hair and slid down my back to join the other at my hips, where he gripped me tight and pulled me closer to his hard body. His leg went back between mine for a moment before he pulled back slightly and took half a step back.

My eyes shot open. I had felt something right before he pulled away. Low against my stomach, he was hard. I couldn't help but think of it like evidence. He liked me as much as I liked him. Was that bad? We were in a bar—it probably was. *Holy crap, I* did that. I lifted my head and grinned up at him.

He shook his head slightly; a slight smile crossed his face. "What are you doing to me, Sabrina?"

"I...don't know," I whispered.

"I forgot my manners. You're making it hard for me to act like a gentleman. I'm sorry, darlin'," he apologized. But he didn't let me go. He took my hand back into his, and we continued dancing.

"It's okay. You don't have to be sorry for anything." I dipped my chin into my chest and let out a silent gasp of surprised pleasure and amazement. Clearly, I was never getting over this.

He chuckled softly and smiled at me. Holding my hand, he escorted me back to my booth. Jackson and Everett were there with their beers. They made room for Wyatt and me to join them. I slid in and Wyatt sat across from me.

Willa strolled up to take my and Wyatt's order. "What'll it be, you two?"

"May I have water?" I asked. I didn't want more alcohol. I wanted to remember every single detail about this night.

"Just a beer for me. Where are you going to park tonight, Willa?" Wyatt asked before she could turn around and leave.

Park? What?

She shot him a *shut up* look. He raised his eyebrows and sat back in the booth.

"How do y'all know each other? And park? Are you sleeping in your car?" I had to know.

"We know each other from Nashville." She shoved her little waitress notebook in her apron, put her pencil in her ponytail, and glared at Wyatt.

Wyatt's eyebrows got higher as he looked at her. He seemed to want her to tell me what was going on. He turned to me. "Her ex was my partner on the police force in Nashville."

Everett and Jackson just sipped their beers their gaze flicking between us like they were watching a tennis match. "I can't believe I don't know what's going on right now," Jackson said, causing Everett to laugh.

"It must be killing you," Wyatt teased him.

"Willa," I interrupted their joking. "You've been in Nashville this whole time? Did something happen with Tommy?" I couldn't believe she had been so close and not reached out to me.

"No, just for the last few years. And we're divorced," she admitted. There was so much more she was not saying. Her eyes were screaming to drop this topic. I would have to wait until we were alone to push. I decided to drop the Tommy subject when I considered that she may not want to talk about it in front of Wyatt and the others.

"Park?" But I was not going to let that go. I was not about to let her be homeless. "Are you sleeping in your car?"

"I have a camper van. I live in it. The long-term campsites here in Green Valley are full. I've been staying in a Walmart parking lot in Maryville until one opens up."

"You can stay with me," I offered.

"You really should," Everett added. "It's not safe to be alone like that."

"I've been alone for a long time. I think I can handle it," she shot back at him. "And, Sabrina, I can't stay with you." She took a step back and started to head for the bar again.

I stood up to stop her. "If you don't want to stay in the main house, you could park out by the barn. There's a trailer hookup right next to it. You can plug in. We have a satellite dish—so there's Wi-Fi and you could have electricity, running water." I grinned as I sweetened the offer.

Her eyes widened. She wanted to say yes. "Are you sure?"

I nodded. "Absolutely."

"Thank you. I won't get in the way."

"Willa, stop being crazy. You've been to my house a million times. You practically lived there before."

She closed her eyes. Sadness clouded her features for a brief second before she wiped it away. "I want to tell you everything. Just—later okay?" she whispered.

I nodded. "Yes, we'll talk later. I'll give you the gate code. You remember where the barn is? Just drive around the garage and you'll see it."

She passed me her notepad and I wrote the code down.

"I have missed you so much," she whispered. She gazed out at the dance floor looking lost.

"We'll catch up. Everything will be all right, you'll see." I watched as she headed back behind the bar.

I spent the rest of the night dancing with Wyatt. I danced with Jackson and Everett too. And when Willa had a break, she joined us. I stayed at Genie's until it closed. I, Sabrina Louise Logan, stayed at a bar until closing time. I bet Sienna Diaz would stay at a bar until closing time—I had done something she would do, and it was fun. So much fun. All I had to do was get out of my head and forget to be embarrassed. It seemed so simple when I thought of it that way. Yet, I knew it was far from simple.

Wyatt had told me I was beautiful and kissed me goodbye at my Jeep. And just like dancing, kissing required being out of your head. If I hadn't been so wrapped up in Wyatt, I might have freaked out and bungled our kiss. Instead I lost myself, followed his lead and it was *wonderful*. My lips tingled whenever I remembered it.

I smiled as I drove through the black iron gates at home with Willa following behind me in her camper van. I waved to her as she passed me by to head back to the barn. My best friend was back in town and I would do everything I could do to make her stay.

I unlocked the door and hurried inside when I heard one of the kid's cell phones ringing in the living room. I rushed to the coffee table and picked it up. My father had a rule: no cell phones in their rooms overnight.

Who could possibly be calling Ruby at three in the morning?

I swiped to answer.

"Baby girl, don't hang up on me no more. Your daddy needs your help," a slurred voice said.

Michael.

I hung up on him and blocked the number. My blood boiled. Ruby barely knew him. He'd been out of her life for good by the time she was six years old. And he'd never come back into it. Cora saw to that. Sure, Cora would hook up with him from time to time—Harry being the result of one of their hookups—but she never let him get to the kids. He was unreliable and unpredictable. And apparently on drugs again.

I wouldn't let him get to the kids either.

Don't you worry, Cora, I won't let him hurt your babies.

CHAPTER THIRTEEN

WYATT

I squinted against the early afternoon sunlight. I was on patrol, cruising around the area surrounding the Dragon Biker Bar a few miles outside of town. The bar also acted as the headquarters of the Iron Wraiths, Green Valley's most notorious biker club. The Iron Wraiths' organization had been shaken up recently when their president—as well as some other key members—were arrested. But they were still dangerous. Probably even more so because of the chaos that surrounded them.

I frowned when I saw Michael Adams drive into the parking lot. I slowed to a stop at the side of the road to observe. After slamming the door of his beat-up old Dodge Neon and looking around the lot, he darted to the entrance of the bar. Nothing good ever happened at the Dragon Biker Bar. Which meant Adams was up to no good—just like I suspected.

I sat back in my seat and reached for my coffee. I sipped and watched as he entered the bar. What the hell was he doing here? He was no biker. I knew he was a gambler with a drug problem; maybe he was here to join a game or score some drugs. Cocaine, I would guess, from the way he acted at the Piggly Wiggly.

My thoughts drifted back to last night at Genie's and a smile crossed my face when I remembered kissing Sabrina on the dance floor. She was beautiful and sweet and tasted like sunshine. I shut those thoughts down. Losing focus on this job was foolish.

My mind had just begun to wander back to Sabrina once again when I saw her park, get out of her black Jeep, and start walking to the front door of the bar.

What the hell?

I sat forward sharply in my seat. Hastily slamming my coffee into the cup holder, I opened my door and got out. There was no way a girl like her should go anywhere near a bar like this. What was she thinking? I jogged through the dirty, trash strewn parking lot in her direction. It felt like my heart had flown out of my chest at the sight of her. It hurt.

I had no claim on her. All I had was this rabid attraction that wouldn't go away. An obsessive want that pumped through my blood and kept distracting me from—shit, from almost everything. And last night when I held her in my arms, *possibilities* had run through my mind like wildfire. I wanted her.

I had no right to tell her what to do or where to go. But there was no way in hell I would let her step one pretty little foot into that bar.

No fucking way.

I quickly headed her off and stopped in front of her. Obviously not paying any attention to where she was going, she crashed right into me, wobbling on her black stiletto heeled boots. Shoes like that in a place like this? She couldn't even run away if she needed to.

"What are you doing here?" I hissed as I steadied her with my hands at her elbows.

Her hands stopped to rest on my chest as she brushed against me. My heart returned to my body and raced beneath her palms.

"Wyatt?" She looked up at me surprised. Her gorgeous mouth formed an O as she quickly looked away, around me toward the bar. The light breeze blew an errant curl into her eyes and I brushed it aside so I could see her better. Those beautiful hazel eyes shone silvery green in the sunlight, but they weren't taking in her surroundings at all. I hadn't snuck up on her. I'm a big guy and by no means was I making my presence a secret. The lights were flashing on my cruiser for fuck's sake.

"You can't go in there." I stated the obvious. Every protective instinct in my body was screaming at me to drag her away, to take her home, to just *take her*. She was *mine*. I would let no one harm her. The thought of it made me crazy, irrational. I had to quickly remind myself that she wasn't mine. Not yet anyway.

A soft gasp escaped her as she looked over my shoulder toward the bar. "Why not?"

"This place is dangerous. You will get hurt."

She bit her lower lip. It was red, pouty, and luscious. *I* wanted to bite that lip. I needed another taste of her, just one little taste. My head tilted down, and her head tilted back in response. For a kiss? I leaned in closer, like she was gravity and I was falling into her.

I could fall for her.

I shook myself out of her pull and stepped back. This was not the time. And absolutely not the place. "I'm not trying to boss you around or control you, Sabrina. But this place is dangerous, you can't go in there. It's full of Wraiths."

She stepped back and peered around me. "But I have to talk to Michael. I need him to sign papers for me. I followed him here." She started walking toward the bar again.

I did not want to manhandle her or force her to stop, but what kind of cop—what kind of man—would I be if I let her go in there? I stepped around her again and stood in her path. "What do you need? Let me help you." I had to make her understand the danger she was putting herself in.

She searched my eyes. We heard glass breaking and boots stomping from inside the bar. She jumped toward me and gripped my shirt. I held her waist and pulled her closer.

I used the radio on my shoulder to quickly call for backup. Jackson was close by—he'd better get his ass here right quick.

"Go on, tell me," I encouraged her. Then I took a quick glance behind us. Whatever was going on inside the bar hadn't spilled into the parking lot, and it probably would not. They usually kept their shit inside and away from potential witnesses and prying eyes. Still, I took her hand and walked us back toward her Jeep. I had to get her out of here in case something serious was going on in there. If it were serious, then all bets were off, and it would spill everywhere.

"I have to get him to sign the adoption papers and I have to make him leave Weston and Ruby alone," she said and tugged her hand out of my grasp. She stopped walking with me. Again, she took a step toward the bar. "My father is too old now to handle Michael. I just want to talk to him for a minute. I can't let him try to take Harry away from me." I gaped at her back as she once more headed to the bar.

After the Piggly Wiggly altercation I pulled Adams' rap sheet. Michael Adams was a selfish, useless piece of shit. There was no way he'd sign anything for her. Over the years he'd been picked up several times for a variety of petty shit—fights, drug possession, illegal gambling, drunk and disorderly. Nothing had ever stuck enough for him to do any real time, just a few months here and there.

"Sabrina." She turned around eyebrows raised expectantly. "I can't let you go in there, darlin'," I said and crossed my arms over my chest.

"I have to do something. I can't just wait around for Michael to agree to sign the papers again. My father's attorney is as old as my father—he can't do anything either. Michael called Ruby's phone at three in the morning. I won't tolerate that. What if he tries to call her again? He already won't stop bothering Weston—he was calling him starting at six this morning. What if he tries to get to Harry somehow?" She took a breath and a determined look crossed her face chasing her fearful expression away. "When my sister died, I vowed I would always protect her kids. I vowed it to her on her death bed, Wyatt. I can't just hide from Michael. What kind of aunt would I be if I let him keep messing with them?" She was the picture of defiance, if defiance took the form of a pissed off, hissing kitten. Or a shy librarian.

"You should stay away from him entirely. Especially if he's here. In fact, you should never come here, no matter what," I countered. Frustration colored my tone of voice, making it sound harsher than I intended. I took a step toward her.

She flinched and leaned away from me. "I'm not some scared little mouse, Wyatt. I have to protect the kids. Plus, Harry will officially be my son soon. I'm the only mother figure he's ever had. What kind of mother doesn't protect her own child?"

That hit me where I lived—my daughters' own mother had abandoned them. I understood Sabrina's motivation, but she was going about it all wrong—getting herself hurt or killed wouldn't accomplish anything. "I think that's great. I understand where you're coming from, but…" I took a quick glance behind us, then attempted to guide her toward her Jeep again.

She sidestepped me and stood firm.

I huffed out a frustrated sigh. "Sabrina, come on. Look around you, damn it. Pay attention to where you are—" Blaring sirens cut me off. I spun toward the bar to make sure no one was heading out here to investigate. The noise inside had died down and luckily no one had come outside.

She jumped at the sound from Jackson's cruiser as he pulled up and got out, his boots crunching the gravel as he approached.

"Sabrina? What are you doing here? Have you lost your mind?" Jackson questioned her. He removed his sunglasses with a flick then shot me an incredulous look. "What the hell?" he mouthed.

Hurt suffused her expression as she whirled to look at me. "You called the police on me?" she accused and stepped back. Had the fact that I was in uniform escaped her? I *am* the police. How did she survive with her head in the clouds like this?

"Not on you. Didn't you hear what was going on inside the bar?" My worry for her caused my words to come out as an exasperated shout.

"Sabrina, we can't let you go in there," Jackson added. At least he managed to keep a gentle tone. *Good cop. Bad cop. Damn it.*

"Oh my God." Tears filled her eyes along with awareness as she looked around the parking lot. Her eyes got bigger as they drifted across the rows of parked motorcycles. "I'm so sorry. Oh my God. I have to go—" She spun on her heel and stumbled across the gravel as she ran for her Jeep. She started it up and drove away.

I stood there and watched her until she was gone.

Fuck.

I wondered if I'd just ruined my chances with her. She was...different. Shy, but also strangely brave despite her obvious anxiety. Delicate but determined. I'd pushed her too far. But what else could I have done?

"What the hell, Monroe? Why would she be here?" The sound of Jackson's voice snapped me out of my thoughts.

"She wanted to talk to Adams," I said. "She's going to adopt Harry and he won't agree to sign the papers. He's been bothering the older kids too. Let's get out of here."

He turned to leave. I followed him to his cruiser. "Oh. Well, coming here is—" He shook his head, his eyes squinted against the morning sunlight. "I mean, what in the fuck was she thinking?"

"I don't think she was thinking of anything but the kids," I answered.

"I could understand that, kind of. But this is the Wraith's territory. She is definitely too much work for me," Jackson finished this last thought under his breath, but I still heard it.

He slapped my shoulder, got into his vehicle, and took off. I walked the remaining distance to my own cruiser parked on the street, wondering if he was right. Was she too much work? She'd made a reckless decision today and I had two daughters to consider.

CHAPTER FOURTEEN

SABRINA

What was I thinking?

I could have gotten myself killed. I could have caused Wyatt or Jackson to be injured by an Iron Wraith. Bikers scared me. What had possessed me go to their lair? No, it was a club—except the Wraiths didn't have Jax or Opie to make it sexy.

I am so stupid.

I sat at the stop sign that led into town. I wanted to turn down the road that led home and go hide. I wanted to skip work so I wouldn't have to face anybody, but I couldn't do that. I felt like I had come a long way, and I didn't want to go back to my loneliness and books.

Where do I go from here?

I heaved out a sigh and turned into the library lot to park my Jeep. Even if I had lost my chance with Wyatt, I still wanted to keep the goals I had set for myself. That was important to me—maybe even more important than dating Wyatt. Or dating anyone else, if it came to that.

Life was much simpler when it was just me and my books.

I trudged through the parking lot to the library. I was scheduled to work lunch today, a short shift in the middle of the day. It wouldn't be right to make Naomi or Mrs. MacIntyre cover for me again. I still felt like crap for the last time I left them in the lurch.

Extreme emotions were kicking me out of my usual run and hide response to stress today. Anger at Michael caused me to go to the Dragon Biker Bar and now guilt was making me go into work.

My date with Wyatt was supposed to be this week—our first official date. Though I felt like I could count our time at Genie's as a date. I couldn't shake the feeling that now it wouldn't happen.

The possibility that I would lose my chance with him hurt my heart. But I didn't know him well enough for this to be a true heartbreak, did I?

I felt wretched. Uncomfortable and sad, and unsure of what to do about it. I knew I screwed up by acting like a big, crazy dummy at the Dragon Biker Bar. I was worried about the kids, angry with Michael, and not thinking straight.

Should I call Wyatt and apologize? Text him? Or just wait and see if he showed up at the ranch to pick me up? I didn't know the rules. I had read one million romance novels and they weren't helping me right now.

"Hello, Sabrina," Mrs. MacIntyre called from behind the counter, shaking me out of my angst-ridden thoughts.

"Hi, Mrs. MacIntyre." I stashed my things on the shelf in her office and grimaced as I checked the to-do list. *Blarg.* I wanted to go home. I had a stash of Kit Kat bars in the freezer ready and waiting for an occasion like this.

"I hate to leave you alone, but I have a meeting about the library budget to attend. Naomi will be back in an hour."

"It's no problem at all. I'll get to work on this list." I smiled brightly and hoped she hurried up and left. I needed to be alone with my thoughts. Or rather, I needed to be alone so I could search my purse for chocolate.

"Thank you, dear." She packed up her things and headed out.

I loaded up the book cart with returned books then headed out front to do a scan of the library. There were always loose books on the tables that people didn't check out or bother to put away. *Rude.*

Halfway through my check, I squealed and jumped a foot when Ruby popped out of the stacks in the back.

"Boo," she said deadpan, with a sardonic smirk.

"What are you doing back there?" I headed her way with a smile.

"Did you know you can catch leprosy from an armadillo?" she asked, apropos of nothing I wanted to know about.

"Uh, yeah. Over half of all armadillos carry it. And it's believed that humans gave armadillos leprosy first. I ordered a crap ton of books about armadillos for Cletus Winston a few years ago," I informed her. Was she getting crazy ideas from Cletus? Maybe producing that podcast was a bad idea.

"Huh, okay. Well, I heard—overheard—him talking about it and I just need to know where to get them. Like, where would you buy an armadillo? Everything I found online seemed kind of sketchy. And how many would I need? I want to know the odds."

"Odds? What odds? And do you really need me to tell you that you shouldn't try to buy an armadillo online?" I grabbed hold of the book cart and shelved a few books while I stood there.

"The odds of catching leprosy from an armadillo. If Dad had leprosy to worry about, maybe he'd leave us alone again and sign the dang adoption papers for Harry."

I dropped the books back to the cart and gave her my full attention. "Oh, Ruby, I'm so sorry—" She looked away. I knew better than to try to smother her with comfort right now. We'd both start crying and I'd end up pissing her off. I'd wait until we were home to dive bomb her with hugs. Logic and facts would be a better approach right now. "Dad is working on getting a restraining order against him. I blocked his number on your cell phone. And Weston's too. And I followed him to the Dragon Biker Bar earlier today. I was unsuccessful in talking to him though." My father had told me to ignore Michael and let the attorney handle everything. I had promised him I would try. My father would also be upset with me when he found out where I went today. I sighed.

"Holy crap, Sabrina. You went there? Are you nuts?" The vulnerability left her expression as she stared at me with her mouth agape.

I twisted my lips to the side. "Apparently. Wyatt and Jackson stopped me from going inside. I think I pissed Wyatt off and I don't know what to do—"

"You probably just worried him. Remember when you yelled at me when I was trying to bake mud pies in the oven and almost set the kitchen on fire?"

I laughed. It was easy to laugh about it now when we were all alive, and the smell was gone. "I remember that," I said as I grabbed another few books to shelve.

"Well, you didn't want me to get hurt so you reacted like a screaming nutjob. Hollering for everyone to run out of the house while you sprayed everything down with the fire extinguisher. You weren't angry, you were worried. See?" I pushed the cart and followed her out of the stacks and toward the tables in the center.

"I get what you're saying. But you were a little kid when you did that. I'm a grown woman, I should have known better. Hey—what are you doing out of school?"

She flopped her backpack down and sprawled in a chair at one of the tables with a huge grin on her face. "I'm cutting. I didn't feel like sitting around school today."

"You can't just cut school whenever you feel like it." She had never cut school before. Me and Dad would know it. Weston had gone through a rough phase his sophomore year—due to his loser father's antics—whenever he cut school, we got a phone call right away. Thankfully he was better now.

"Sure, I can. I have a 4.5 GPA. I'm the president of like, everything. I've already earned credit for college. I could graduate early if I wanted to."

"You make it hard to argue with you sometimes, Ruby." I slid into the chair across from her and tousled her hair.

"It's like arguing with Google, isn't it?" she said with a smug smile.

I grinned at her. "Yeah, kind of. Plus, you're cutting to go to the library. You're my mini-me."

"We're two nerds in a pod." The smug left her expression as she grinned back. "It's my night to pick up the chicken at Genie's. Give me a ride later?"

"Sure, I get off at three. Walk straight back to school and I'll pick you up," I told her. Even though her mood had lightened, I would still insist we talk more in depth later. Their father was a constant sore spot in their lives, and I was sick of him.

She rolled her eyes. "Okay. I have a test last period anyway."

She got up to leave but turned back around when she made it to the door. "You know what you should think about?"

"What?"

"You're afraid you pissed Wyatt off, and you went to the Dragon Biker Bar like a crazy person, but you're here at work instead of hiding in your bed at home. That's progress, Sabrina." She smiled at me and took off.

I smiled to myself. *Small victories.* I'd take it.

After my uneventful shift at the library, I picked Ruby up and once again, pulled into the parking lot at Genie's to pick up the chicken. I wasn't nervous this time. What could possibly be worse than the last time I was here?

"You've had a rough day. I'll do the talking," Ruby offered as we entered. We didn't bother to hang our jackets on the hooks; we weren't going to stay long.

I turned back to look at Ruby. "Thanks." Scanning the interior my gaze snagged on a booth and my heart lurched. I stopped and took a huge step backward, crashing into Ruby.

"What? What is it?" she hissed and caught me by my arms before I landed on my butt on the floor.

There *was* something worse than running into the Winston brothers in Genie's Bar. Running into the Monroe brothers was infinitely worse. There they were, sitting in the booth we'd shared the other night. The only Monroe brother I'd officially met, besides Wyatt, of course, was Everett, but they all looked so much alike it was crazy. Tall, dark, and handsome, every single one of them. I could use the various characters Henry Cavill had played to describe them. Everett was Henry Cavill as Superman, when he was all beardy and hot during the oil rig scene—like he'd been working hard and needed a beer after a long day. The oldest brother, Barrett, resembled Henry Cavill in *Mission: Impossible—Fallout,* with a beardy mustache, curly hair on top, a button down shirt open at the throat and the sleeves rolled up. Forearms—mmm. Garrett was obviously the youngest. Think of Henry Cavill in *The Tudors* era. Garrett was jeans and a T-shirt, flirty smile hot. No sign of Wyatt though—clean cut, sexy, Henry Cavill as Clark Kent.

Ruby peered around me where I stood at the edge of the lobby. "Holy Hufflepuffs, Sabrina," she whispered. "It's a total plethora of man candy over there. Too many hot guys at one time—I don't think I can take it. My eyes are on overload." She turned to leave.

What?

I was the one who runs away. This was confusing.

"Sabrina!" Willa shouted my name and waved to me from behind the bar.

I grabbed Ruby's arm and pulled her along behind me. I contemplated ignoring them when three Monroe heads whipped around to look at me. But I waved to them anyway. I didn't want to be rude. Plus, progress, dang it.

Everett waved back with a raised eyebrow of concern. Great, he probably knew all about my Dragon Biker Bar experiment in idiocy earlier today. I sighed and smiled weakly at him.

Ruby and I took a seat at the bar. "I heard all their middle names are William," she whispered to me out of the blue and completely random.

I shot her a look and nodded. It was true. They had been named after their father and every other Monroe man from generations past. Their mother had to put up a fight—they almost got stuck sharing it as a first name. Instead she gave them matchy first names that none of them were thrilled with. Wyatt had told me that fun fact during our epic three hour and thirty-seven-minute phone conversation.

"Hey, y'all. Hang on a sec. I need to get their order first." Willa tipped her head to the Monroe booth. They must have just got here.

"Okay," Ruby said without looking up. She had pulled her cell phone out of her pocket.

I spotted Genie come out from the swinging doors behind the counter and watched warily as she made her way down the bar. The look on her face told me to brace myself. Willa switched directions and stood at my side, just like a best friend should.

Genie slapped a hand on the bar with a judgy grin. "Girl, tell me you did not go down to the Dragon Biker Bar. Your daddy is going to have a cow—"

"Please don't tell him, Miss Genie," I interrupted.

Ruby laughed without looking up from her phone. "He probably already knows," she said.

"How? How in the heck does everyone know what I did?" My mouth dropped open because UGH.

Willa put her arm around me. "It's Green Valley, Sabrina. Everyone knows everything."

Genie finally gave me a real answer. "I heard it from Patty who heard it from Julianne MacIntyre down at the library who heard it from Wyatt's momma. Julianne ran into Becky Lee at the Piggly Wiggly when she was picking up her sandwich on her lunch break. And everyone knows Becky Lee Monroe always listens to the police scanner while she does her gardening, bless her heart." Genie froze and looked up. "Garrett Monroe, I see you listening in. Don't you go tellin' your momma I blessed her heart, you hear?"

"Yes, ma'am, I hear. I won't say one word." Garrett snickered and picked up his menu.

Genie scrunched up her face and nodded. "Well, I have to finish up in back. Willa, go and get their order."

"Yes, ma'am." Willa saluted Genie and headed over to the Monroe table.

I sighed and tried to make myself turn invisible so I could eavesdrop on Wyatt's brothers.

"We should have gone to Daisy's Nut House. I want hot chocolate and pie for dinner, not fried chicken and beer." I heard Everett say.

Gah! I was going to give myself a headache straining to look at them from the corner of my eye.

"I'm sorry, but we're fresh out of pie and cocoa. Hot chocolate is for kids anyway, Everett." Giving up all pretenses, I turned all the way around in my barstool to see a smirking Willa standing by their booth, notepad in one hand, the other on her hip.

Eff it, I wanted to see what happened. I could take a lesson from Willa. Before she hooked up with her a-hole boyfriend (now ex-husband) Tommy, she was a master smart-mouth and could flirt a guy into submission like nobody's business.

"Never underestimate the power of a good cup of cocoa, Willa." Everett looked up at her and pinned her with a big, gorgeous smile. *Wow.* "Hot chocolate and a well-timed nap are key ingredients to a perfect day." He put his menu down to give her his full attention.

Her lips parted as she studied his face. "That sounds perfect," she whispered. Then she grinned. "It also sounds like something my grandpa would say."

I elbowed Ruby who was staring at them with an open mouth. Their banter had even managed to draw a teenage girl away from her phone. It was like a rom-com in the making. We exchanged a look. They were totally flirting. Go, Willa.

"So, what can I get for you boys?" she finally asked them.

"Beer and fried chicken," Everett answered without looking away from Willa's smiling face.

"Sounds good. Us too," Barrett superfluously added.

"We have two more joining us in a bit. Will you bring extra plates and stuff?" Garrett asked.

"Sure thing," Willa said and walked back our way.

"Willa! Oh. My. God," I mouthed. She shook her head with her eyebrows up. I got the message—I would grill her about Everett later. "How was the apartment hunt? Any luck today?" I asked once she took her place behind the bar. She was still trying to find a place to rent. She had gone apartment hunting in Maryville today.

She frowned. "No. Nothing but waiting lists. I'm on a few more, but it will be months."

"You need a place to rent?" Everett yelled. "My tenant just moved out. You're welcome to it." Clearly, he was not above eavesdropping either. He *soooo* liked Willa, I knew it.

Willa's eyebrows shot up. "You mean, live with you?" she yelled back. She held a finger out to us, then walked back to their table.

Ruby and I turned our stools around to watch. I allowed myself to get involved in their flirt-fest. It was a good distraction from the angsty thoughts I had been drowning in earlier. Plus, I knew myself—there would be plenty of dwelling and obsessing and angsting out later. It was better to do it at home, where the Kit Kats and wine lived.

"Not really. It's my house, but it has a walk-out basement with an apartment in it. One bedroom, one bathroom. So, not really like living together, more like neighbors," Everett informed her.

"But you're the landlord?" she grilled him.

"Well, yeah." He grinned at her.

"Huh," she said.

"Oooh, take it, Willa. Then you can stay in town for sure," Ruby butted in.

Everett grinned. "Give me your number, Willa. I'll call you and you can come take a look when it's cleaned up," he offered.

Willa didn't answer. She had her thinking face on.

Everett sensed her hesitation and added, "Bring Sabrina, or whoever you want. No pressure, I haven't listed it yet. I still have to get the cat hair professionally vacuumed out of the rugs and air out the patchouli and weed stench."

I watched her smile at him; it was her flirty smile. "You should know, up front—I won't clean the oven unless I move, or something catches on fire in it. And I've been known to burn water."

"Believe it or not, I've seen worse," he said and grinned broadly at her.

"Thank you, Everett. Wyatt has my number. I'll go and get your order put in." She turned around and headed back toward Ruby and me.

"He likes you and you were totally flirting with him—" Ruby whispered.

"I'm a bartender. Innocuous flirting is part of my job. It's habit," Willa insisted. She was fully in denial over the sparks that had flown between her and Everett.

I rolled my eyes at her and almost fell out of my stool when I saw Wyatt and Jackson, still in uniform, enter the bar.

Wyatt noticed me right away. "Sabrina," he said, voice gruff and eyes uncertain as he started walking toward me.

"Wyatt, hi—"

Then their radios started going off. Jackson rolled his eyes. "We have to go." He waved to me and turned around to leave. He waved to me. Did that mean he didn't hate me?

"We'll talk later, Sabrina," Wyatt said in a tone of voice that gave no clues as to what in the heck we'd talk about later. He turned and followed Jackson out of the bar.

What was that supposed to mean? And when would "later" be?

In romance novels the phrase "we'll talk later" always meant trouble. Since romance novels were my only frame of reference for romantic relationships, I got worried.

Was Wyatt going to break our date? Did his ex-wife move back to town with a secret baby? Had he just found out he'd inherited a billion dollars?

I didn't know what to expect, and the uncertainty might just drive me crazy.

"It'll be okay, Sabrina," Ruby whispered and took my hand.

I hoped so.

I liked Wyatt a lot. And even though it had only been a short time since I'd met him, I would be heartbroken if I lost my chance.

CHAPTER FIFTEEN

SABRINA

Sometimes I couldn't sleep. I had been that way since I was a little girl. Thoughts would swirl in my brain of things I'd lost, things I wanted to find, things that refused to give me peace. I'd toss and turn and wreck my covers, never to get comfortable, only to get up and wander the house like a dead-eyed, stumbling zombie. Tonight was one of those nights. I was torturing myself over my stupid decision to go to the Dragon Biker Bar and I couldn't manage to stop my racing thoughts. I was also torturing myself over Wyatt and what would happen between us. He had not called me. Was our date still on? I had been too scared to call him myself and find out.

I got out of bed. There was no way I would go back to sleep now.

Harry was upstairs, tucked up tight in his bed. My father was home. I didn't need to check on him; I heard him snoring from the hallway when I checked Harry before I went to bed. I knew better than to check on Ruby and Weston anymore. Their teenage attitudes demanded 'privacy.' I understood that. I used to be that way too, once upon a time before Cora died.

I was in the main kitchen, pouring hot water over a tea bag. On nights like this, I found solace in a hot cup of tea and my sister's favorite mug. As I sipped, the warmth hit my system like a cup full of comfort. Cora and I would drink tea together when we were up late. Insomnia was probably a family thing—or maybe just a sister thing—because we'd always laugh together at the crazy sounding snores my father would fill the quiet house with.

As I shuffled through the kitchen, my feet grew cold on the wood floor. Collapsing on the edge of the sectional in the living room I watched the pre-dawn moonlight filter through the windows cast everything in a dark silvery glow. I scooted to the corner of the couch and sank into the cushiony seat, tucking my feet under my booty to warm them.

I stared outside and watched as the sun and moon fought for dominance. The sun won and early morning light filled the porch. My feet hit the floor when I saw movement there.

It was Weston, slowly rocking by himself on the porch swing. Now, I respected and understood the desire for privacy. This wasn't the time for it though. Rocking alone on a porch swing before dawn demanded checking on. I sat my empty mug on the coffee table and headed outside.

"What are you doing out here, Weston? Did you sleep at all?" I asked when I reached him.

"I broke up with Lizzy," he answered without looking at me.

I sat next to him on the swing. "Why did you decide to do that?" It surprised me. Weston loved Lizzy. He'd been dating Wyatt's niece since ninth grade. He'd once told me he wanted to marry her someday.

"She got into UT, early admission. She'll be gone in January and she isn't interested in trying long distance. She said we're too young and she wants to be free to experience college. Her parents got divorced because they were together since high school and got sick of each other. At least, that's what she told me. She was afraid to even talk to me about it. I think she was planning to just *go.*" He finally looked at me, the hurt in his eyes painful to see. "Wyatt told me. I saw him at Daisy's Nut House. He mentioned the great news about Lizzy —and I had no clue. He told me to ask her about it because he didn't like the idea of her blindsiding me." He turned back toward the emerging dawn and stared into the distance.

"I am so sorry. But maybe this breakup doesn't have to be forever. Maybe it could just be you two taking a break." I wished I could hug him and take his pain away like when he was a little kid, but this was a heartbreak that a hug from his aunt couldn't fix. He'd been through too much for someone his age.

His shoulders shrugged up and didn't come back down.

I wanted to help him, and I didn't know how. Weston had always supported her dreams. I couldn't understand why Lizzy would think he wouldn't be happy for her. I was also sad about Wyatt and hearing his name said out loud hurt my heart. Weston pulled me into a sideways hug. He must have sensed my misery matched his own.

"I like Wyatt. He's a good guy," he finally said.

"Yeah, he is. But I'm afraid I blew it," I confessed.

"How?" He turned to look at me.

"I went to the Dragon Biker Bar to see your dad. Wyatt and Jackson James stopped me. Wyatt was mad, and he was right to be. It was stupid."

"I can't believe you went there. Wow. Don't do it again, no matter what Dad does, please?"

"I won't. I learned my lesson. Let's go to Daisy's and get breakfast to cheer us up," I suggested. "Pop is going to watch Harry this morning because I have to work early."

"Good idea. I'm already dressed, but I should shower and change. I wore this yesterday. I got home last night and kind of just sat here."

"Oh, Weston." I hugged him. He needed it, and so did I.

He pulled back and shook his head. "No more sadness. It's for the best, anyway. Lizzy needs to do this, and I won't be the one who holds her back. It wouldn't be right. And you're right; it doesn't have to be forever."

This apple had fallen so far from the tree it was on another planet in another galaxy in an alternate universe made up of nothing but future romance novel heroes.

"You got it, Weston. No more sadness for us. Shower, change—I will too—then we'll go. Ruby might even be up in time to go with us."

"I doubt it. She was on the phone until late last night spreading the news around." At my confused look he smiled. "Trent Buckley asked her to the homecoming dance."

I clapped my hands and squealed a tiny bit. "I'm happy for her. She was hoping he'd ask."

"Heads up. She's going to ask you to take her to the mall to go dress shopping. I know you don't like crowded places." How hard must it be for him to be so happy for Ruby when he is going through a breakup? He was such a good boy…man? Gah, he was growing up so fast it made me want to cry.

"I'm trying to be better about stuff like that. As of last week, I'm pretty much making decisions that are the opposite of my normal instincts."

"Then maybe you can come to the homecoming game and see me play."

"I will. Harry said he wants to go. And I really want to see you play. I'll think about it. Or maybe I should *not* think about it and just go."

"I'd go with the second option. Thinking is overrated. When you think too much, you sacrifice too much. If I were a selfish prick like Dad, I'd still have a girlfriend. At least until January, anyway."

"Yeah, maybe, but then you'd be a selfish prick, and we'd all hate you. Just be you, Weston. *You* are awesome." I bumped his shoulder with mine when we reached the doorway.

He laughed and opened the front door. "You are awesome too, Aunt Sabrina. Going to the Dragon Bar was dumb, but it took guts, and you did it for us. You're still alive; don't beat yourself up too much."

"Thanks, Weston." I liked his perspective better than my own. My perspective was mean.

"Let's get a move on. I have a sudden craving for a huge ass stack of pancakes," he said.

"Me too, and I need an iced mocha the size of my head. I've been up for way too long."

"Shoot, Sabrina, I didn't sleep at all. And I have football practice later, ugh."

We went into the house and headed to our respective rooms to get ready for the day.

When I finished, I grabbed my purse and headed out to meet Weston.

Ruby was on the couch reading a book. "Hey, Ruby. Congratulations on your homecoming date," I said.

"Thank you." She beamed. "He called me last night. We talked for hours and hours." She stood up and twirled around the living room just like Maria in *The Sound of Music.* She stumbled to a stop and grabbed my hands. I had never seen her like this—ever. It was the cutest thing. "Oh. My. God. We have to go shopping, Sabrina." I exchanged a sideways look with Weston who shook his head with a grin. "Oh! Or maybe I can wear that prom dress Mom made for you when you went to the junior dance? Is it in the attic?"

"It's in the attic. And I think it's a great idea, Ruby. I'll get it down later."

"*Eeeep*! I'm going to get my purse from upstairs. Be right back." She ran up the stairs with more energy that I'd ever had in my entire life.

Weston sighed at my side. "I'll tell her about me and Lizzy later, okay? I don't feel like talking about it anymore today."

I hugged him again. Ruby had added a strange contrast to the collective mood in the house. It felt weird to be so happy for someone when your heart was possibly about to break like mine, or had already broken, like poor Weston's. The only thing I could think to do was hug it out. We pulled apart and headed for the door after Ruby came bounding down the stairs.

"Let's all go get breakfast. Daisy's awaits," I said. I took my Jeep and Ruby rode with Weston.

After we arrived at Daisy's, Weston and I found a table in the corner while Ruby took off for the doughnut case to talk to Cletus, who was busy perusing Daisy's finest. I quickly took a seat against the wall and opened my menu to hide behind. Old habits die hard. I peeked out. Weston's eyes were closed. Was he asleep?

"Wake up!" Ruby dashed up behind him and put her hands on his shoulders, giving him a little shake.

He sat up in his chair and almost fell out of it. "I'm awake," he breathed before opening his eyes.

I shook my head at Ruby. I raised my eyebrows and gave her a look I hoped communicated that she should be nice. She didn't know about Lizzy yet and I didn't want her to feel guilty about giving Weston a bunch of crap for being tired. Over the years, Ruby and I had perfected the art of wordless conversation.

She returned my look and nodded. She snatched up a menu and sat next to Weston. "I'm not getting doughnuts. I don't know if I want pancakes or an egg white omelet."

"Why on earth would you want an egg white omelet? *Ew*." I scrunched up my nose. Daisy's made great food, but egg white omelets were gross, no matter where you got them. *Ew* and yuck and slimy and nope.

She looked at me. "I want to lose some water weight. I want to look nice in my homecoming dress."

"Don't be stupid. You don't need to lose weight," Weston said, face buried in his menu.

Yeah, Weston! I internally cheered. Hearing that from me would be typical. Hearing it from her brother might actually make it sink in.

"Weston is right. Get pancakes, or a normal omelet. Don't worry about water weight."

"Fine, you're right. I like Dr. Pepper too much to go on a diet anyway."

My eyes dropped back to my menu but I jumped a foot out of my chair when Ruby began waving wildly, grinning from ear to ear. I looked in the direction she was waving, and I was pretty sure the feeling that coursed through me was the out-of-body kind when I saw it was Wyatt she was waving over to our table.

I wanted him to come over here. We needed to talk. But I also didn't want to talk. Being in limbo was better than rejection, even though limbo felt horrible.

I glanced over my menu at him. Holy crap he looked good. That uniform did things to me. Things I had no business feeling when I was sitting at a table with Ruby and Weston. Things they were probably old enough to read on my face. In fact, I knew Ruby had figured out exactly what I was thinking when she elbowed me with a smirk. Luckily, Weston had once again shut his eyes and fallen asleep in his chair.

"Sabrina." Wyatt's smile was hesitant as he approached our table.

Weston's head snapped up and he blinked. "Where am I?"

"Daisy's," Wyatt answered with a sympathetic smile and sat down.

"Wyatt?" Weston's face showed his confusion.

"I think you should go home, Weston. You need to sleep," I said.

"I'll go home with him and make sure he stays awake while he drives," Ruby said and stood up pushing Weston's shoulder to get him moving faster while giving me a significant look.

Weston stood up to follow her. "Bye, y'all."

"See you tonight," I said.

They left. Now I was alone with Wyatt, and I didn't know what to say. So many contrasting feelings pulsed through me leaving me confused. The top two were embarrassment and self-doubt. I was fighting hard just to force myself to stay in my seat and not run away from him.

"How are you?" he asked me. I studied his face; the small smile that crossed it gave me no clues to his thoughts.

"I'm fine." I couldn't stop twisting my napkin. I let it go and sat there blinking at him. "I'm just tired. I couldn't sleep last night."

His expression softened and his smile disappeared. He didn't answer; he just sat there and looked at me like *he'd* like to be the reason I was up all night. His eyes burned into mine. It reminded me of the way he had looked at me at Genie's Bar when we danced, right before he kissed me. Something intangible existed between us, I was sure of it. His gaze reminded me of how Leonardo DiCaprio's looked at Claire Danes in *Romeo + Juliet*—hot and full of longing. Sure, after that first hot gaze in the beginning of the movie the whole thing turned to crap and they died at the end. But that first look was everything.

I swear I could feel it, him wanting me, and I wanted him too. I didn't know what I'd do with him once I got him, but I was dying to figure it out. Okay, that was a lie—I had a top ten list of things I wanted to do with him written down in my journal. I had a good imagination. Plus, I'd been reading romance novels since I was twelve.

"Next time you should call me. I don't care how late it is, I'll help you sleep."

"Okay," I breathed. He said next time. That must mean he wasn't mad and wanted me to call him. Right? Maybe I should ask why he didn't call me. I opened my mouth to speak but I couldn't form the words. I shut my mouth and picked up my napkin again.

Thud. Boom. Pow. Those were the sounds my brain just made as it ping-ponged from one confusing thought to the next. My feelings for him felt huge and overwhelming. The risk of being hurt was terrifying.

"Hey, y'all. Sorry for the wait, are you ready to order?"

Both our heads swiveled comically in response to our waitress's simple question.

Wyatt recovered first and answered, "A large coffee and an egg white breakfast sandwich for me. To go."

To go. Disappointment flooded through my veins, dashing the hope that had flowed only a moment before. "Uh, an iced mocha for me, and a chocolate croissant, please," I murmured.

I was probably wrong about everything. I was projecting my out of control feelings onto him. He probably thought I was just a sad, crazy girl with a pathetic crush. Also, an egg white breakfast sandwich? *Ew.* We could never be breakfast buddies. I felt an embarrassed flush crawl up my neck to heat my face. I felt like I was shrinking, and my head pounded. Maybe all we had was a first look. Just like Claire and Leo in the movie. *Dang it.*

I was stuck between wanting to know how he felt and wanting to stay right here in this terrible limbo. Was he giving me mixed messages, or was I just mixed up?

As we waited for our orders an awkward silence descended between us. Not at all like that first day when we were silent in my

Jeep as he drove into town. This time there were words unspoken between us. I had "I'm sorry about The Dragon Biker Bar. I'm not really a total idiot" on the tip of my tongue to say but was too embarrassed to let it out.

I glanced at him; he was fiddling with his cell phone. Preoccupied with whatever he was seeing on the screen. I sighed and pushed my glasses up with a fingertip.

He looked at me and opened his mouth to speak but the waitress bringing our orders stopped him. Instead he said, "I'll see you later, Sabrina." That small impersonal smile crossed his face before he turned and left.

I had lost my courage. "Okay, later," I said to his retreating back.

Later? As in the generic "see you later" that everyone says? "Later" around town? Or "later" as in Saturday night for our freaking date?

This was not a movie and it was not a book; it wasn't even a love song. Those things had a beginning, middle, and end—a pattern. Life was unpredictable and scary, and I couldn't help but wonder if it was worth it.

I sipped my coffee and stared out the window, watching as he drove away in his patrol car. I wanted him to drive out of my head too, but he wouldn't leave.

CHAPTER SIXTEEN

SABRINA

I had spent the rest of the day with no sign of Wyatt. I never saw him "later" and we hadn't "talked" at all. I had no idea what to expect.

Saturday mornings at the library were either slow or crazy and there was usually no in between. I typically preferred slow, but the thought of a crazy day sounded good for a change. It would keep my mind off Wyatt and the potential rejection I would face tonight. I could keep my mind on the best ways to prevent awkward interactions with library patrons instead of obsessing about whether or not our date would happen.

I had stopped contemplating what to wear tonight. I was thinking about what kind of ice cream to pick up at the Piggly Wiggly on my way home from work instead. It didn't matter that I'd only known Wyatt a short time. I had already halfway fallen for him and my heart was just waiting to finish breaking—or falling, hopefully. Either way it turned out, I was gonna need some freaking ice cream.

I smiled at Mrs. MacIntyre as I stowed my things in her office.

"I have a meeting, dear. Can I trust you to handle the library by yourself again?" she asked.

"Yes, you can trust me. I'll be fine."

"I'm proud of you, Sabrina. I saw you saying goodbye to everyone at story hour the other afternoon. You've been spending more and more time helping patrons and less time avoiding them to do other library tasks. It hasn't gone unnoticed. Keep it up."

"Thank you, I will." I returned her smile as warmth coursed through me. It felt good that she had noticed. I didn't even feel like running away to go hide from her compliment. I felt like I had earned it. Maybe the horror section would become just another shelf of books instead of my favorite spot to hide out in. Every day since I had met Wyatt had been a step forward. Even the time when I had called off work and hid in my bed was a step forward—instead of the relief I normally would have experienced, I'd felt guilty. Meeting Wyatt was the spark I had needed. But even if that little flame I had found with him flickered out, I would find a way to keep this fire of self-improvement burning. Somehow.

Mrs. MacIntyre grabbed her things and left with a wave.

I smiled to myself and scanned the library. A few teens were at the old computers in the corner, Jackson was in my usual haunt in the horror section looking for something scary to read, and Everett sat in the red rocking chair in the children's section with Makenna and Melissa next to him on the floor, listening to him as he read them a story.

"Hi, Riri, hi!" Harry called as he and Ruby made their way through the small lobby. Harry ran around the counter and threw himself into my arms. I picked him up and smacked a kiss on his cheek.

He laughed and wiggled to get down.

"Hey, Aunt Sabrina," Ruby said. "Harry wants to sit in the purple beanbag and read *Harry Potter*. Our copy at home is not good enough." She laughed and plopped into one of the chairs at the tables in the center of the library. Ruby was watching Harry until my father finished at the senior center.

"Hey! It's Mak and Mel! I like them!" Harry shouted excitedly and ran for the story area.

"Harry!" Melissa shouted back, stood up, and met him at the edge of the solar system rug. "You're here at the library! Sit with us.

Uncle Everett is reading *Fancy Nancy* and she is a ballerina in this one."

I laughed as Mel did a little pirouette before she took her place on the rug again.

"Sit here, Harry." Makenna patted the floor between her and Mel indicating he should join them.

Everett looked up from the book and waved to me. He looked harried; his hair was in a messy man-bun, and the hair tie was a pink glitter scrunchie. Mrs. Monroe must be sick or something. Wyatt had told me she usually watched his girls while he worked.

I saw Jackson approach the checkout counter with his books. I gripped the edge of the counter and held on. My heart started to pound a nervous echo I could feel in my ears. I wanted to dart into Mrs. MacIntyre's office and invent an emergency so I could hide from him, but I fought the urge. I owed him an apology for the trouble I almost caused at the Dragon Biker Bar and I was determined to give it to him. "Hi, Jackson."

He grinned and slid his books across the counter.

"I'm sorry—for, uh..." I drifted off as I struggled for words. This was important; I had to do it. I felt like it would be a big step forward for me. I needed to look Jackson in the eye and say I was sorry. I inhaled a huge breath.

"It's okay," he said before I could try again.

My eyes shot to his. "You aren't mad at me?"

"I'm not mad at you, sweetheart." His eyes held mine as he smiled at me.

I released the huge breath I was holding and smiled back at him. "Thank you. I won't do anything stupid like that again—probably."

"It was very stupid," he agreed. "But it was also brave. Funny how those two things go hand in hand sometimes."

I laughed softly. "Yeah, big feelings seem to keep pushing me out of my comfort zone." Why was it so much easier to talk about this with Jackson? Probably because I didn't have a super massive crush on him like Wyatt.

"I'm glad." He winked at me. "Comfort zones are boring." His wink didn't give me all the feels that Wyatt's did, and I still couldn't believe I had completely overlooked his potential. He was adorable, blond, sexy-hot, and some lucky girl would get—uh, lucky when she caught his eye. Plus, he loved Stephen King and that made him awesome. It had also made him my friend, I hoped.

"You're right, Jackson."

Suddenly there was a commotion in the children's area. "My tummy hurts, Uncle Everett—" echoed across the library just before the retching started.

Jackson spun around, Ruby stood up in alarm, the teens at the computers ran out the front door, and I grabbed the small metal garbage bin that sat at the side of the counter and made a mad dash toward Mel.

I managed to thrust the garbage can under her face just before a wave of red vomit blew forth. It smelled a lot like frosting as it filled the can.

"Oh, shit!" Harry cried and crab walked backward to crash into the shelf against the wall. Harry had a sensitive gag reflex and an extremely picky appetite; he threw up often. I could probably become a professional puke catcher if I wanted to make a career change. But I also had a tendency to curse whenever barf was involved—which Harry had picked up on—so keeping my job in the library was probably for the best.

"I told you it would made her sick, Uncle Everett," Mak said, matter of fact.

"But—I didn't let her eat any," Everett stammered. He looked a little green as he stood there and stared at Mel and me in horror.

"What did she eat?" I asked, hopefully it was just a full tummy and not food poisoning or something worse. I pulled Mel onto my lap on the floor when she finished throwing up. I pushed the curls out of her face and smiled down at her. "You'll be okay, honey," I murmured.

She closed her eyes and rested her head against my chest.

"Red velvet ladybug cupcakes," Everett whispered. "This is so gross." His hand got caught in his man-bun when he tried to run it through his hair, so he threw his arms out to the sides instead.

"I called Wyatt," Jackson said from the edge of the children's area a safe distance away from the epicenter.

"Red frosting makes Mel sick," Mak informed me. She had found a book to read and sat down in Everett's spot in the rocking chair. "She took them into the bathroom, Uncle Everett. I told you to check on her."

"I did check on her," he argued. "She said she had to go potty real bad."

Mak looked at me, eyebrows up. "Mel is sneaky."

"Shut up, Mak," Mel whispered. She wrapped her arms around my waist and snuggled closer, cuddling herself into me.

"Are you sneaky, honey?" I grinned down at her upturned face.

She scrunched up her nose and shook her head.

Harry peered over my shoulder down at Mel. "She looks kind of sneaky, Riri."

Ruby picked up the garbage can. "I'll hose this out. Can I go out the back, Aunt Sabrina?"

"Yes, you can. Thank you, Ruby. My keys are on the counter up front."

"Men can't handle it when it gets real." She smirked at Everett as she passed him with the garbage can.

"It's probably because of the patriarchy," Mak said without looking up from her book.

Jackson barked out a laugh from behind us, just as Wyatt came running through the front door.

"Where is she?" The concern in his voice touched my heart. What a good dad. What a good, hot, sexy dad.

"I've got her. I think she's okay now," I called to him.

I looked up as he sank to his knees across from Mel and me.

"Thank you, Sabrina." A small smile crossed his face as he reached for Mel and she pulled herself closer to me instead of going to him.

"I like Sabrina," she said.

"I like you too, angel," I told her and smoothed her bouncy curls back only to watch them spring forward again into her face. *Adorable.*

"I'm sorry, Wyatt. I didn't know she couldn't eat red frosting. I feel terrible." Everett knelt alongside Wyatt. "I'm sorry, Mel," he added.

"It's okay, Uncle Everett. You told me not to, but they were pretty and delicious, and I love ladybugs. I think it was worth it," she sighed.

"Hey, Wyatt. Take the girls home," Jackson said. "I'll go into the station and cover the rest of your shift. Will you hold onto those books for me, Sabrina?"

I nodded and Wyatt thanked Jackson as he left.

"She needs Grandma Essie's rainbow soup," Harry declared. "Grandma said it will cure what ails you. Throwing up is very ailing. I always eat the soup after I barf. We should bring her some later." He nodded sagely.

"I want the soup. I need the soup. I am feeling very aily, and rainbows sound delicious." Mel looked up over my shoulder and answered Harry.

"I'll bring you a Creeper plushie too," Harry said decisively. "Don't worry, they only explode in the game. Do you like Minecraft?"

"Uh...maybe she just needs to go home and rest, Harry," I protested.

"We have soup in the freezer," Ruby butted in as she entered with the hosed-out garbage can and a smug smile that she shot in my direction.

Wyatt grinned at me, complete with the eye-crinkle and the dimple. "Would you like to come over later? Bring Harry and the soup and I'll make grilled cheese to go with it? It looks like I won't be able to take you to the Front Porch tonight. Not after this. Everett won't be able to handle it if she blows again. And my mother is down with a migraine."

"Hey!" Everett looked offended for a minute. "Nah, you're right. The sight of those cupcakes coming back up almost made me throw up too. Like the blueberry pie barf-o-rama in *Stand by Me*."

"Well..." I started, but Ruby cut me off.

"She'll be there, with the soup and Harry. I'll go home and defrost it right now. Come on, Harry." Ruby held out her hand.

Harry rushed over and took her hand. "Bye, Mak and Mel. Bye,

Sheriff Wyatt. Bye, Sheriff Wyatt's brother Everett. Bye, Riri. I will see you tonight."

"Bye, Harry." I waved as Ruby led him out of the library.

I guess we were going to have dinner with Wyatt and his girls tonight.

Our date was broken just like I thought it would be. Only I wasn't sad about it at all.

CHAPTER SEVENTEEN

WYATT

Dinner at the Front Porch had turned into dinner at my place. I cringed when I remembered the mess I'd left the house in this morning. I had a few hours to straighten up. God, what did a sweet girl like her want with a guy like me? Divorced, raising two daughters alone in a house that I couldn't even manage to keep clean. I was a deputy sheriff, not someone prestigious like her orthopedic surgeon father. I couldn't give her the kinds of things she was probably used to having. The kinds of things my ex-wife had wanted so badly that she was willing to lie, cheat, and abandon our daughters to get.

I glanced in the rearview mirror. Mel had fallen asleep in her booster seat with her head tipped back and mouth wide open and Mak was reading one of the books she'd just checked out. "Wait until we get home to read, ladybug, or you'll end up getting carsick," I told her. One barfing daughter was all I could handle at a time.

"Okay, Daddy." I heard the book snap shut. "I'll help you clean up when we get home. I like Miss Sabrina. Can she be your girlfriend now?"

I tried not to react in a way that would give her too much hope. But I couldn't help but smile at the thought. I was thrilled that the girls seemed to like her so much. "I like her too, and I don't know yet. How would you feel about that?"

"I would like it. I think Mel would too. Miss Sabrina was nice when Mel threw up, not all grossed out like Mom gets." My heart sank. My ex-wife was not a warm person. Even when they were babies, she was never the type of mother to cuddle and coo over the girls. I had done my best to give them all the hugs, encouragement, and love they needed but I always feared it wasn't enough.

What would it be like to have someone like Sabrina to come home to? Someone sweet like her, to warm my house and fill it with love. Someone to warm my bed at night. Someone who would let me love her.

When I first saw her in the back of that Jeep I thought, *that's her*. I thought I'd found the one for me. Crazy, right? To have such thoughts at first sight. Thoughts like that would get me into trouble if I wasn't careful. I couldn't let myself take a leap before I got a good look at what I was jumping into.

I pulled into my garage and shut off the engine.

Mel woke up when the truck stopped. "Daddy, I'm sleepy. Can I watch *Fancy Nancy* and wear your robe on the couch?" Mel loved to wrap up in the old flannel robe my mother had bought for me when I left for college.

"Sure, you can."

I laughed as Mel unbuckled herself and ran to the door. "My tummy is empty. I need rainbow soup and Goldfish crackers." She crossed her legs and bounced up and down in place, "Hurry, Daddy. I have to peeeeeeee."

I rushed to the door and threw it open in front of her after I unlocked it. She darted in and ran for the bathroom.

"You shouldn't let her watch *Fancy Nancy*. She tricked Uncle Everett and locked herself in the bathroom with, like, five cupcakes. I told her not to do it," Mak informed me. She was like a little mother, more than a big sister. Guilt filled my mind when I thought of all the growing up she had to do after the divorce.

I heaved out a sigh. "Okay, I'll talk to her. Again." Mel was a sneaky little thing and cupcakes were her kryptonite. She'd do anything to get her hands on one—or five, apparently. Even risk throwing up. Red food coloring was also her kryptonite.

Mak entered the house, hung her backpack and jacket on the hook, and immediately started filling the pink toy box with the toys that had not been put away last night...or the night before...or ever. "Thanks, Mak."

She turned and beamed at me. "We should make dessert, too. I want Miss Sabrina to like it here."

I want her to like it here too.

"Sure, I think we have banana pudding stuff. How's that?" I couldn't bake for shit, but I could mix stuff in a bowl and assemble it.

"Good. Everybody likes banana pudding," she answered and stuck her hand out for a high-five. We smacked palms and I headed down the hall to change clothes.

"I'll be right back to help," I called.

Between Mak and me, we got the house picked up, the table set, and the banana pudding made. Mel lounged on the couch watching cartoons the whole time. Sometimes it was just easier to let her be. I tried to save taking the easy way with Mel for emergencies because it wasn't fair to Mak. Having dinner guests was not exactly an emergency, but it was important. Plus, she did throw up today—even if it was her own fault.

"How much longer?" Mak asked once we'd finished.

"Any minute now." We grinned at each other when we heard the knock at the door.

"They're here!" Mel screamed from the living room before running toward the front door and throwing it open.

Sabrina stood there with Harry. She was in jeans and a snug red sweater. It took a lot for me to take my eyes off that sweater. Every other time I'd seen her she was in various skirts and loose cardigans, high-heeled shoes, and headbands. Her white Converse sneakers and softly tousled hair were... She was gorgeous, and I was struck dumb. Was this what she wore when she wasn't at the library? Because, yes please. I wanted to get my hands in those black waves that flowed like a shiny midnight river over her shoulder. I wanted to feel those jeans-clad legs wrap around my waist as I kissed her. I wanted...too much, too soon. She was an irresistible mixture of sexy and sweet. But I sensed that she was still mostly sweet. I wanted to be the one to discover that sexy side and flip the balance. I just wanted her. *Stop it, Monroe.*

"Harry! Come watch cartoons!" Mel yelled and tugged Harry into the house.

"Maybe Harry doesn't want to watch cartoons, Mel. Maybe he wants to play video games with me," Mak said from the edge of the entryway.

"I like cartoons and I like video games too," he said with a huge smile lighting up his face. He turned and looked up at Sabrina. "They like cartoons and video games just like I do, Riri. What do I do?"

She tousled his hair. "You can do both. Maybe cartoons first, since Mel asked first? Does that sound okay with you, Mak?"

Mak nodded. She had grown shy at their arrival.

I stepped back, reaching for the bag she was carrying. "Come on in. Let me take that for you."

"Thank you. We just need to heat it up." She stepped inside and closed the door behind her.

"Follow me." I grinned at her and headed into the kitchen to put the soup on. I opened the bag and pulled out a plush doll that was sitting on top. It looked like a green penis with a face. "What's this? Did the Incredible Hulk lose something?"

She blushed. "Oh, it's for Mel. It's from Minecraft. It's a Creeper. Harry wanted to give it to her." Sabrina called him over and handed him the Creeper.

I was used to girly toys. Barbie dolls and Beanie Boos and Shopkins that hurt when you stepped on them with your bare feet. I found myself wondering what it would be like to have a little boy around. Would Harry be interested in things like tossing a ball out in the yard or catching fish at Sky Lake? I knew there were girls that liked that stuff too. I just had two girls that were not.

"Oh, yeah. Mel, I brought you a present because you threw up in the garbage can. It's a Creeper. It will blow up the barf germs." Harry handed it to her and made explosion sounds.

"Thanks." Mel took it and examined it with a scrunched-up face. "Um, I don't know if I can love it though, Harry. It's not cute like my other plushies. It's not even ugly-cute like my Ugly Doll."

"Just try your best," Harry advised.

Mel hugged it to her chest. "I will try so hard. I'll put it with my Beanie Boos. They can help it be cute. Y'all, come on!" She ran off down the hall to her room. Harry and Mak followed her.

"Hello." I smiled at Sabrina. It felt like so long ago when I'd kissed her at Genie's Bar. I wanted to do it again. I wanted to erase that awkwardness that had sprung up between us after that morning in the parking lot of the Dragon Biker Bar.

"Hi," she breathed. Her head tipped forward and her smile softened.

I reached out for the curve of her waist and pulled her closer with both hands. Invisible strings pulled us closer until her palms met my chest and slid up and my lips met her lips to press down for a quick kiss. We closed the distance between us until I could feel her against me. I wrapped my arms around her and hugged her. I hoped I wasn't being too forward, but I couldn't help myself.

She pulled back and stepped out of my arms. "I guess this means you aren't mad at me?" She studied my face obviously waiting for me to answer.

My eyebrows shot up. "I'm not mad at you. Why would you think that?"

She turned red. "Um, we barely talked at Daisy's and you said we had to talk when I saw you at Genie's. And I went to the Dragon Bar and, uh..."

"I'm sorry I made you think I was mad at you. My mother texted me when we were at Daisy's to tell me she had a migraine. I had to get Everett to watch the girls—I should have just told you. And we do have to talk, it's important. We have to talk about situational awareness and personal safety. I want to make sure you stay safe, Sabrina."

Her eyes got huge. "That's it? That's what you wanted to talk to me about?" Then she laughed and kept on laughing. She covered her mouth and looked away. "I drove myself crazy. I thought you..."

I touched her cheek and gently turned her face to mine. "What did you think?"

"Um, never mind what I thought," she whispered. "I guess I was wrong."

"I'm sorry, darlin'."

"It's okay. Now," she murmured.

"Good, because we have to reschedule our date. I owe you dinner at the Front Porch."

"Oh, you don't have to take me there. Maybe we can go to Daisy's or Genie's. The Front Porch is so fancy it makes me kind of nervous."

I smiled at her. Huge. The Front Porch was too fancy for her? It was too fancy for me too. Maybe I didn't have to worry about giving her what she was used to. Maybe she wanted something *I* could offer her. "We can go wherever you like. I just want to spend time with you."

CHAPTER EIGHTEEN

SABRINA

I didn't know what to think. So I decided to stop thinking. He wasn't mad at me now and he never had been. That was what I decided to take away from our conversation in the kitchen. I'd take that and the kiss and hold on to the feelings they gave me to use whenever I doubted him. Or myself.

Dinner went by just fine. We were eating food Harry was used to, so he didn't have a problem with it. The girls were sweet and adorable and did their best to make Harry and me feel welcome. Now we were all in Wyatt's living room watching *The Princess Bride* and I was about to combust with the lust that burned through my body like the fuse on a stick of dynamite. I was lusty and giddy and in danger of making a fool of myself.

The kids were sprawled out on the floor, submerged in piles of pillows and blankets. Wyatt was next to me on the couch, his hard thigh close to mine and his arm draped across the back of the cushions. He wasn't touching me with that arm or that thigh, but I could feel his warmth against my skin. It would take nothing at all for me to just lean to the side a bit and press myself against him. I wanted to so bad. I found myself wanting a lot of things right now. I wanted to be alone with him. I wanted to crawl into his lap and kiss him. I wanted all the things I'd been dreaming about and used to be so scared of. But I didn't feel scared right now. I felt amazing. Something about Wyatt felt right. Something about him had unlocked something in me and made me feel free to be myself. Or maybe it was just the combination of me being ready for a change and running into the right person. I didn't even care. I just wanted to hold on to this feeling. It felt a lot like hope.

"Harry, don't look." Mel surged out of the blankets and covered Harry's eyes as the rodents of unusual size appeared on the screen. "Oh, no, Mak! My hands are busy, cover my eyes!" she shrieked.

Mak sighed and sat up to cover Mel's eyes.

"Do I need to cover your eyes?" Wyatt whispered to me with an adorable flirty sideways smile.

I turned to him and nodded. Covering my eyes equaled touching and I was all for that.

He chuckled and let that arm on the back of the couch drape over my shoulders as he placed his warm palm over my eyes. Thankfully, I was wearing my contacts. I took the opportunity to lean into his side. Now my thigh pressed against his, his arm was around me, and I was definitely going to combust because this was even awesomer than I thought it would be.

He moved his hand from my eyes but didn't move his body away from mine. We watched the rest of the movie like that. Until I grew used to being next to him, comfortable and warm. He reached over and took my hand. As he held it against his leg, I realized that I was no longer nervous around him. My heart pounded like crazy. My face flushed and I grew flustered, but it was not out of fear or embarrassment. It was out of anticipation and desire. I was both comfortable and exceedingly *uncomfortable* around him. I couldn't help but think the uncomfortable part would go away once we knew each other better. Maybe after we spent more time alone.

He lifted my hand to his mouth, turned it over, and kissed the inside of my wrist. I felt his lips linger on my pulse point. The little fluttering pulse in my wrist soon flooded my blood elsewhere and I squirmed in my seat. My eyes drifted shut and I wanted more. I wanted more of his mouth on my body and I was not particular about where he should put it.

"I should stop. The kids..." he murmured.

"I think they're asleep," I quickly whispered in response because I didn't want to stop, not yet.

He grinned and took a quick glance at the floor to confirm my observation. Then he turned my hand again and brushed soft, sweet kisses over the back of each finger before placing my hand on the back of his neck and pulling me into his body. Ripples of warmth flowed through me as I melted against him. My breath caught in my throat as his hands drifted up and down my back. For the first time I understood what it meant to have a man's touch light you on fire. I was burning up.

His fingers sifted into my hair and with a gentle tug he tipped my face back. I watched his eyes drift shut and his grin fade away as his face dropped to mine. He kissed me, warm and soft, claiming my mouth with his until I was left in a happy haze of pleasure. He pulled back; I opened my eyes to find his eyes on mine, sweet and sexy with that crinkly perfection at the corners I adored.

"Is this okay?" he asked softly as he swept my hair over my shoulder.

"Yes, Wyatt," I whispered. Then he kissed me again—deeply, sweetly, completely. Restless pulses of pleasure darted through me as our kiss deepened and his tongue entered my mouth to tangle with mine. *Holy Hufflepuffs, he was a good kisser.*

We were lost in each other, in this perfect moment where nothing existed but me, him, and this beautifully epic, probably life-changing kiss. His heart had found mine. More than our lips and hands connected us; we were in one of those rare moments when two people communicated with their souls. I pulled away to look at him and I knew he felt the same. My skin prickled with awareness as my heart opened up to let him inside. I pulled back with a sigh as I recalled my father's warning to be careful of falling too fast.

He let me go, but first placed a soft kiss on my forehead. "I like you here." He framed my face with his palms then I swayed into him again to rest my cheek against his broad chest.

"Thank you for inviting me." My words were muffled but he heard me just the same. "I should probably get Harry home. It's late." I sat up and looked into his eyes as he smiled at me.

"I'll help you get Harry into the car," he whispered.

"Thank you."

We stood. I gathered our coats and Wyatt scooped Harry up off the floor. Once Harry was secure in the back of my Jeep, I turned to Wyatt. "I had a great time tonight. Your girls are amazing, your house is adorable, and I like you so much." I shut my eyes. God, I had turned from not talking at all to a compulsive oversharer. What was wrong with me?

I'd read a lot of books. I used to look for answers in books when I was too afraid to live my life. Books were full of helpful facts, even fiction. But if you weren't pairing your reading with living then the facts were useless. Was this what a relationship was? Having a hand to hold and feeling like you had somewhere to belong? Because I felt that way right now.

He didn't say anything. He just slammed his mouth to mine.

I ran my hands up his chest, loving the way his muscles felt under my palms. My hands came to rest on his cheeks as his mouth opened and his tongue swept between my lips to move against mine.

He was delicious and I wished we weren't outside. I wished I didn't have to get Harry home and into bed because I didn't want to stop kissing him.

After another moment he pulled back. He held me and studied my face.

I pressed my fingertips to his lips. Then I threw my arms around his neck and my body back into his. He wrapped his arms around my waist and buried his head in that sensitive spot where my neck met my shoulder, a spot that I hadn't known before this moment would drive me crazy with his touch. My head tipped to the side so he could reach it better. His breath drew goose bumps across my skin before his lips pressed a kiss there. I held tight and breathed him in. I couldn't get close enough. I wanted more of this feeling—I was soaring and every time he touched me, I flew higher.

I waved goodbye to Wyatt as he stood on his porch watching me go. My heart fluttered with the memory of being in his arms and my thoughts kept drifting back to his sweet kisses. As I got closer to home, I couldn't help but wonder how it would work if we went further. Where would we live? Would he be willing to leave this adorable house and move his girls into the ranch someday? I couldn't take Harry away from my father, from Weston and Ruby. My life was not completely my own and neither was his. Was it possible to add anyone to it and take care of Harry the way he needed me to?

CHAPTER NINETEEN

SABRINA

Tonight was the night. Our second attempt at a first date. We were meeting at Genie's, to have dinner, dance, and whatever else. The possibility of *whatever else* was what I was a little bit nervous about. We had been texting and talking on the phone all week long, but I hadn't mustered up enough courage to tell him I was a virgin. He could probably figure it out if he thought about it—whenever I talked about my life it was like a giant context clue that shrieked VIRGIN ALERT on repeat like an obnoxious, blaring alarm clock—but did men really think that hard about stuff like that?

I finished applying my lipstick—MAC Diva (I wish)—and stepped back to examine myself in the mirror. I had traded my regular library nerd-wear for the skinny jeans Ruby helped me pick out when we were back to school shopping and a silky black tank to wear under my leather jacket. I was also wearing sexy underwear; it was green and lacy. Green was Wyatt's favorite color. Sexy underwear made me feel sexy, but it also made me more nervous. I never said I made any sense. I slipped on Cora's red boots for luck and tried to stop thinking about my panties.

I drove to Genie's and recalled the time when I'd come here to find Willa. I almost felt like a different person now. I was still shy, and I always would be, but that sickening dread I always felt whenever I left my house was gradually dissipating. The more I made myself do, the less I felt it. I was nervous, but not terrified, and for me that was huge.

I pulled into a spot and got out. No hesitation this time as I crossed the parking lot to enter the bar. Wyatt had planned to drop his girls off with his mother and meet me at the edge of the bar, near the booth in the corner.

I spotted Willa behind the bar slinging drinks and looking like a hot, blond, female version of Tom Cruise in *Cocktail*. Okay, she looked nothing like Tom Cruise, but she could flip a bottle up in the air and catch it like a badass. Genie was there, too. She waved to me as she filled glasses with the beer on tap behind the bar.

I sat in a stool and waited.

"Flamin' Dr. Pepper?" Willa called to me with a huge smile on her face.

"No, thank you. Just a beer please."

"Coming right up." She slid me a beer. "When is Wyatt supposed to get here?"

I glanced at the clock on my phone. "Any minute now."

She grinned at me. "I'm so happy for you, Sabrina. Wyatt's a great guy." She patted my hand and headed down the bar to help another customer.

I sipped my beer and waited.

Willa and I had caught up a lot since she'd come back to Green Valley, but I still didn't know everything she'd been through while she was gone. I knew she was divorced. I knew her husband was a giant a-hole. But I had already known he was a bossy a-hole before she left. Mostly we just spent time talking about me, the kids, her job here at Genie's, and the fact that she was about to move into the apartment in Everett's basement next week.

I finished my beer and glanced around the bar. I got up to stand on my tiptoes and scan the area. *Where was he?*

I didn't want to order another beer and I didn't want to keep checking the time on my phone like a loser. I should text him. Just a little text to see if he was okay.

I'm at Genie's. Are you running late?

I added a smiley face emoji and a friendly red heart so I wouldn't seem like a crazy, hostile nag. I hit send.

Oh my gosh, I shouldn't have added the heart. He would think I want to marry him right now and have his babies. He would think I was in love with him like a stalker or something. I inhaled a huge breath and tried to calm my racing thoughts. I did want to have a baby. And sometimes I thought about what it would be like to marry Wyatt. Did he know that I practiced signing Sabrina Louise Logan-Monroe in my journal? Was he against hyphens? Had he figured out what my thoughts were and decided that escape was his only option? I mean, he hadn't texted me back yet.

I put my phone in my pocket and waited.

Willa came around the bar and glared at the man in the stool next to me until he got up and walked off. "I'm on break," she announced and took his seat.

I tried to smile at her but the only expression I could muster up was a raised eyebrow look of panic. She covered my hand with hers and pressed down to stop me from tapping it on the bar.

"You're going to be fine, Sabrina."

"He's late. He's not coming. He hates me, I know it." The words burst out of me before I could filter them.

"He doesn't hate you. No one hates you. There is nothing to hate." She smiled sympathetically and held my hand.

I froze. Of course, there was nothing to hate. I had been *nothing* for years. It was easy to be nothing.

Now I was something. I was a girl waiting for a boy in a bar and it was scary.

I wanted to be more than that.

I am more than that.

I was a daughter, an aunt, and a friend. I was an assistant librarian and a responsible driver. I could make the most kick-ass brownies in the world, and don't play Monopoly with me—I'll kick your butt. And yes, I was also a girl waiting for a boy in a bar, but I was so much more than that. And Wyatt was one of the people that had helped me see it.

"You're right. Something must have happened. I'm going to call and see if he's okay."

"Good idea."

I pulled my phone from my pocket and called.

It sent me straight to voice mail.

"No answer," I said.

"Wyatt wouldn't stand you up. I'll call Everett," she offered.

"Oh, you have his number, do you?" *Go, Willa. Everett is a catch.*

"Shut up." She smiled and rolled her eyes. She pulled out her phone and held up a finger as she waited for him to answer. Her eyebrows went up. "He's not answering either."

"Well, we're all out of numbers to call. How long do people wait for a date? I don't want to be rude."

She laughed. "You're so crazy. He's the one who's late and you're sitting here worried about being rude."

I shrugged. "I can't help it."

"Good, don't change completely. I'd miss you."

Tears filled my eyes. I leaned over in my stool and hugged her. "Thank you."

She pulled back and looked me dead in the eye. "But if he doesn't have a good reason for this, you let him have it. Life is too short to put up with shit from any man."

"Okay. I will let him have it if I need to. I will take no shit."

"Good for you."

"I think I'm going to head home. If he shows up, will you tell him?"

"Absolutely. And I'll stop by in the morning. We can either eat a shit-load of ice cream for breakfast or go get pedicures. I'm there for you either way."

"I'm so glad you came home, Willa."

"Me too."

She got up and headed back behind the bar while I retrieved my jacket and drove home.

Ruby and Weston were in the living room watching a movie, boxes of pizza spread open on the coffee table in front of them.

"Hey," I said as I flopped down on the sectional and reached for a slice of pepperoni.

They exchanged a look.

"Aren't you supposed to be out with Wyatt?" Ruby asked.

"He didn't show up." I took a huge bite of pizza, then flopped it back in the box. I didn't have an appetite after all.

"He stood you up?" Weston sat forward. "I can't promise I'll succeed. In fact, I may die if I try it. But, for you, I'll attempt to kick his ass."

I shook my head as I finished chewing. "That won't be necessary. Something probably happened. It will be fine," I insisted.

"What's going on? What is up with you? Why aren't you freaking out?" Ruby questioned me.

"He's a good guy," I explained. "Something probably happened. I'm sure he'll call me later and apologize. And if not, then I will be okay. I am more than just a girl in a bar."

"Yeah. You are. Absolutely." Ruby studied my face as she reached for another slice of pizza. She tossed it back in the box and glared at me with suspicion. "Who are you and where is my Aunt Sabrina?" She turned to Weston. "We shouldn't have watched that body snatcher movie earlier. I am freaking out."

Weston laughed.

"Riri! You're home early." Harry jumped over the back of the couch and hugged my neck.

"I sure am and I missed you."

"I missed you too." He cuddled into my side. "Let's watch *Harry Potter.* Can we?"

"Sure, it's been two days," I answered. "I was starting to forget some of the dialogue."

Ruby laughed and snuggled into my other side. Weston grabbed another slice of pizza and settled in to join us.

We watched the movie.

I tucked Harry into bed at nine o'clock. Hours after my date with Wyatt was supposed to start and I still hadn't heard anything. Was he okay?

I said goodnight to Ruby and Weston and headed down my bookshelf-lined hallway to my little apartment off the side of the house. I changed into yoga pants and my favorite Smash-Girl T-shirt.

What would Sienna Diaz do?

Would she cry if the man she was falling into serious like with stood her up? Was that okay? Tears filled my eyes. I tried to blink them back, but they wouldn't stop.

I spun around as Ruby entered my room with a knock.

"I knew you were upset." She ran in and hugged me.

"I can't help it. I—"

"Shh, no matter what, you'll be fine. We're all here for you. I'll help Weston kick his ass. Or maybe I'll just call Cle—never mind. You'll be okay. I'll make sure of it. Pop is upstairs. Do you want to talk to him?"

"Nah, I'm okay. I love you, Ruby."

"I love you too." She squeezed me close again then pulled back to smile sympathetically at me.

"I think I'm going to go for a walk. I don't feel like being cooped up in here just thinking and wondering and being miserable."

"To the pasture?"

"Yeah, you know me."

"I do know you. That's how I know you're going to be just fine."

I slipped on my Chucks, grabbed a hoodie, and grinned at Ruby. "I'll see you in the morning, sweetheart."

CHAPTER TWENTY

WYATT

Tonight could not have gone worse. I was supposed to meet Sabrina at six o'clock for our date at Genie's. Instead I spent the evening in an emergency room in Maryville with Mel and her sprained wrist. She had fallen off the slide on the playground at school. In my crazy rush to get to the hospital I'd lost my phone. I did not have Sabrina's phone number memorized. Who memorizes phone numbers anymore? I was not able to call her, and I was late—so, so late. Over four hours late.

My mother agreed to stay with the girls so I could swing by Sabrina's house and attempt to get her to forgive me for tonight. My mother was a romantic and nosy as hell. It didn't take much to convince her. The girls were asleep when I left and wouldn't even notice I was gone, hopefully. How could I manage this—a potential relationship—when I had the girls to take care of?

Sabrina had texted her gate code to me weeks ago, when I'd asked her out the first time. I punched it in and drove through. I parked my truck in front of the house, relieved to see the lights on downstairs.

It was bad form to knock on anyone's door this late at night, but I didn't want her to think the worst of me. I hated the thought of it. It was killing me to think I'd hurt her feelings.

I knocked softly. I shifted from side to side like a teenager picking up his first date. I shook my head and took a deep breath.

The door flew open. It was Ruby. She stood there and glared at me with her eyebrows up. Weston came up behind her.

"Hey, Wyatt. You're kind of late, bro," he said with a glare to match his sister's.

Ruby continued to glare at me.

I flinched when she narrowed her eyes. Damn, she was scary for a sixteen-year-old girl. "Mel sprained her wrist. I was at the emergency room and I lost my phone," I said in a rush. I didn't want Ruby to slam the door in my face or attack me like a teen demon.

I didn't have to worry though. Once I finished explaining, she lost the malevolent look and smiled at me. "Oh, well, that's different. That's good—not for poor Mel—but for you. I have to go and text Cletus," she muttered and ran off.

"Cletus? Winston?" I asked.

"She was planning something with itching powder. I don't know. I only heard one side of the conversation. I find it's best not to rile Ruby up too much," Weston advised. "Sabrina is out back. She was kind of upset earlier and went out there to think. Just drive around the garage, go past the barn, and keep on going until you see the old horse pasture. You'll find her out there."

"Thank you, Weston."

"I know how it is. Relationships—they're tough, man."

"How're you doing?" I had heard he and Lizzy had broken up.

"I'll live." He grinned at me. "Go get her."

I nodded and got into my truck.

The moon sat low in the distant sky, gleaming huge and orange, shining almost as bright as the sun. I drove slow over the gravel road and kept my eyes peeled for Sabrina.

I drove a bit more before I spotted her down a slight slope, sitting in the middle of an open field. I cut the engine and made my way to her.

"Sabrina, it's Wyatt!" I shouted as I approached.

"It's the Harvest Moon, Wyatt. I forgot it was tonight. Isn't it amazing?"

"Yeah, it's beautiful. I'm so sorry, Sabrina—"

"Don't."

"Okay." I stood there and studied her face, trying to discern her features in the dark. I wished I'd left my headlights on or brought a flashlight. Or knew where my fucking cell phone was so I could use the light on it.

"This is my favorite spot in the world. I always come here to think."

We were in an old horse pasture. It was a wide-open space, bordered by trees on one side and the Great Smoky Mountains National Park on the other side. She pointed to the distance, and I saw the dark silhouettes of the trees up high in the mountains. The dark muted their colors to varying shades of gray and black with the ever-present mist filtering down through the trees toward the pasture. In the daylight this place would be amazing—colorful and bright. It would have been pitch dark tonight if it weren't for the golden glow of the Harvest Moon.

"This used to be one of the pastures for the horses," she told me. She turned and looked up toward the mountains. "I love it here." She leaned back on her elbows before lying flat on her back in the grass. "Isn't it beautiful?"

I stood there and looked at her—hair splayed out on the grass like a dark halo around her head, her sweet face relaxed and smiling up at me. "Yes, more than anything," I answered.

"Wyatt," she murmured and held her hand out.

I sank to my knees and took her hand. I stretched out next to her with my other arm bent under my head. "I didn't mean to stand you up." I moved to my side, resting my head on my hand so I could watch her face as I explained. "I was at the hospital in Maryville with Mel. She fell off the slide at school and sprained her wrist. She'll be fine. But I wasn't fine; I was all worked up with worry and I lost my phone. I couldn't remember your number to call you. Please tell me I haven't screwed everything up with you."

She turned to her side, matching my position. "You haven't messed anything up with me," she said, making me smile. "At first I assumed you stood me up because I did something to make you not want to go out with me. But then I realized I have to stop thinking like that. You've done nothing to cause me to assume the worst. You've always done the opposite and made me feel like it's okay to open up. And honestly, my feelings got in the way of my logic. I'm sorry I assumed the worst about you—I won't do that again. And I'm glad Mel is going to be okay."

Compelled to touch her, I brushed her hair over her shoulder with my free hand letting it sift through the soft strands. "Thank you, Sabrina. I don't want to screw this up. I wanted to go out with you tonight. I want to try again with you, but I don't want to keep letting you down. It's been twice now. I know that this kind of thing will happen again. My girls are my life." Looking into her eyes made my chest constrict with need. I saw her shiver as the slight breeze picked up again. I wanted to wrap her up in my arms to keep her warm. Instead I trailed my hand down her arm to link our fingers between us on the grass.

"They should be your life. They deserve that, and I wouldn't like you so much if you felt differently," she said decisively. "I want to try with you too, Wyatt. We both have responsibilities. You have your girls and I have Harry and I'm sure I'll have times when I have to drop everything and take care of him—"

"Can we have an understanding between us? Can we take it slow?" I asked.

She squeezed my hand. "Yes. I don't want to give this up."

My eyes traced the deep curve of her waist, down her long legs and all the way back up again over her full breasts to her beautiful face—I wanted my hands to follow that same trail. What I wanted from her was the opposite of slow. What an idiot I was for suggesting slow.

Instead of touching her I let her hand go and sat up.

I didn't quite understand why I held myself back. Why I was

having such a hard time succumbing to this moment—other than I strongly believed that the rest of my life could be lying on the grass next to me. I didn't want to mess it up like I had with most everything else.

She sat up next to me and I chuckled, nervously, like a stupid kid. She leaned against my side and looked up at me. "Everything will be okay, Wyatt."

I closed the distance between us and took her mouth. I swept my tongue out to taste her bottom lip. I needed to be close to her. I needed a taste of her. I wanted to taste her *everywhere*.

She moaned into my mouth and darted her tongue out to meet mine. "Wyatt." It was breath, not voice, and it drove me crazy.

I lost my mind and all my barely leashed control. I lifted her by the waist and pulled her forward to straddle my lap as I pressed myself up against her warmth. She made a sexy little sound in the back of her throat as her body relaxed over mine. That felt good, but I wanted her underneath me. I scrambled to my knees to lower her to her back on the grass and followed her down to cover her body with my own.

She wrapped her arms around my neck and captured my mouth with her sweet lips. And I took from her what I'd wanted since I'd met her. But I didn't need to take it—she generously gave it—yielding her body to mine. Opening her mouth to let my tongue come inside, wrapping me up in her long, long legs, and sliding her fingers into my hair to hold on tight, to not let me back away from her. As if I could, now that I'd gotten started.

I let one hand sink into all that soft midnight hair to support the back of her head against the grass, supporting my weight on my forearm. I let my other hand run up and down the length of her body, over the supple curves I'd been dying to touch, to rest on her hip and grip the softly rounded flesh. I caressed her hip, then up over her ribs to swipe over her nipple with my thumb and cup her full breast in my palm.

She gasped against my mouth and arched into me, pressing her breast further into my hand.

Her grip on my neck tightened, as did her legs around my waist. She raised her hips upward, seeking the friction I knew we both needed. I thrust my hard length against her once…twice. She moaned against my lips. God damn.

My lust filled brain wanted to take, take, take—get her clothes off, get inside her, make her come, make her mine. But the part of me that knew I could fall in love with her someday told me to stop. To slow the hell down because there was no way our first time together should be on the grass in the middle of a horse pasture without even a blanket to keep her off the cold, hard ground.

I want her. I fucking adore her—and I really need to be inside of her right now.

I disentangled from her soft warm body and sat up. Hard as a fucking rock and half-insane with lust, I sat there, panting like I'd just run a six-minute mile.

My head was filled with images of fireworks and stars, planets realigning in the universe, that enormous Harvest Moon illuminating us from up above like it was there just for us, and the feeling that everything in my life had shifted into place so I could be right here at this moment—exactly where I needed to be.

I scrubbed a hand down my face. I'd never had a kiss like that in my life. It had laid me bare.

"I won't take you on the grass, Sabrina. I won't do that; you deserve better than that," I growled more to myself than to her.

"Okay, Wyatt," she whispered. She was smiling at me from her back in the grass.

I grinned sideways at her.

"But I don't want to leave," she said. "It's beautiful out here tonight. Will you stay with me? For just a while longer?" She sat up and leaned her side against mine.

I wrapped an arm around her. "Yes, I will stay with you," I whispered.

A soft smile crossed her face. "Thanks," she murmured before letting her eyes drift closed and darting her tongue out to wet her lips in anticipation.

I took a moment. I really needed more than a moment to regain my control, but I didn't want to keep her waiting.

Just kissing. No more touching. Just keep your dick away from her.

I met her lips with mine—slowly. Soft and gentle. Her hand found the side of my cheek, caressing a warm pattern that led down to my neck and into my hair to hold me to her mouth. I returned that soft touch and wove my fingers into her silky hair letting the soft strands fall through my fingers. My hand eventually came to rest against her throat. I liked the feel of her pulse beating against my palm.

We stayed like that—barely touching, softly kissing—taking only a small portion of what we needed from each other. Until the breeze picked up, and I felt her shiver against my side.

"I'll drive you to the house; it's late," I said against her lips. Then kissed her one more time.

"Okay, in a minute." She drew back and kissed my dimple, which made me chuckle. She seemed to have an affinity for it.

A strong gust of wind kicked up. Leaves stirred on the grass and blew against us.

"I guess we should probably go," she said with a disappointed grin.

"I want you to meet my parents," I blurted. *Shit, was it too soon?*

She beamed at me. "I would love to."

"What are your plans for the homecoming game next Friday? My family always goes. We could all sit together. Then you can meet them and not have to worry about too much conversation." I was excited by the prospect of moving forward with her, moving her deeper into my life. But at the same time, what if it was too much for her? Was I rushing things?

"It's like you know me or something." She laughed and I let out an internal sigh of relief.

"I know how to pay attention when it's important," I whispered in her ear.

"Weston wants me to go to the game. I've never seen him play. Harry and my father are going. Maybe we could all hijack a row and sit together. What do you think?"

"Sounds good." I tugged her close and lowered my face to kiss her again. I couldn't get enough. I wondered if I would ever be able to get enough of her.

We held hands on the walk back to my truck where I couldn't help but back her up against it to kiss her one more time. She grabbed onto me, kissed me back and the one more time lasted a lot longer than I'd intended.

CHAPTER TWENTY-ONE

SABRINA

Homecoming was a big deal in Green Valley.

I took in a huge breath. I could do this.

You've got this.

I always hated it when people said that.

I've got nothing.

I had nothing but the feeling that this teeming crowd would eat me alive. There were people everywhere—milling about in the parking lot, chatting, and walking toward the stadium. Green Valley loved its football team. Even regular Friday night games were always packed full of people.

This was like a test for me. Like when Luke Skywalker faced Darth Vader. Would Luke turn to the dark side and rule the universe at Vader's side? Or would he stand on his own and do the right thing? When I faced the huge Homecoming crowd tonight, would I turn to the scared side and hide under the bleachers alone? Or would I sit by Wyatt and his family and act like a normal human? Okay, maybe it was not the same kind of test...

This was a huge deal for me. This was a giant bunch of people, talking, laughing—probably judging. And I was about to voluntarily submerge myself within it. I tapped my foot on the floor and fiddled with the zipper on my jacket.

What would Sienna Diaz do?

This night was so huge, even my bravery mantra failed me. I didn't care what Sienna Diaz would do right now. Sabrina Logan wanted to hide on the floor in the back seat.

I was about to officially meet Wyatt's parents tonight. Meeting the parents was a massive thing, a relationship thing, a boyfriend/girlfriend thing. I wanted to meet them, but I couldn't help but wonder what had possessed me to agree to do it at a football game. Less conversation was a plus. Being surrounded by a crowd of people was a massive minus.

I looked over at my father in the driver's seat, still diligently trying to find us a parking spot close to the stadium. Harry was in the back seat playing a game on his tablet, oblivious that I was up front silently fidgeting and freaking the heck out.

My therapist once gave me a list to use when I needed to ground myself and talk myself down from an anxiety ledge.

One thing I could taste.

Did the taste of fear count? I reached into the center console and stole one of my father's lemon drops.

Two things I could smell.

I guess fear still didn't count. I caught scent of dry leaves and fireplace fires wafting through my open window. I also caught a whiff of my minty shampoo when I fluffed my hair in the mirror. I shut the visor and looked out the window.

I had always been terrible at this—this exercise gave me anxiety. But going through the list would not leave me huddled in the fetal position on the floor of the back seat, so it was preferable to the anxiety creeping up on me. I twisted my lips and turned on the radio.

Three things I could hear.

Besides the voices from the one million people outside, I could now hear *Firework* by Katy Perry. I turned it off. I sucked on my lemon drop and reconsidered the radio as the noise swelled from my window. Maybe turning the radio back on with the volume up would mask the sounds of the people outside. Maybe getting this song stuck in my head would be good. I should try to be a freaking firework and let my colors burst.

Dad turned to me and gave me a smile full of sympathy before returning his eyes to the parking lot. "You'll be okay, sweet pea."

One more thing to hear. "Hey, Harry," I called to him in the back seat.

"Hey, Riri," he answered back. My name from Harry's lips. The most perfect sound in the world.

Four things to touch.

I rubbed my palms down the length of my denim covered thighs and gripped my cell phone. I know what I *wanted* to touch. I wanted to touch Wyatt. I still hadn't gotten my hands on that booty. I decided that could count. This was my internal monologue; I could count whatever the eff I wanted. I just needed one more thing to touch—I bumped my head on the window when we passed Wyatt, standing by the ticket booth. Ouch. Moving on…

Five things to see.

I peered out the passenger window. I saw Jennifer Sylvester—no, it was Jennifer Sylvester-Winston now. She had married Cletus, and they were holding hands and walking toward the gate. Jenn and I used to hide behind the big kids' legs during choir practice at church. She was just as shy as I was back then. We'd communicated solely through our held hands and big eyes as we huddled together and tried to avoid being noticed. I waved to her. She smiled and waved back. Maybe I'd go into her bakery sometime and say hi.

My father passed the ticket booth again. Wyatt was still there texting on his phone. He was wearing a brown leather jacket with the sleeves pushed up, and a navy blue and yellow Green Valley High School football T-shirt stretched snugly over his wide chest.

I was wearing jeans and a GVHS T-shirt too. I had to borrow one from Ruby. I was bustier, so it was just a little bit tight. I had my brown leather bomber jacket on as well; we had inadvertently matched our clothes. So, what if it was a football game and there were hundreds of people in T-shirts exactly like ours? That made no difference to fate.

I declared my list done. I hated to admit it worked, no matter how annoying it was.

My father, oblivious to anything except finding a good spot, kept right on driving. I leaned back into my seat and shut my eyes. We would be driving around this lot forever. My father always wanted to find a well-lit spot up front and that was just not going to happen. We would end up parking on the street next to a dumpster full of criminals. I didn't even care. I just wanted to get out of this car and go see Wyatt.

"Jackpot," Dad said a few minutes later.

My eyes popped open. *Finally.*

Whoa, he did it. While we were not in the front of the lot, we were safely ensconced in the middle, right next to a tall light post. I turned and gave him a sideways smile. He smiled back. We got out of the car and headed off to meet Wyatt.

I needed to concentrate and try to remember all the football crap I'd read about on the internet. Like what a touchdown was, and that Weston was the quarterback, and Wyatt had been a defensive—uh, something. Damn it. He tackled people. I saw one of his college games on YouTube. Tackling looked painful, but also strangely hot. Football pants were very tight, and I had watched Wyatt play football on YouTube longer than I intended to last night.

I was getting love drunk—I could feel it. I froze in my tracks, pulling Harry to a stop when my nerves got the best of me. My father smiled down at me and took my hand with an encouraging squeeze. Harry was busy just looking around. He was handling this evening far better than I was. All the things I had thought of to say to Wyatt's family tonight flew right out of my head.

I walked again, faster this time. Harry giggled and jogged to keep up, and my father laughed as he lengthened his stride to match mine.

Wyatt hadn't seen us yet.

"Wyatt," my father called out.

His head snapped around and a smile lit up his face when he caught sight of us.

"Hi, Sheriff Wyatt," Harry waved and yelled.

Wyatt grinned and waved back as he headed in our direction.

I said nothing because I had lost my words. All I could see was him.

"Are Mak and Mel already here?" Harry asked Wyatt.

"Yep, they're inside, saving our seats, and they are excited to see you." He turned to my father. "I already got tickets; we can head inside." He reached out a hand and shook my father's.

"Sabrina." He grinned at me. "Are you ready?"

I smiled. "Yes." *No. Maybe. Sort of.*

He chuckled and took my hand. "You'll be fine, darlin'. Stick with me."

Wyatt handed our tickets to the kid at the gate and we headed to the stands. Homecoming started earlier than regular Friday night games. The sun was just going down. The tall stadium lights surrounding the football field burned like midnight suns, casting everything in a bright golden glow.

"Look." Harry pointed. "Lizzy flipped over." He stopped and stared, then looked up at me with excitement on his face. I looked where he pointed. The cheerleaders were stretching and dancing and doing flips on the track on the side of the field. Lizzy waved at us.

"Hi, Lizzy, hi!" Harry shouted at her.

She ran over and gave him a hug. "I'm gonna miss you, Harry, when I go off to college." She sniffed then looked at me. "I'm sorry, y'all. I didn't mean to hurt Weston, I..."

"It's okay, honey," my father answered before she could finish her thought. "College is important and y'all are just too young to be in a serious relationship."

I nodded my agreement. "And we're happy for you, Lizzy. Congratulations."

"Thank you," she whispered.

"Good luck tonight, sweetheart." Wyatt hugged her goodbye before she ran back to rejoin the cheerleaders.

"We got here early. We're almost up front, right by the fifty-yard line," Wyatt informed us and pointed to where his family was sitting—third row back, dead center.

My father had turned away to chat with one of the people that had come up to say hi to him.

Harry excitedly held up a hand. "Shh, I can hear Ruby and the band. Do you hear it too?"

We could hear the band warming up from somewhere close by. Ruby said they would march in to their fight song.

"I hear it, Harry." I smiled at him. He was so excited, and I was so proud of how far he had come since the school year had started.

"They are playing 'On, Wisconsin!', the official fight song of the Wisconsin Badgers, and the battle cry of Arthur MacArthur Jr. in the battle of Chattanooga at Missionary Ridge, in the Civil War. It is one of the most popular fight songs in the country. It is in the public domain. So, I can sing it wherever I want to, and no one can sue me," Harry informed us.

"Wow," Wyatt said.

"Harry likes to read history books. He likes facts and quotes," I explained.

"'Destiny is that which we are drawn towards and fate is that which we run into.' Wyatt Earp, right, Harry?" Wyatt said with a smile.

"You remembered!" Harry was pleased.

It astounded me that Wyatt remembered that—from the day we met.

I smiled up at him.

He touched my nose with his index finger and grinned at me.

Boop.

"There they are. Let's go. It'll be starting soon," my father announced and started waving to Wyatt's family.

Mel spotted us. "Hey! Harry, hi! Harry, over here, look at me!" she screamed and waved as she jumped up and down in front of her spot on the bench. Everett caught her before she tumbled forward into the row below. He stood her up on his legs to sit on his shoulder. She laughed, thrilled at her high perch, and waved both hands over her head at us.

Harry laughed and returned her wave.

Wyatt shook his head. "I told you she was excited to see you, bud. Come on." He held his hand out. Harry took it, and they jogged through the crowds and up into the stands. My father and I followed close behind.

"Hi, Miss Sabrina," Mak greeted me once we'd caught up to Wyatt and Harry.

"Hi, sweetheart," I said softly.

"Hey, y'all," Wyatt's dad greeted as he stood up. "Roy, good to see you." Wyatt's father and mine shook hands and his mother stood up to hug my father. Jeez, he really did know everyone in town. Wyatt's brothers waved at us from their spots farther down the row.

I took a deep breath and smiled at Wyatt's family. The good thing about being in a crowd this large was that it was loud. I quit worrying about chatting with his family and instead concentrated on smiling at them without crazy eyes.

I shook his parents' hands and smiled when Wyatt introduced me. Then Wyatt held his hand out to me with a grin on his face. I took it and he pulled me down the row to sit next to him and the girls. Everett and his other two brothers, Barrett and Garrett, were on the end, close to the staircase on the other side of the bench. We took up an entire row of the bleachers. My father sat by Wyatt's father on the end of the row, and they chatted together with his mother.

I settled into the bench with my hip and thigh pressed all along the length of Wyatt's. My heart pounded a fast staccato and my stomach dipped and swirled like an internal roller coaster.

How was I supposed to sit like this for the whole game and not die of a heart attack or have a spontaneous orgasm?

He leaned over to talk to Mak and Mel. His arm went around me, and he placed his hand on the bench next to my hip.

He was so warm, so handsome, such a good dad, and a good man.

Holy crap. This is it. This will be how I die—dead of an effing swoon at age twenty-seven.

I inhaled a deep breath and got a lungful of Wyatt. His head was in front of mine as he spoke to his daughters, telling them to behave. I could smell his shampoo. I could also smell his soap or cologne or whatever it was that made him so yummy—or maybe it was just *him.* Maybe it was his pheromones that drove me crazy and got my own pheromones all riled up. Whatever it was, I wanted to take a bite, or a lick, or just move in and live inside of him so I could smell him all day.

He pulled back a bit, his face near mine. Only inches away. *Holy Hufflepuffs.*

"You doing okay?" he whispered.

I nodded. "I'm fine, Wyatt. Thank you."

He stared into my eyes for a second while the crowd did all the crowd stuff—laugh, talk, yell, cheer. Whatever.

He leaned forward and pecked me on the lips. He followed that move with a grin.

I poked his dimple, and he laughed.

"Where's your mom?" Mel said to Harry.

I gasped softly and froze.

Wyatt's eyes darted to the kids.

"My mom lives in heaven," Harry answered. "But it's okay because I have Pop and Riri. She's going to be my mom for real soon."

"We don't have a mom either," Mel said.

"Our mom has a new family," Mak added.

"Riri takes care of me. Maybe she can be your mom too. She's real good at it. I know how to share. Love grows when you give it away. My Pop says that sometimes."

Don't cry. Don't cry.

"You can't just get a new mom, Harry. You have to get adopted or something," Mak said.

"I'm getting adopted by Riri," he explained.

Mak's eyebrows rose, and she looked at me with questions on her sweet face.

We all jumped when we heard a whistle, followed by a drumroll from the percussionists. The band had taken position at the edge of the football field and began playing the fight song. As they played, they marched onto the field and divided into two lines on either side of the goal posts to stretch down the football field. The cheerleaders lined up next to them with their navy blue and gold pom-poms waving in the air.

Harry stood up. "I can't see Ruby."

Mel stood next to him. "I'll help you find her. What does she look like?"

Harry pointed to me. "Ruby looks like Riri."

Mel squinted her eyes and studied the band. "They all have hats on, and their clothes are all the same. Just watch everybody Harry, then you'll see her for sure," Mel advised.

I grinned at her. I couldn't argue with that logic.

Wyatt chuckled. "There she is." He spotted her before I did. Luckily, she was facing our side of the field.

"Hi, Ruby! Ruby, hi!" Harry yelled and waved.

"She can't hear you," I whispered into his ear. He was doing remarkably well with the noise. I couldn't believe it.

"Okay," he said. I put my arm around him as we watched.

The drum major whistled again, and the band quieted as the announcer's voice filled the stadium over the speakers. Harry flinched when the speakers crackled. I pulled him closer into my side. "It's just the speakers," I said into his ear.

"Welcome to Green Valley High School's homecoming game!" the announcer shouted. The crowd went wild; the screams were deafening. Harry turned into my body and buried his face into my chest.

"You're okay, Harry. It will be just fine," I told him. "If you turn back to look, Weston will come out soon."

He looked up at me, some of the fear left his expression and he nodded and turned around.

Mak had traded places with Mel, who was now on Wyatt's mother's lap. She took Harry's hand and held it. "It is too loud," she said. "We don't like it either."

"You okay, ladybug?" Wyatt said to her.

She gave him a look, then glanced pointedly at Harry. "Yeah, Daddy, I'm okay." She was trying to make Harry feel better.

I am now officially in love with Wyatt's daughters.

I smiled at her, then we all turned our attention back to the field as the announcer started calling out the players' names. They ran through the rows the band had formed and stood on the opposite side of the field.

"And here's your quarterback: The shark of the Green Valley High School Football field—Weston Adams." Tears filled my eyes when I saw Weston run across the field to join his teammates on the other side.

You should be here to see this, Cora.

I blinked the tears away before they could fall. Wyatt put his arm around me and squeezed my shoulder.

The band moved again to form a waving flag across the football field, the majorettes and color guard pulled red white and blue streamers through the rows the band had created, and the cheerleaders stood on either side, pom-poms still in the air and flashing navy and gold under the lights.

"Look at that." Harry excitedly turned to me as he pointed out to the field.

"Amazing," I agreed.

"In the crowd tonight, we have a special homecoming treat for y'all. One of Green Valley High School's most accomplished alumni. He started right here on this field and went aaallll the way to the University of Tennessee Knoxville's football team. Give a cheer for Green Valley's own Wyatt Monroe!" The crowd roared in response.

I glanced at Wyatt. He had turned bright red. His smile was tight as he gave a quick wave. He really did not like the attention. I leaned into him and he gripped me tighter.

Harry and Mak cuddled against me, Harry in front of me, and Mak at my side. I wrapped my arms around them both as we listened to the band play "The Star Spangled Banner." The band marched off the field and took their place in the stands, one section over from us. The referee tossed a coin and some other stuff happened, the game started, and I lost interest. I guess I agreed with Ruby on this one—the band *was* more entertaining.

Wyatt and his brothers, however, did *not* lose interest. It was cute how they cheered and discussed the game.

"Weston is good," Wyatt praised.

Harry moved to sit between me and Wyatt. Wyatt and his brothers explained to him what was going on. It kept Harry focused on the game and not on all the noise in the stands and the crackling speakers blasting out the announcer's voice.

Mel was dozing off on Becky Lee's lap, which I could not understand one bit. My ears were ringing from the noise.

Since my dad and Wyatt's parents were busy becoming best friends at the end of the row, that left Mak and me. I didn't have time to dwell on finding the right thing to say because somehow, I was in the moment, instead of obsessing about what could go wrong.

The game was a close one. The teams had been trading the lead back and forth the whole time. Every so often Wyatt would explain what was going on or I would check the scoreboard. I'm not a complete football idiot. Halftime was long over. The show the band put on only solidified my opinion on the band versus game debate—not that I would ever let Ruby or Weston know what I thought.

I almost fell off the bench when Wyatt, his brothers, and Harry yelled, "Go, go, go," and cheered loudly. My eyes snapped to the field. Weston had the ball; he was running for the end zone.

"If he makes it, then we'll win!" Wyatt explained.

Mak and I cheered and jumped up and down with the guys as Weston dodged two boys from the other team before they could tackle him.

"Go, Weston!" I screamed, surprising myself. I had no idea I had that in me.

Harry looked up at me with a huge smile on his face. I beamed back down at him. The crowd was going berserk. I held Harry's hand and stayed close to make sure he was okay with the deafening noise.

I noticed the band had already left the stadium. Ruby would miss Weston's potential big moment.

Suddenly two boys from the other team tackled Weston and

landed on top of him. Right by the goal posts. Why would they do that? He was in the end zone. Hadn't he already scored?

Harry gasped, then he screamed, "Noooo, Westie!"

Oh no, oh no.

"What the hell?" Everett yelled.

I pulled Harry close to my body. I felt his head tip up to look at me, but my eyes remained glued to the field. The two boys got up, but Weston did not move. He was still and quiet on the ground, with the ball in his arms. Until it rolled to the side to land in the grass.

I looked up at Wyatt. He glanced down at me, concern etched in his features. "He'll be okay," he whispered.

I was not convinced.

"Westie. Get up, Westie!" Harry screamed and lunged forward. I caught him around his waist before he could fall. He covered his face with his hands and burst into tears. I sat down and pulled him onto my lap. Mak cuddled into my side and looked up at me, eyes wide with concern.

"It'll be okay, honey," I told her.

I glanced down the row to my father. He was trying to move into the crowded aisle to get down to the field. People had frozen where they were, even standing on the steps between aisles, in order to see what would happen.

"I need to get down there," he said, frustration filled his voice.

Weston still had not moved.

"We'll get you down there," Everett said. Wyatt's three brothers stood and passed in front of us to help my father get down to the field.

"Tighter, Riri. Harry's scared hugs please," he sobbed. I squeezed him as tight as I could against my body.

Weston or my father were always the ones to give Harry the 'scared hugs.' They were bigger and stronger than me and could hold him tighter than I could. Tears filled my eyes as they bounced between a scared and melting-down Harry in my arms, to Weston on his back on the field, and to Wyatt's huge brothers escorting my father down to help.

"I'm trying, Harry. Shh, he'll be okay. It will be just fine," I whispered as I squeezed him with all my strength. His arms flailed before he gripped his fists into my T-shirt.

Wyatt's parents scooted closer to us. "What can we do?" Becky Lee asked me.

"I don't know," I answered.

Mel had awakened. "Is Harry gonna be okay?" she said from Becky Lee's lap.

"He will be. Big feelings are still hard for him to handle," I explained.

Harry was writhing and sobbing in my arms. I was struggling to keep hold of him. "Tighter," he sobbed.

"I'm trying, Harry. I'm squeezing as hard as I can. Weston will be okay." *Please be okay.*

I squealed when Wyatt scooped me up to sit sideways on his lap. He wrapped his arms around me, over my arms and covered my hands with his to help me squeeze Harry tighter. Harry moved his face into Wyatt's chest and huddled into him. We were both in a warm cocoon, safe in Wyatt's arms.

I glimpsed what my future could be, and for a moment it scared me—what if I lost it?

He lowered his head to whisper to Harry, "Weston will be okay. Your grandpa is down there with him right now."

I turned my head; he had finally made it to the field. Thank goodness for the Monroes. Had we been here alone…

I turned back and met Wyatt's eyes. He smiled softly at me. "He'll be fine, Sabrina. It's just part of the game sometimes."

I nodded at him. "Okay, Wyatt." My eyes darted back down to the field. My father was kneeling over Weston, examining him. The coach waved something under Weston's nose, and he sat up. It looked as if he took a huge breath in. Maybe he had the wind knocked out of him? Relief filled me and a huge sigh left my body.

"Weston is sitting up. Look, Harry, he's okay," Mak said and patted Harry on the shoulder.

Harry sat up on my lap, leaned sideways against my chest, and looked up at me with confusion clouding his features. He turned to face Wyatt.

"Weston is okay?" he asked in a trembling voice.

Wyatt smiled at him. "He's sitting up, look."

Harry twisted around and looked.

"Are you okay now, bud?" Wyatt asked.

Harry nodded. "Yes. I am okay now." He twisted back and examined Wyatt. "You're good at scared hugs and you are warm too. Thank you."

"You're welcome." He cupped Harry's cheek and wiped the remaining tears away with his thumb.

He would have to wipe up my heart next because it had melted. Warmth filled me, but not from the heat coming from Wyatt's big warm body. It was the kind of warmth that burned through a person and blazed a permanent trail.

The crowd cheered as Weston stood up. And since my father was down there to examine him, I had no doubt he really would be fine. My father wouldn't let him up if that weren't the case.

My first football game could not have met a more dramatic end—injuries, meltdowns, dramatic exits from the field escorted by the handsome Monroe brothers. And I was pretty sure I had fallen in love with not just Wyatt, but his entire family. But *especially* with Wyatt.

He pulled me closer and kissed my temple. Mak grinned at me with a knowing look.

Harry sat up, clambered off my lap, and sat down next to Mak on the bench. She grinned at him and bumped her shoulder against his.

"Football games are boring," Mel said with a yawn. "We should have gone to Chuck E. Cheese instead."

Wyatt laughed and the vibrations moved through my body still snuggled on his lap as if it belonged there. I moved to get up, but his arms tightened around my waist to keep me still.

We were so close I felt his breath move my hair and his lips against my ear as he murmured, "Do you think football games are boring?"

Um, that would be no. Not anymore, I didn't. I'd watch a whole lifetime's worth of football games for the rest of eternity if I could do it from Wyatt's lap, holding his hand, and pressed into all that warmth.

I turned my face to his. "I'm not bored," I answered. His face was right there, close enough for me to kiss. *And I wanted to, so bad.*

He grinned and whispered, "Do you want to get a drink with me? We could go to Genie's. The girls are spending the night with my parents." His hand released mine to travel up my spine, before moving my hair aside and resting it on the back of my neck. His other arm remained across my waist, hand on the outside of my thigh, gripping it in his big warm palm.

I couldn't think with his hands on me this way. At least I couldn't think of anything I *should* be thinking about. Nothing G-rated or appropriate in the presence of the kids or his parents was going through my mind at all right now, yet I still did not want to move.

"I would love to. My father drove tonight. He'll take care of Harry."

"Good. Let's go check on Weston and your dad, and then we can get out of here."

I nodded. Best idea ever.

When we made it down to the field, we found out that Weston did indeed have the wind knocked out of him. But it wasn't until Weston himself reassured us that he had never even been unconscious that my fear went truly away. Harry had run to him with big smiles, and Weston promised him they would build Harry's new Lego set when they got home.

With our worries for Weston finally put to rest and the girls and Harry safely off with their grandparents, Wyatt and I said our goodbyes. And I would bet the rest of our night would definitely not be boring.

CHAPTER TWENTY-TWO

WYATT

I should have realized how bad the traffic would be. Everyone was leaving the parking lot after the game, not trying to get back in like I was. Sabrina had needed to use the restroom before we left and instead of both of us waiting in the long line, she told me to meet her in the parking lot with my truck. When I finally made it back into the lot, it was mostly deserted. It had taken me longer than I expected to get back to her and I was worried she would be waiting for me.

I pulled closer to the restrooms just in time to see Michael backing Sabrina across the sidewalk. Rage filled me as he grabbed her arms and shook her. I slammed my truck in park and jumped out just as I heard her yell, "Let me go!"

Never, not once, had I deviated from my law enforcement training. But I found myself wanting to abandon all of it and charge Michael when I saw his hands on her. I did not want to respond as a deputy sheriff. I wanted to react as Sabrina's man and beat the shit out of him. I sucked in a huge gulp of air then let it out as I charged toward them. Michael let her go and sneered at me. He knew I was a cop. He probably expected warnings, rational behavior, or maybe he thought I would read him his rights instead of shoving him away from Sabrina and into the chain-link fence. He bounced forward and took a swing at me while I reared back to dodge it. But I wasn't fast enough; he managed to land a light tap on my chin. I shoved him back into the fence again and held him there. I was glad he'd hit me. It would make it worse for him after he was arrested. It was hard to keep my temper under control. I wanted to hit him.

"Put your hands above your head," I ground out. I could feel the muscle in my jaw pulsate, I took a deep breath to try and let some of the tension go. My body strung tight with anger. I let him go halfway hoping he'd take another swing.

Michael glared at me. But he did what I said.

"Turn around and hold on to the fence," I ordered.

He complied and I patted him down.

"Sabrina, call 911. Tell them who I am. Get in my truck and lock the doors." I glanced at her; she had wrapped her arms around her middle. Her face was pale, and she trembled as she stood there.

She nodded and took her phone from her pocket as she headed to my truck.

"Don't move. You are under arrest." I pressed Michael harder into the fence and read him his rights.

Jackson must have been on another call because a few other deputies arrived moments later to cuff Michael and take him in.

Sabrina rushed out of my truck and ran to me. "Are you okay?" she cried. "I wish you didn't have to get involved with this. I'm so sorry, Wyatt. Will you get into trouble for shoving him into the fence? We're trying to get a restraining order against him, but it hasn't gone through yet. He kept calling me the weak link of the family. I'm not a weak link, Wyatt, I'm not..." Her voice shook, she reached out with a trembling hand to touch my jaw where that idiot had hit me.

She was scared, and I was angry. But not at her. Never at her.

I leaned into her touch. *So soft.* I wished that I could have done more. I wished I could have pounded that fucker's face right into the back of his skull for touching her and not lose my job over it.

"Stop. He barely connected. I'm fine." I pulled her into my arms. She needed to stop talking so I could calm down. "You're with me. That means if one of us is going to take a punch, it sure as hell won't be you." I pulled back to look at her. "Look at me, Sabrina. I can take it. I get that you can take care of yourself, but there are ways I'm better suited for taking care of you and this is one."

"But you shouldn't have to."

I grunted and pulled her closer in response. I couldn't think of adequate words to make her understand how serious I was.

"Let's get out of here." I caressed the back of her neck and guided her closer to my truck.

She looked up at me, eyes still filled with fear. "Michael is completely irrational. I can't let him get anywhere near the kids, Wyatt."

"It won't happen. Even if you didn't have me, you've got your dad. Just look at what he did tonight. We've arrested him—again. There is no way a judge would ever grant him custody, or even visitation."

"You're probably right. But it's still hard not to worry." She reached out and touched my jaw again. "You're getting a bruise." She frowned.

"Don't worry about it. It doesn't even hurt. And besides, what high school football game ends without a fight in the parking lot? Your first game is complete; you got the whole experience."

"I don't want to go to Genie's anymore. Can we go somewhere quiet?" she asked. My attempt at humor had not helped her relax.

"Sure thing. Let's go." I took her hand and led her back to the truck. I helped her inside and shut the door.

I decided to take her home with me. After tonight's scare, we both needed reassurance. Maybe it was too soon to take her home but it felt right. I knew she trusted me, but I wanted more. I wanted to make her mine. I wanted to sink so completely inside her that she would never be able to let me go.

CHAPTER TWENTY-THREE

SABRINA

Wyatt pulled into his garage. I took a huge breath and tried to relax. I was about to be alone with Wyatt in his house. On the drive here Wyatt held my hand, helping me to shake off most of the panic Michael stirred up. Now I was left with two problems. My squealy girl urges and my ever-present desire to run home and hide. I glanced at Wyatt after he cut the engine. His sweet smile and tender look chased my run and hide compulsion away, and I smiled back. And when he took my hand and kissed my palm, I realized I was where I belonged. Taking a deep breath, I promised myself I would not say 'yay'. There would be no fist pumping, and I would definitely not do a victory dance.

He exited the truck and hurried around to open the door for me. He seemed to enjoy being a gentleman—opening doors, holding my hand or elbow, helping me with my coat, getting in Michael's face to defend my honor, and just generally making me swoon.

He took my hand and tugged me gently out of the truck and into his arms. I fell forward onto his chest and wrapped my arms around his neck. My feet had yet to hit the garage floor; he was holding me up with his arms around my hips.

"Hi," he said as he let me slide down his body until my shoes touched the floor.

"Hi," I breathed as my hands slid down his hard chest.

"Let's go inside. We can put on a movie or talk. Or we could sit on the couch and I could just hold you until you feel better."

I followed him inside. I didn't want to talk or watch a movie. I wanted him to hold me. Then kiss me, undress me, and make me his.

I thought of all the ways he fit into my life and made it better. I wanted to be with him all the time and I never stopped thinking about him when we weren't. Since the day I met him, everything about Wyatt had drawn me in. His first instinct in any situation was always rooted in kindness. He was understanding and empathetic. He never got frustrated when I got nervous or afraid or lost my words. If there was such a thing as soul mates, then he was mine. I hoped I was his.

The way he was with Harry at the game tonight had pushed me over the top. I had never been in love before, but I knew how love felt. I figured if you added wanting to have sex with someone to all the regular love feelings, then you would be *in love*. All these things added together made me realize I was in love with him—it seemed logical.

But was love logical?

He tossed our jackets to a chair in the corner. Then he took my hand and tugged me to the couch that sat in front of a window. The curtains shifted, followed by an indignant meow.

"You have a cat! I didn't see him last time I was here." Another soft meow sounded from the window behind the couch, and then his head popped up. He was big and orange; he reminded me of Garfield. He jumped gracelessly onto the couch, then to the floor to flop over onto his side in front of my feet.

"There he is." Wyatt chuckled.

"Hey, kitty." I knelt and scratched his soft belly and he started purring. I looked up at Wyatt. "He's cute. Harry loves cats. What's his name?"

"Uh, it's Princess Buttercup," he answered, eyes darting everywhere else but to me. Was he blushing? Oh my gosh, his cheeks were red.

A hot dad with a cat named Princess Buttercup—my heart couldn't take much more. It was only pure luck that allowed me to giggle instead of pass out from the wave of lusty giddiness that smacked me in the face. "You didn't name him, did you?"

"Ah, no. Mel named him. It looks like he likes you. Can't say I blame him." He held his hand out to help me up. I took it and stood in front of him.

Princess Buttercup took off toward the hallway. My eyes drifted closed as Wyatt's face finally lowered to mine and our lips touched. Softly at first, then with more intensity.

He pulled back, kissing me on the forehead. "Something to drink?" he offered.

"No, thank you." I didn't want him to stop kissing me. I wanted to keep going until I was his and he was mine and we were lost together in what we could be.

He took my hands and led us to his couch where he pulled me down to sit next to him. "Movie?" he asked. Why did he keep putting on the brakes? Perhaps he thought I was still afraid from the run-in with Michael and didn't want to take advantage of me.

"Sure," I said. I had to tell him I was a virgin. There was a big flashing sign in my brain that said tonight was the night. I was more nervous about telling him I was a virgin than I was about losing my virginity. That was weird, but it also said a lot about Wyatt and how comfortable I felt around him.

He put his arm around me and pulled me into his side.

I snuggled closer. This was nice. I stared down his jeans covered legs to his booted feet on the coffee table. My legs, also in jeans, stretched out next to his. He dug the remote out of the cushions but set it aside when I wrapped my arms around his neck.

He turned and kissed me again. My mouth opened under his to seek his tongue. He obliged and deepened our kiss. We sat there kissing and touching. He held me tight and soon my heart was racing with desire and not whatever residual fear remained from the incident with Michael. Maybe he was right to take this slow.

"I have to tell you something," I whispered against his lips.

"Tell me," he whispered back between soft kisses.

"I—um, I'm a virgin, Wyatt." I sat back and took a deep breath. This was a make or break moment. Nothing was in my brain right now—no thoughts at all. I hovered on a precipice I had never experienced, ever. Like the entire course of my life was about to shift depending on what he said.

He studied my face. "I kind of thought so," he finally said.

"It's pretty obvious, right?" My cheeks heated and I lowered my eyes to the floor.

He lifted my face with a fingertip. "I think it's sweet, and I'm a lucky man. And I want you in my bed, Sabrina. Are you sure you're ready for this? It doesn't have to be tonight." He leaned in to me and touched my lips with his.

It was the sweetest kiss I would probably ever receive. I felt tears pricking behind my eyes and I blinked as my heart flittered in my chest like the wings of a hummingbird. I moved back to look at his face and nodded. "Yes, I may be a virgin. But I'm also a twenty-seven-year-old woman. I'm pretty sure I've been ready since I met you," I confessed on a whisper as my blush intensified. But unlike my confession before, I didn't look away from him.

His lips quirked to the side as his eyes warmed on me. "Then, can I have you?" he murmured.

I smiled at him. "Yes."

He stood up and took my hand. He led me down the hall to his bedroom and tugged me inside, shutting the door behind us.

He gestured to his bed. "Sit down, darlin'."

I sat on the edge of his bed.

He reached behind his neck and pulled his T-shirt over his head letting it fall to the floor.

My eyes widened as I took him in. He really was beautiful. His chest was broad, and it tapered down to a majestic set of abs I wanted to taste. I reached for him, but he stepped back.

"Let me see to you first," he said.

"What?"

"Let me take care of you, it will make it easier." He knelt in front of me. His big chest spread my legs apart to rest against his body on either side. His hands framed my face and he kissed me—deep and possessive— his tongue in my mouth and lips slanted over mine left no doubt about his intentions. I was his and he was going to take me.

My hands traced down his back, over warm skin and hard muscle. Then lower until I was at the waistband of his jeans. Then even lower to that booty, I gave it a squeeze and he chuckled against my lips. *Wow.*

I gulped as his hands slid behind my knees to pull me closer. He lifted my T-shirt over my head before leaning down to take my nipple into his mouth, through my bra.

Oh, God...

I whimpered. I arched my back and he sucked harder, wetting the now stiff peak with his tongue. It felt good, but I wanted the bra *off.* Like a mind reader, his hands slid behind me to unhook it and toss it aside. He watched my eyes as he licked up my breast with the flat of his tongue and sucked my nipple into his mouth once again. Bare skin, hot mouth...I gasped and arched my back—it was involuntary.

"Does that feel good?" he murmured against my skin.

I nodded. It was all I could do.

I didn't even need to *feel it,* just watching him *do it* was almost enough to blow my head right off the top of my body. Seeing his dark head bent against me, his tongue darting out to taste my skin, that look on his face, the intensity in his eyes...the want, the need...

He reached down and removed my shoes, then tugged my jeans down my legs, all the while kissing and laving hot, wet attention over my breasts and neck. His hands reached the lacy waistband of my underwear and pulled them down.

"Lift."

I lifted.

"Lie back, up against the pillows."

I scooted back until my head was on his pillow. I watched him toss my undies aside as he removed his pants and kicked them off, leaving him in black boxer briefs—boxer briefs that did nothing to hide the huge erection he was sporting.

I barely had time to think or ponder or freak out before he put a knee to the bed, dipped his head, and crawled up my body to put his mouth on me.

Right there.

"Oh my God, Wyatt." My knees fell to the sides as I arched my body toward his mouth. His magical, beautiful, so, *so* capable mouth.

"Ohmygod," I repeated. Because. *Oh. My. God.*

Seriously. OH MY GOD.

"Ooooohhhhh," I moaned and arched higher. I felt tempted to grab his head and hold it there because I might die if he stopped. *Would that be rude?*

He chuckled against my sensitized skin but didn't take his mouth away. Chuckling made his lips twitch, and that made it even better.

"Please, Wyatt," I groaned. He reached around and held my hands, interlacing our fingers. Then he tugged them down my body to press my hips against the mattress and hold me still.

Suddenly, I wanted him to move away, to stop, it was too much.

It was almost scary how *too much* it was.

I had never been able to make myself feel like this, not even with the shower head. And I had a freaking great shower head.

"Stop," I said. He immediately stopped. "Wait, no, don't stop." I changed my mind. Stopping was terrible.

He lifted his head. The sight of Wyatt looking up at me from between my legs would be embedded on my brain for the rest of my life. "You sure? We can stop," he said.

I shook my head. "I'm sure. Please don't stop." I watched him lick his lips, then a slow, wicked grin crossed his face before he swirled his tongue around, right at the top, then down my slick skin to enter me with it.

"*Guhrggh,*" I said. Don't worry, I knew what it meant. It meant, *holy forking shirt this is amazing and must happen at least once a day, every day for the rest of my life, or I might die from withdrawals.*

His tongue moved back up to circle, while he let go of one of my hands to slide a finger inside me. It felt good. It felt great...then he added another and curved them while he softly, ever so gently thrust them in and out.

I was *right there.* All I had to do was let go and fall.

"Wyatt. Oh, God, oh please..."

He said something, but his mouth was still busy being awesome so I couldn't really tell what it was.

I moaned. His hand held me down as I writhed beneath him. Cresting that final peak, I exploded into a million sensations, each more delicious than the last.

At some point he'd removed his underwear. I hadn't noticed; I was caught in a hazy pleasure vortex. Love and lust swirled inside me along with amazement and the sense that I finally had a place to belong. I opened my eyes to watch him slide open a drawer on his bedside table and pull out a box of condoms. He dumped the box and grabbed one. He quickly sheathed himself and covered me with his body. I wrapped my legs around his waist and my arms around his neck and held on—I never wanted to let go.

"Can I?" he asked against my neck, his hot breath tickled my skin.

"Yes. Yes. Yes." Holy crap, I felt good. I was sure it would only get better once he made me his.

He slid himself up and down my center, then slowly pushed into me. He held himself still above me once he was all the way in.

I let my legs fall from around his waist to lie open. I felt pressure, a little pinch, but no pain. It felt strange at first, but then it felt good—it felt *right.* It felt beautiful to be connected to Wyatt. Like we were where we were meant to be—with each other, to each other—just like I imagined it would feel.

He pressed sweet kisses to my lips. "Am I hurting you?" he murmured between them.

"No, it feels good."

He nodded, sweat beading up on his forehead, his eyes blazing into mine. I wanted to feel him against me, skin to skin. I reached for his shoulders to pull him closer, but he held himself back. Was he afraid he would hurt me?

"You can move, Wyatt," I whispered. "I'm yours. Please."

At that, he rocked into me, rolling his hips to thrust gently at first, then with more intensity as I learned to move with him, to match his movement with my own. He was so beautiful above me—muscular and hard, yet gentle with the care he took with my body.

I loved how he took care of me. How he made this experience beautiful and right and so *special*. Tears filled my eyes.

"Sabrina…" he whispered and captured my mouth with his. He laced our fingers together and held them over my head as his thrusts grew more frantic and I grew restless beneath him. I rocked my hips upward faster to get what I needed as he ground himself against my body to give it to me.

"Wyatt…"

His eyes closed as he followed me over, then collapsed on top of me, giving me all his weight for a second before rolling to the side and pulling me to rest against his chest and wrapping his arms around me. I wound my arms around him in return, feeling his smooth skin beneath my palms as I held him close.

We stayed still there, holding each other. We were different. It felt like we had become something more. Every new experience I had with him felt like a beginning and I wondered if it always would—if every time we took a step forward together it would be as magical and wonderful and amazing as this one. *I hope so.*

"Are you okay?" He kissed the top of my head.

I nodded against him. "I'm perfect. I don't think I've ever been better in my life." I tipped my head back to look at him.

"Me too," he said.

He smiled down at me, that yummy dimple in full effect. I leaned up and kissed it, and his smile turned into that devilish grin that undid me when he was, you know—grinning down lower.

"I'm going to get rid of this condom. I'll be right back."

Standing at the edge of the bed with his back to me, I committed the sight of Naked Wyatt to memory. It was that beautiful. I might have drooled a little bit. I let my eyes wander down to my number one favorite Wyatt part—that glorious badonka-booty that I had become hopelessly devoted to while watching his Stop and Go video on repeat like a perv. I got a handful of that booty tonight and the experience immediately went on the highlight reel of the life and times of Sabrina Louise Logan. I watched as he opened a dresser drawer and pulled out some green plaid pajama bottoms. He opened another drawer and tossed me a T-shirt with a grin.

"Thanks." I smiled and slipped it over my head, sniffing it as I pulled it over. It was all April Fresh and Wyatt. After my head popped out of the shirt, I turned around to see his heated eyes on me as he stood in the doorway.

"I'll be right back," he said.

"Okay," I whispered and watched him walk away with a sigh that could only be described as dreamy.

I took this chance to look around. I was not above superficial snooping. The bed was big and there was a stack of large pillows in the corner by his dresser. I stood up and grabbed the pillows. I flipped his quilt down and propped the pillows against the dark wood headboard.

I smiled as he reentered the room and sat next to me in the bed.

"Come here," he said.

He didn't have to ask me twice. I went. His hands were magic, his mouth was even better, and the rest of his body was a playground I wanted to visit every day—twice on the weekend. But even better than all of that was *him.* He took care of me; he protected me. I felt cherished and special.

"I can't get enough of you," he said as he pulled me against his chest. I was on my knees between his legs as he reclined against the pillows by the headboard. His wandering hands traveled up the back of my thighs to squeeze my bottom.

I bent down to kiss him.

"I love your body," he murmured. "You're like an hourglass." His hands came around from my bottom to caress over my hips, and up under his T-shirt to travel over my waist, my breasts, then back down. Over and over, like I mesmerized him—like he did really love my body.

"I love your body too," I whispered. I loved looking at it, but I loved what it could do to mine even more. I let myself collapse against his chest. He wrapped me in his arms and kissed me.

He slid down until he was on his back and I was stretched out on top of him. "We should wait a few days. I don't want to hurt you."

"Okay," I agreed. I didn't want to stop, but I felt tender. Waiting was probably smart.

He shifted me to his side. Then he gathered me close like he never wanted to let me go. "Can you stay with me tonight?"

"I can stay."

"I suspect that eventually I'll want you to stay with me always."

My head jerked around so I could see his face. "You say the sweetest things..." I whispered. With every word that came out of his mouth my feelings grew.

"It's the truth," he whispered back then pressed a kiss to my forehead. "This is fast. I know it is. But I can't help the way I feel about you."

I lifted my head from his chest to look at him. "I feel the same way about you. Since we feel the same way—it shouldn't matter if it's fast. I mean, are there rules?" God, I hoped there weren't rules. If there were, I was sure I had broken them all by now. I kept switching from overly candid to quiet, from blushing to bold—back and forth like a wackadoodle pendulum. It was a wonder I was here in Wyatt's bed right now.

He laughed. "Not that I'm aware of."

I grinned. "Okay. Then we can do what we want."

Lifting his head, he kissed me. "I just want you. Every day, all the time. You're mine now."

I ducked my head into his chest overcome with emotion. "Yes. I want to be yours."

He kissed the top of my head and flicked the covers over us. "Sleep, darlin'." I felt him sigh; my head rose and fell with his breath. Replete with pleasure, my heart full of smiles, I fell asleep.

CHAPTER TWENTY-FOUR

SABRINA

After the homecoming game and Michael's arrest the weeks that followed were spent steadily falling head over heels for Wyatt Monroe. He called me every night before bed, and we texted each other throughout the day whenever we had a chance. We stole time to have lunch together. I brought Harry to his house for dinner a few times and it was sweet how well the kids got along together. He'd been out to the ranch with the girls as well and it seemed as if they liked it. Everybody got along. Everything was perfect.

Except for at the library. I had overheard Naomi and Mrs. MacIntyre talking about budget cuts and that maybe the library was at risk for closure. I tried to push it out of my mind as I walked up the path to the front door.

"Hi, Sabrina," Mrs. MacIntyre called out from behind the counter. She was bustling about, filling up one of those cardboard office boxes with papers and manila folders.

"Can I help you with anything?" I rushed around the counter to store my purse in her office then logged into the computer to sign in.

"Thank you, but I've got it. I'm out the door. It hasn't been busy today. In fact, we have no patrons at all right now." She shouldered her purse, snatched up the box, and rushed to the door. "Bye, dear.

Don't forget to set the alarm when you leave," she called as she hurried out.

"I won't. See you tomorrow."

I slid out of my coat and added it to my purse. That was weird; she wasn't usually in such a hurry. I guess my life was not the only thing changing around here.

I tidied up the non-existent mess behind the counter which comprised straightening stacks of papers and filing one folder. I pulled out the box of books on hold and spotted the new Stephen King on top. I left a voice mail for Jackson letting him know he could pick it up. I finished leaving messages for the other patrons and then grabbed the broom and the book cart so I could shelve books and sweep along the way.

There was nobody here. Sometimes afternoons could be slow, but this was nuts. I was in the stacks sweeping dust into the pan when the bell over the door announced someone's presence.

I stepped out to see Michael standing in the doorway.

"Can I help you?" I said out of habit. Then I shook my head to clear it. "Why are you here?"

"To talk to you. I want the kids back, Sabrina." He swiped under his nose with a hand as he stood there.

"Why? You've missed their whole lives. You've never even met Harry. Why now?" A jolt of fear shot through me, followed by anger, then the realization that Michael stood between me and every available phone in the library—not to mention the exits. Crap.

"It's none of your fucking business why. They're mine and I want them back." He didn't look right. His eyes were red and glassy, and his body twitched and shook with manic energy.

"They're people. Not your property. Don't you care what they want?" I tried to reason with him, to stall him, hoping someone would enter the library.

"You don't know what you're messing around with!" he shouted and stepped farther into the library.

"No!" I yelled back at him. For a moment, brave anger and the desire to protect the kids emboldened my heart. "You don't know who *you* are messing with. You know what you are?"

"Yeah, I'm the asshole in this scenario. Shut your mouth, Sabrina. I don't want to hear your useless opinions."

"No, I won't shut my mouth. I don't do that anymore. You're a disappointment, Michael." I gasped after the words shot out of my mouth. Then I stood taller. I had kids to protect. I beat back the fear; I couldn't afford to let it take over right now.

He froze, and his eyes snapped to mine.

"Cora loved you. We all loved you. You were part of our family. She gave you chance after chance to be a good husband and father, but you kept blowing it. It's too late now. Taking the kids won't do any good. They don't know you and they don't want to know you. Cora would be beside herself—she would hate this. You know it and you're still doing it. Shame on you."

He flinched and drew back as if I'd slapped him. He looked stricken for a second, but then that arrogant asshole mask he constantly wore replaced the small glimpse of humanity that had managed to break through for a brief second.

"Fuck you, Sabrina!" he yelled. Anger radiated out of him as he stood there and glared at me, shaking and swaying where he stood.

"You need to leave," I pleaded. "Just go. Leave me alone." Why was I pleading with this loser? I started to get mad. He had called me the weak link of my family after the homecoming game. Maybe I was a weak link in the past but I wasn't anymore and he could not use me or intimidate me to get what he wanted.

This wasn't like what happened in the Dragon Biker Bar parking lot. I hadn't sought this out. He was here. He was in my space acting like a big jerk and making threats. Eff this.

He stalked toward me. I stood firm.

"Sit down, Michael. Sit in that chair and listen to me, please. We can talk about this." I pointed to the table and chair next to him.

I flinched when he picked up the chair and tossed it out of his way to continue stalking toward me. Mrs. MacIntyre was going to be so pissed. You can't throw chairs in the library.

"Pick it up and sit down!" I yelled at him. I threw the dustpan I held in my hands at him. No, that was stupid. I picked up a hardback copy of *Moby Dick* from the cart behind me and threw that. Because Michael was a dick, I was sick of his crap and eff him, dang it.

He stared at me like I'd lost my mind.

I hadn't lost my mind. I'd lost my freaking temper for once in my life.

I reached behind me to the cart and hurled a copy of *Crime and Punishment* at him. It hit him in the chest then fell to the floor with a thump.

He flinched and stumbled back a step with his hands on his throat.

I grabbed another book and threw it, then another, and another. He backed up after each one. I pulled the cart behind me and continued launching the books at him. He continued flailing backward, stumbling and cursing at me the whole time until he finally turned and bolted toward the door.

The door which had just opened to let Jackson James inside. He stared at me openmouthed as I continued lobbing books at Michael.

Michael had turned his head around to look at me as he tried to make it to the door. "I'll sign your fucking papers, Sabrina. Stop throwing fucking books goddammit." He reached the lobby area and unfortunately for him, crashed smack dab into Jackson James. Michael bounced off Jackson's impressive—yeah, I said it—chest and landed on his butt on the floor.

God bless Stephen King. If it weren't for his new release and the power of a friendship birthed through a mutual love of horror novels, I may well have run out of books to throw at Michael's stupid ass.

Then what would have happened?

I can't kick anyone's ass. I'm an assistant librarian for Filch's sake, not a ninja.

"What the hell?" Jackson grabbed Michael, hoisted him up, spun him around, and pushed him up against the front window. "Stay still, dumbass."

"Arrest him. He came in here all rude and threatened me again. He threw a chair! That's against library rules! Arrest him, Jackson."

"You're under arrest, Adams."

"She threw the books. Arrest her too!" Michael hollered.

I stared at Jackson with my eyes bugging out.

"Yeah, okay." Jackson turned to wink at me. "We'll talk about that at the station, Adams."

My eyes got bigger and my jaw dropped as Jackson cuffed him and recited that Miranda stuff.

Jackson used the radio on his shoulder to call Wyatt.

"He'll be here in a minute, sweetheart. Don't you worry."

"I'm not worried. Thank you, Jackson. Oh! wait a minute!" I rushed around the counter and grabbed my purse out of the office. I pulled out the adoption papers and ran back to Jackson and Michael. "Here." I thrust the papers toward Michael.

He just stared at them. "Fuck you, Sabrina."

"You said you'd sign them. And fuck you too, Michael."

He looked to the side and huffed out an angry breath. "What happened to you? I thought you'd cave and get all scared like you used to and go running to your daddy, and then I could get the kids."

"Ruby said you wanted child support," I accused.

His face hardened; he didn't answer.

"You're their father, stupid. My father could have gone after *you* for child support all these years. Don't you know that?"

"He doesn't know that, Sabrina," Jackson answered for him. "His brain is fried from all the drugs he takes. Give me the papers. When he sobers up, we can probably have one of the public defenders go over it with him. Shit like this has to be notarized anyway."

"Thank you, Jackson."

He grinned at me and led Michael outside. I watched through the window as he put him in the back of his patrol car.

I saw Wyatt park his cruiser and get out. He spoke to Jackson for a minute then came inside. Relief filled my body—along with the shakes. Tears pricked behind my eyes and I didn't understand it because I'd managed to kick some serious ass just a few minutes ago.

His eyes swept up and down my body. "Are you okay? Are you hurt?"

"I'm okay." I lurched toward him and he caught me.

He swept me up against his chest and wrapped me up in his arms. "I couldn't get here fast enough," he whispered.

"I'm really okay," I whispered. I pressed myself against him. He was so warm, and I couldn't stop shaking. Why was I shaking?

He pulled back slightly and studied my face. "What happened?"

"Michael showed up. He was acting crazy; he threw a chair, so I threw books at him. He didn't touch me this time."

"Were you alone here?"

"Yes. Mrs. MacIntyre was supposed to work today. When I got here, she was in a rush to leave."

"Call her now. You're not staying here. We're leaving. Let me take care of you." He walked me over to the counter, picked up the phone, and handed it to me.

"I don't need to leave. My shift just started. I'm fine."

He smiled softly. "Darlin', you're shaking. Call her."

Wyatt held my hand as I called her. Mrs. MacIntyre instructed me to close the library. To lock the doors, set the alarm, and get out of there. Once I'd hung up the phone, he instructed me to call my father to take care of Harry. "Get your stuff, Sabrina. I'm taking you home," he told me when I finished my calls.

All I could do was nod and follow his lead.

Wyatt took me to his house and led me inside. I was in a daze. My body felt tired, but my brain wouldn't stop racing through everything that had just happened.

"I feel so tired, Wyatt. Like all of my energy has been drained away."

"Adrenaline crash. It's normal. You can take a nap in my bed. The girls will be home soon. I'll cook dinner and you can eat with us when you wake up. I'll text your dad and let him know you'll stay here with me tonight. Let me take care of you, Sabrina."

"Okay," I whispered. I didn't have the strength to go home. I didn't have the strength to even stand here anymore.

"Come with me."

I followed him to his room. He gave me one of his T-shirts. He pulled back his covers and switched on the bedside lamp.

"Change your clothes. I'll stay with you until you fall asleep. We can talk about everything when you wake up."

"Okay, I can't think straight to talk now."

He kicked off his shoes and undressed. I followed suit then slipped his T-shirt over my head.

I watched him pull on a pair of sweatpants and a white T-shirt then get into the bed. He held an arm out to me. I still felt shaky; I wanted him to hold me. I was lucky Jackson showed up when he did. I didn't want to think of the things Michael could have done. My mind raced with jumbled thoughts, and I couldn't stop my imagination.

"Thank you for taking care of me, Wyatt."

"Always, darlin'." He pulled me deeper into his arms and held me tight as I rested my head on his chest. He stroked my hair, and I felt the shakes dissipate. He was so warm, so strong. I couldn't help but feel safe when I was in his arms. I felt myself drift off, and I allowed myself to succumb to sleep.

My eyes jolted open. It had to be hours later. I was panting as I struggled to see in the darkness.

"Daddy! Come here!" Mak yelled from the doorway to Wyatt's room. I looked around. Light no longer filtered in through the slatted blinds on his window. How long had I been asleep?

I tried to focus but Wyatt's cat was on my chest, purring and butting his head on my chin. My eyes adjusted and I looked up; Mel was sitting in the middle of the bed holding my hand. She squeezed it when she noticed my eyes were open.

"You were dreaming," she told me and patted my cheek. "Princess Buttercup is good at finding bad dreams. He always wakes me up when I have them. He purrs and meows in my ear. Then when my eyes open, he licks my face." Her head tilted to the side and she grinned at me.

I felt Princess Buttercup's rough tongue lick my chin. Then he meowed and ran off. I guess his work here was done.

I heard footsteps pounding down the hallway.

"What's going on?" Wyatt asked as he rushed over and sat next to me on the edge of the bed. He brushed the hair back from my forehead. "Are you okay?"

"She was having a bad dream," Mak answered for me. "I was reading in my room and I heard her making noises. When we came in here, Princess Buttercup was trying to wake her up."

"I don't know what I was dreaming about," I whispered.

"I always have bad dreams about zombies and witches," Mel whispered back to me. "I was holding your hand in case you were trying to get away from scary things in your dream. I was going to pull you out of it. But then you woke up." She smiled; she had lost her other front tooth since the last time I'd seen her. I laughed softly when she stuck the tip of her tongue through the gap.

"I used to have bad dreams about the flying monkeys from *The Wizard of Oz*," I told her.

"Then I hope you weren't dreaming about those. I couldn't have pulled you away if the scary things were flying." She looked at me with worried eyes.

"Daddy made spaghetti," Mak said. "Do you want to eat dinner with us?"

"I would love to eat dinner with you."

"Girls, go wash up. Let's give Sabrina a chance to wake up."

They cleared out.

Wyatt pulled me up and into his arms. "I shouldn't have left you alone in here. I'm sorry."

"The stress of it is probably hitting me. And probably relief, too."

He cupped my face. "We can talk about it. You can tell me anything."

"I think Michael is finally going to sign the papers. He thought he could intimidate me into talking to my father and letting him have his way. I'll tell you more about it later when I get my brain function completely back," I joked.

He kissed me, then pulled back when we heard the girls yelling.

"Daddy! Mel got spaghetti on the floor!"

"Shut up, Mak! I'm hungry."

"Daddy! Mel is eating spaghetti off the floor!"

I giggled softly. He probably didn't think it was cute. Maybe if we got married someday and I had to deal with the spaghetti on the floor, I wouldn't find it cute either. But now? I found his girls adorable and hilarious.

Wyatt shut his eyes and groaned. "Please don't let this evening be a deal breaker."

"Just you wait. Harry has been on his best behavior around y'all so far. He can get complicated sometimes. Especially with food. Nothing can touch—you already know about that—but it's only one of his many rules."

His lips quirked to the side. "Divided plates are preferable to spaghetti on the floor. Just saying."

I burst out laughing. "Perhaps. But when a kid insists there is a difference between Goldfish crackers out of a box versus out of a bag or refuses to eat an entire plate of food because a pea rolled into the mashed potatoes, it can get dicey."

"Fair point. My girls will eat anything. Even if it's been on the floor—even if it's *still on* the floor."

I hugged his neck. "Oh, Wyatt, I feel like you get me."

"I do get you. And, it's been too long—I need to get *in* you again. Soon." He kissed my neck, then gently bit it.

Holy crap. I shivered. His hands traveled from the back of my neck, down my spine, and around my waist.

"You should stay here with me tonight." His breath was hot against my neck as he whispered.

"I could—my dad can take care of Harry. But what about the girls?"

"I told them we were together, that we're dating. But they don't have to know you will sleep here, not yet anyway." His hands continued their meandering pattern across my body, distracting me from thoughts of anything but being with him tonight.

"How will I get home in the morning? I don't have my car," I breathed.

"The school bus gets here at seven fifteen. You don't even have to get out of bed until they're gone. Then I'll drive you to the library to get your Jeep. I'm off tomorrow." He pulled away and winked at me.

"Perfect. It's pretty quiet out there. Should we worry?"

"Shit," he whispered. "Yeah, I'd better check on them."

"I'll be right out. I need to put my pants on."

With one last blazing look, he turned and left the room.

CHAPTER TWENTY-FIVE

SABRINA

Dinner with his girls went great. Spending time with them drove all thoughts of Michael and the library right out of my head. I decided to let it stay out of my mind and think about it tomorrow. The girls were cute and funny and seemed to enjoy me being there. In fact, Mak asked if we could have a sleepover. Wyatt winked at me when they weren't looking.

We tucked the girls into bed. I'd said goodbye to them like I was going to go home. Wyatt took my hand and led me into his bedroom, shutting and locking the door behind us.

"I want you," he stated with an adorable sideways grin. He let go of my hand, reached behind his neck, and pulled his T-shirt off. "Unless you would rather talk about today?"

"I don't want to talk at all," I answered and stared at his gorgeous chest.

He grinned and tossed his shirt at me.

If a person could really get heart eyes, I would have them right now. Wyatt without his shirt was beautiful—broad and strong, sculpted and *delicious.*

I took my shirt off and threw it at him. He caught it with a laugh and tossed it aside to join his on the floor.

He kicked off his shoes, so I toed my socks off. His eyes grew hot as he unbuttoned his pants and pushed them down and I followed suit with my jeans. He was in tight white boxer briefs and I was in pink cotton undies. He tipped his head and eyed my bra with an expectant grin. I laughed and took it off, letting it fall to the floor. Now we were even.

He took a big step toward me and grabbed my waist, hauling my body against his and banding an arm around my hips to lift me to my toes.

My breasts pushing against his chest, I groaned and held on to his neck. Every single time he put his hands on my body, delicious swirly feelings grew low in my belly. But also in my heart. I was twisted up in knots that only he could untie and I loved it. His hands slid into my panties to push them down my hips. I kicked them aside when they fell to my feet.

His lips slammed into mine, and I melted against him as he devoured my mouth and sucked on my bottom lip. I could hardly keep up with him he was moving so fast. His big hands held my hips and bit into my bottom to guide us backward toward his bed.

He walked over to the edge of his bed, then let me go. I tumbled to the bed, and he followed me, knee between my legs, to cover my body with his.

"Can I try stuff?" I murmured against his lips as I pushed at his chest. I wanted to be on top. I was dying to try it out. I wanted to get lost in him. I wanted to forget this entire day.

"What stuff?" he asked.

I turned red. "Um, can I, uh…"

"How about this: do whatever you want to me. I'm yours." After rolling to his back he scooted up the bed to lean against the headboard with lowered eyebrows and a devastatingly sexy smile. He stretched each arm along the back of it and winked.

Wow. I stared at him with big eyes.

"Get to it then, darlin'," he encouraged.

I bit my lip. All I could do was stare. It was like Christmas morning and my birthday, a pile of presents and a chocolate cake, all wrapped up in the most beautiful man I'd ever seen wearing nothing but tight white boxer briefs and a devious smile. Until he lifted his hips and removed the briefs. He stroked himself once before returning his arms to the headboard with a grin that was also a dare.

I had no idea where I wanted to start. At the top, for a kiss. Or at the middle, where I could give a kiss of a different kind. I was dying to try that out. I'd been reading about this stuff for years in romance novels and I was finally *doing* it. Saying 'yay' out loud would probably be weird, so I kept quiet.

I tilted my head with a grin and crawled up his outstretched legs to kiss him once on his gorgeous lips before I made my decision.

His eyes on me changed. His hot, lust filled gaze warmed to reflect the depth of his feelings. "I don't know what I'd do without you," he whispered. His arms left the back of the bed to enclose me.

"You'll never have to find out," I murmured against his lips.

His hand tangled in my hair. The kiss grew deeper as his tongue entered my mouth to meet mine. His other hand moved from my back to softly caress between my legs.

"I want you now. I want this." His eyes flashed into mine as he gently entered me with his fingers.

My head dropped back, and my body arched against his. I sank down on his hand and let him fill me, but I wanted more. I grabbed his hand and placed it back on the headboard. His eyes glinted as his chest rose and fell rapidly with barely contained lust as he let me take control.

I smiled at him. I wasn't trying to tease him, but he was so sexy. So big and hard beneath me. And the way he looked at me…

He made it safe for me to be this way—coy and flirty, sexy and wild. All of it was because I trusted him. I felt safe with him.

I ran my hands up and down his chest and abs. I watched as his muscles flexed and released beneath my palms. He was so warm, so beautiful, so *mine.*

I scooched backward, bent low, and took him into my mouth. I'd read about this. I knew what to do.

I watched as his jaw tensed, his eyes blazed, and every muscle on his body flexed as he sucked in a huge breath. His hand stayed gentle in my hair as he watched me take him with my mouth and tongue.

"Sabrina," he growled as his hips thrust gently up.

I released him and sat up on my knees. I watched as he rolled a condom down his thick length.

I crawled forward again. I held his cock in my hand as I rubbed my slick center up and down the hard length, then sank down. His eyes dropped closed and his head fell back, mouth opened in a silent groan as his hands dug into my thighs encouraging me to ride him faster, harder.

But I moved languidly. Slow and steady. I wanted to savor; I wanted to keep this feeling. "This is nice," I groaned against his mouth.

"Mmmm," he answered before burying his face into my neck, placing his hands under my thighs and flipping me to my back.

"God, Wyatt!" I squealed.

"Baby, shh…" He put his hand over my mouth—which drove me absolutely crazy. It felt like I was doing something forbidden, something secret, something naughty. Low in my abdomen heat swirled and twisted.

"I can't be slow," he grunted. "I need you too much." He rose to his knees and his hand slipped between our bodies to swirl tight circles with his thumb right where I needed it as he moved inside of me.

"Please." My head pressed into the mattress as I arched up. He fell to one hand above me as he slowed down. His other hand glided up my body to cup my breast and lightly pinch my nipple.

Now who was teasing?

He kissed me. His tongue in my mouth matched his slow strokes inside of my body. "Tell me you want me," he groaned against my lips.

"I do. I want you, please," I gasped.

He pulled out and turned to his back. "Then take what you want."

Immediately I threw my leg over his hips and plunged down on top of him. Now I watched *his* back arch under me as I rode him until we both came. Then I collapsed into an exhausted heap at his side. He turned and gathered me close, kissing the top of my head and sighing into my hair as his hand trailed softly up and down my side.

"I never thought I could feel like this," I confessed.

"Like what?"

I smiled up at him and kissed the underside of his jaw before answering. "Like I can be myself and you will always want me."

He smiled softly. "I *will* always want you. It's so easy to be with you. We make sense together. How would you feel about moving in with me someday? I have four bedrooms. Harry could have his own room."

I hesitated before I answered. I was afraid of this moment. I couldn't take Harry away from my father, from Weston and Ruby, and his home on the ranch. Even though I would be the one to adopt Harry, my father had been there for every step. I couldn't have done it without him. My father was more than a grandfather to Harry; he was necessary to Harry's continued growth.

"I would love to live with you someday. But I don't know if I can take Harry away from the ranch. He—"

"I should have thought of that," he interrupted.

"How would you feel about living at the ranch someday? It's what Logans have always done. It might be weird, but I grew up with both sets of grandparents living there. And Cora and Michael, before he turned to the dark side, and the kids…"

"So, it's kind of a family tradition?"

"Yeah, and the house is so big, we'd have our own wing. The girls could have one too—they could live in the rooms Cora and I used to share when I was a little girl."

"If we had our own wing, then I wouldn't have to put my hand over your mouth when we're in bed." His grin was downright wicked.

I giggled. "You could still do that."

His eyes heated as his hand trailed up and down my back.

"It's something to consider," he said. "I wouldn't want to do anything to hurt Harry's progress."

"It's not always about progress. Sometimes it's about making peace with the ways he will always differ from what most people consider normal. I struggle with that about myself lately. But, anyway, I'm glad you'll consider it."

He flipped the quilt over us. "I'm falling for you, Sabrina—whether or not you think you're normal." His smile was gentle on my face. The weight of his feelings was a comforting presence. But I would have felt it even if he hadn't said it. "I will consider anything it takes to be with you."

My heart.

"Oh, Wyatt, I'm falling for you too."

"Sleep, baby," he whispered against my hair. He kissed my temple then settled me into his arms.

CHAPTER TWENTY-SIX

SABRINA

Tonight was Halloween. I was excited to spend it with Wyatt's girls and only a tiny bit nervous that his mom and Everett were coming too. But Ruby and Willa would be there to fill in whenever my conversational skills disappeared. Wyatt was on duty, but he was supposed to meet us at the senior center when he took his break. Most people in Green Valley went to the community center for Halloween but the senior center stayed open for those who wanted to celebrate but couldn't handle big crowds. We took Harry there every year, and most of his friends from school attended too. It was always a small affair, with a candy cafeteria path and quiet music in the gathering room.

"Are you ready?" Harry shouted from the half-bath under the stairs at the ranch.

"I'm ready, Harry! I am, I am!" Mel shrieked from the entryway. Wyatt's mother had created Mel's dream costume—she was a ballerina ninja princess, complete with a tutu and tiara.

"I'm ready too, Harry." Mak laughed. She was dressed as Hermione Granger even though Harry had insisted that with her red hair she looked more like Ginny Weasley. Harry, the girls, and I had been reading *Harry Potter* together after dinner most nights, either here or at Wyatt's place.

"Look at me," Harry said. "I'm a deputy sheriff, just like Wyatt Earp and Wyatt Monroe. 'Fast is fine, but accuracy is everything. In a gun fight...you need to take your time in a hurry.' Wyatt Earp said that." He pulled his squirt gun from the holster and shot at the front door just as Willa walked through it, splashing her in the stomach.

"Good shot." She laughed.

"Oh, no. I'm sorry, Willa."

"Don't worry, Harry." She stood up straight and got into character. "I'm from the remote desert planet of Jakku, I'm probably dehydrated." Willa was Rey from *The Force Awakens.*

Ruby laughed as she entered from the kitchen carrying the pumpkin trick-or-treat buckets. She was Princess Leia, which was pretty much the best Halloween costume of all time—aside from my own. As soon as she had been old enough to let Cora know, Ruby had wanted to be a different Leia every Halloween. I encouraged her to keep up the tradition after Cora died. This year she was the white robe, doughnut-buns Leia from *A New Hope*.

This year I was Smash-Girl. I felt like a badass and it was time to dress like one.

We all turned as my father's footsteps sounded down the stairs. "I'm headed to the senior center. I'll see y'all there."

"Pop, you're a vampire. But you aren't scary at all," Harry said.

"Yeah, I don't want to scream *or* run away," Mel said, sounding disappointed.

He laughed. "That's right, I'm a friendly vampire. We don't want anyone getting too scared to have fun."

"I heard Big Ben is going to play dulcimer for y'all. It's quite the scandal around town." Becky Lee laughed.

"You betcha," Dad said. "It wasn't easy, but we booked him before the community center could get him for their Halloween party. First time in ten years he won't play there." His gleeful laugh made me smile. "His rendition of 'The Monster Mash' is top-notch." He waved goodbye as he headed outside.

We planned to start the evening at the senior center and then head up and down Main Street to experience Green Valley's Trick-or-Treat Trail. All the shops handed out candy and most of the owners decorated and dressed up. The Trick-or-Treat trail started and ended early so people could have time to attend the community center Halloween party. But we were skipping the community center party this year. It would be too crowded for Harry, and if I'm being honest, me too.

"Let's go, let's go, go, go." Mel hopped up and down. "I need candy!" she shrieked and waved her hands in the air.

"Come on, sweeties." Becky Lee laughed, directing us all to her minivan.

"You don't need any more sugar, Mel. Your head might explode," Mak said as they headed out the front door.

Mel stuck her tongue out. "It will not. Be quiet, Mak."

"Ready?" I said to Harry. "And remember, we can come back home whenever you want, just say the word."

"I'm ready." He smiled.

"And I'm ready to eat all the candy you don't like." Willa grinned at him.

"I only like Hershey Bars and plain Kisses. That's it," he informed her.

"It's my lucky night then. I heard Big Ben's Dulcimer Shop gives out full sized Kit Kat bars."

"Um, no way," I protested. "I have dibs on all Kit Kats in all their various forms—white, milk, and dark chocolate."

She laughed at me. "How could I forget about your obsession? Fine. I get the rest." She patted her light saber. "Don't make me use this on you."

"Willa, you don't need that. You can use the force on her," Everett teased.

"Pretty sure she can only use it for good. Though we won't know for certain until the next movie comes out," Ruby argued.

"Let's go. I have a hankering for a Snickers bar, among other things." Everett grinned at Willa and headed for the door.

There was a cool breeze and leaves were blowing every which way, covering the lawn and gravel drive.

Becky Lee pulled into the senior center lot and we headed inside. Becky Lee started snapping pictures of the girls in the front of the hay bales that were decorated with happy jack-o'-lanterns and smiling scarecrows in the corner of the spacious lobby.

"Get in our picture, Harry," Mak called.

He sat next to them and they all smiled at Becky Lee.

"Hey, ladybugs," Wyatt called from the doorway.

"Daddy!" Mak and Mel yelled and ran to him.

I held myself back from yelling and running to him too. But just barely.

"Look at me, Wyatt. I'm you," Harry informed him and waved his hand in front of himself.

"You sure are. We should get a picture together." Wyatt held his hand out and Harry dashed over to take it.

"Okay, Wyatt." Harry beamed up at him. Both my heart and my panties melted at the sight. I sighed and reconsidered running to him.

"Let's take a picture of all of you together. Sabrina, Wyatt, kids—sit on the hay," Becky Lee ordered.

Wyatt took my hand and tugged me over to the hay bales. He pulled me down to sit at his side while the kids surrounded us.

"This is perfect. Y'all look like one big happy family." Becky Lee grinned and snapped pictures.

It felt perfect. It felt like a dream come true, like everything I'd ever wanted.

"Okay, get up, y'all. Willa and Everett, sit. I want to take a picture of you two."

Everett's eyes got huge as he looked at Willa, whose jaw had dropped.

"Go on now. Sit on the hay. Scoot," Becky Lee ordered.

They took our place on the hay bale and Becky Lee snapped away with her camera.

"Good. Done. Kids! Let's trick-or-treat." She held out her hand and the girls quickly took hold. "Chop, chop."

Becky Lee looked expectantly at Harry. "Come on, Harry. You too, Willa and Everett," she bossed.

Harry looked at me, eyebrows raised. "Can I?"

"Yes," I said with a laugh.

He got up and took Mak's outstretched hand.

Willa smiled at me and shook her head before following them into the dining room. Everett followed behind all with an eye roll.

"My mother is not subtle," Wyatt said wryly.

"She sure isn't," I said with a laugh. "She's sweet."

"My girls adore her. Harry will too."

"I think he already does. He took to her right away, like he didn't have a choice."

"He will fit right in with my family. You will too. They'll love you just like I do," he whispered before wrapping me in his arms and kissing me.

Did he just tell me he loved me?

He'd said he was falling for me the other night. Was that the same thing? Should I say, 'I love you too?' Because I did—I loved him. Or should I wait for him to say the words exactly and then say it back to him? I stood there and stared at him.

Nod and smile while you think.

I smiled at him. Then I nodded even though he hadn't asked me a question.

What would Sienna Diaz do?

I threw my arms around his neck and kissed him.

She'd probably do that, right?

My kisses would have to do the talking for me because I couldn't bring myself to say the words aloud if I was unsure if he felt the same.

"I wish I didn't have to get back to work. I'd rather trick-or-treat with y'all, then take you home later and see what kinds of treats you'll give me." He teased and smacked another kiss onto my lips.

"Wyatt!" I gasped.

He laughed. "I'd better get going. I'll call you later."

"Be careful out there," I said.

"Always, darlin'."

As I watched Wyatt walk away my heart gave a little lurch. I loved him so much. I should have told him.

CHAPTER TWENTY-SEVEN

SABRINA

The sun had just started to go down, but Main Street continued to glow with festive Halloween spirit. Strands of orange and purple lights twinkled in the trees and jack-o'-lanterns flickered ominously from behind their carved-out grins and eyes while white ghost luminaries strung from pole to pole above us lent their soft glow to the Green Valley Trick-or-Treat Trail.

People were in awesome costumes. I saw a lot of Avengers, a few Power Rangers, and Disney Princesses. And some Winstons—Ashley and Drew Runous had dressed up their baby girl like Belle from *Beauty and the Beast*. The sight of that sweet baby girl made me want one of my own. Gah! I think I just caught baby fever. What would a baby of mine and Wyatt's look like? I melted inside when I pictured a tiny baby with chocolate brown eyes just like Wyatt's.

I waved, smiled, and said hi to various tiny costumed humans and their parents as we walked down the street and the kids got their candy from the shops.

Ruby tugged on my arm and pulled me aside. "Look at you," she whispered with a huge smile on her face.

"What?" I laughed.

"Saying hi, waving. You're *in the world,* Sabrina. Not hiding inside your head or a book, or wherever you used to go inside your brain."

"It's no big deal," I lied. It was a big deal. On the outside I was smiling and waving but inside I was still nervous and a little bit afraid. The difference from before was I was willing to try—I wanted more and was working hard to get it. My dad always told me, "The more you do, the easier it will be to do more." And he was right; it was getting easier to come out of my shell a little bit. I would never fully leave it, but I could poke my head out from time to time if I could hide out and recharge when I got home.

"It used to be," she argued. "Before, if I could even get you to go anywhere with me in the first place, you would have had your head in the clouds, like you weren't even present, like mentally or something. You wouldn't have noticed at all if someone tried to speak to you."

"Ruby, I think I got through the last nine years by pretending that they weren't happening. I was always shy, but when your mom died, I let the shyness combine with my grief and lost myself in it. Plus, I'm not exactly having deep conversations with anyone right now. I'm just smiling and saying hello." I decided to be honest with her. I had come a long way and she had always been there to encourage me.

She hugged me. "I understand that. But, Sabrina, I feel like you're *here,* with me. And I'm so glad."

I hugged her back. I was *here* with her and not hiding in fearful thoughts. And I would still have to go home and do my usual—ponder, ruminate—but instead of freaking out and throwing up, I would write my feelings down in my journal and try to leave them there.

"Hey, Smash-Girl! Over here!" I spun around after Ruby poked me in the side and pointed across the street.

A family of masked *Incredibles* were waving at me from in front of the Dulcimer Shop. I needed to go over there anyway, for the Kit Kats, of course. Not curiosity. You know what they said about curiosity—it killed the cat.

I caught Becky Lee's attention. "I'm going to cross the street with

Ruby for a second, we'll be right back. Come on, Harry." I took his hand and we made our way to the other side of the street.

Elastigirl beamed at me as we approached, her dimples practically blinding me. I slowed my pace and glanced over at Ruby who was deliberately looking elsewhere. My Spidey senses were tingling, could it be?

"Hey, the baby is Jack-Jack!" Harry yelled. "Hey, Jack-Jack! Hey, Mr. Incredible! Oh, and two Dashes. Hi, two Dashes!"

Mr. Incredible said, "Hey, little man," to Harry and I recognized him from the library and Genie's Bar. Mr. Incredible was Jethro Winston.

"Knock Knock, Miss Sabrina." I heard that tiny little voice from the library say once we'd reached them—Benjamin. I gulped. Holy crap, I was about to fangirl so hard. There would be *squee*-ing. I may even go down.

"Who's there?" I asked as I gazed at Elastigirl with what I hoped was a neutral, friendly expression. *Hide it, Sabrina. You hide all that fangirl crazy* right now.

"Boo." He giggled.

"Boo who?" Harry shouted. I giggled at Benjamin while at the same time trying to prevent myself from hyperventilating. Ruby grabbed my hand—did she sense I was about to bolt?

"Don't cry, it's just me—and my mom." Harry burst into laughter and Benjamin high-fived him before turning to look up at me. I had finally managed to wrench my eyes away from Elastigirl to pay proper attention to him. "Miss Ruby said my mom is your favorite when we saw her at the Piggly Wiggly yesterday," he informed me.

"I think *you* might just be my favorite, Benjamin. You have the best jokes." I held my hand out for a high-five of my own and he smacked it. He looked up at his mother with an adorable, smug expression.

"Oh, now you're my favorite," Elastigirl said.

Sienna Diaz just called me her favorite. I was literally going to die. Tears formed behind my eyes and I blinked rapidly to keep them from falling. I sucked in a huge gulp of air and tried to smile.

What would Sienna Diaz do?

Holy effing crap. This was unprecedented. And slightly meta.

"I love you," I blurted. *You're so cool, Sabrina...and totally normal. NOT.*

There was no way to express what she meant to me without sounding like a total nut job, it was best that no one ever know.

Sienna Diaz laughed. She reached over and hugged me.

I hugged her back. "Thank you for hugging me. I'm sorry for interrupting your trick-or-treat trail experience," I said when we pulled apart.

"You didn't interrupt us. I interrupted you, remember?" She laughed again. Sienna Diaz had a glorious laugh. And a glorious smile. And she was super nice too. Oh. My. God.

"It was great to meet you. I'm sorry if I got weird," I said with an internal cringe.

"Everyone gets weird around me at first. You'll get over it. I'm just a normal human like everyone else." Her nod was sage as she smiled at me.

"No, you're not," Jethro told her with a grin.

"Let's trick-or-treat some more, Mommy," Andy, the second Dash said.

"We better hit the trail. I'll see you around town, Smash-Girl." Sienna Diaz took her son's hand and they all took off up the trail.

"Bye," I said then turned to Ruby when they were out of hearing distance. "I can't believe this. I just can't believe it. I will never believe it because this is impossible to believe."

"You will. You'll probably see her around town too now that you've joined the world." She grinned at me.

"Oh my God." I was going to have to go home and lie down. I was going to need at least a week to recover from this.

I let Harry trick-or-treat at the Dulcimer Shop—because, full-sized Kit Kats—before rejoining the others. I snatched it out of his bucket and unwrapped it. I took a big bite right out of the middle just to watch Ruby flinch. It made me feel a little bit better.

"Gah! I hate it when you do that, Sabrina," she said and stomped ahead. I chuckled.

"My candy bucket is full. And my feet hurt," Harry complained once we caught up to Wyatt's mom and the others.

"I can't walk anymore," Mel said from her perch on Willa's back.

"Sugar pie, I've been walking for the both of us for the last ten minutes." Willa laughed. "I'm like your own personal candy pack mule. I'm even carrying your bucket. My piggy back tax is a bag of M&M's and a Snickers bar, by the way."

"I'll pay the tax, and you can have the Butterfingers too. They hurt my teeth," Mel offered.

"Mel, I thought I got the Butterfingers," Everett teased.

"No way, Everett," Willa retorted. "Mel and I have just struck a deal. No takesies-backsies, Mel. We'll shake on it when I put you down."

"I'll share with you, Uncle Everett," Mak offered. "And Grandma is going to chop some candy up tomorrow and make Halloween candy cookies."

"That sounds intriguing," I said.

"It's just a chocolate chip cookie recipe." Becky Lee laughed. "It impresses the kids though, especially if you add sprinkles to it. Then you don't have candy cluttering your house and making your kids into hyper little sugar monsters for the week after Halloween."

"Genius," Willa said. "If I ever have kids, I'm coming to you for a list of your sneaky tricks."

Becky Lee's phone rang. "Hello." She listened for a second. She stopped walking and glanced at me. "Yes, she's right here with me."

We stopped too. I froze at the expression that crossed her face. She had lost all color and her hand shook as she held the phone. "We're coming. We'll be right there," she finally said.

"What is it? What's wrong?" I asked, but she was already busy texting someone.

Everett's phone pinged with a text message. He pulled it out and froze just like Becky Lee had.

"Wyatt," she mouthed to me. "We have to go. Right now. Take everyone to the house, Everett."

"Willa, Ruby, can you help?" Becky Lee asked.

"Yes, I'll help watch them," Willa agreed, confusion on her face.

"Thank you, honey," Becky Lee said and rummaged in her purse. She separated her keys, "Here is my house key." Everett took it.

"We'll have fun. Won't we, kids?" Everett said.

The girls looked like they were wondering what was going on.

"Everything is fine. Sabrina and I have to—just—we'll be right back. Later. Don't worry about a thing. Everything is fine," she told them.

"Okay, Grandma," Mel said from her perch on Willa's back.

"I've got Harry," Ruby told me. "I'll call Pop as soon as we get there. I promise."

"Thank you," I said. My fingers dug into my palms as I watched everything unfold as if I were hovering above it all. I felt myself start to disconnect like I used to do as panic filled my mind.

"It's no problem, Sabrina," Everett said. "Go with my mom. It'll be okay." His voice came at me as if from underwater.

I hugged Harry. "Pop will pick you and Ruby up soon."

"Okay, Riri," he answered and hugged me back.

"Come on, kids," Willa said. "Since I'm just the babysitter I have no idea about how many candy bars you are allowed to eat on Halloween or how late y'all are allowed to stay up watching movies."

"Oh, yeah! We're going to get so sick!" Mel yelled as Everett led them up the street to the Monroe house.

"Come on, honey. Sabrina, come with me." Becky Lee had taken charge.

"Wyatt. Is he—how bad?" Why hadn't I told him I loved him when I had the chance? What if it was too late? Tears burned behind my eyes but I blinked to keep them at bay.

"I don't know how bad it is. They won't tell me over the phone," Becky Lee said.

We rode to the hospital in Maryville in silence.

Becky Lee pulled into a spot. "Come on."

I wished I could be like her. Something or someone had hurt her son. Who knew how bad—and she was still in control.

I was not in control. I was hanging by a thread.

I followed blindly as Becky Lee led us to Wyatt. At some point she took my hand. I grabbed on to it, needing something to hold on to because it felt like I would float away. The white halls and the white lights, the beeping and the smells—it took me back to the last time I was here, with my sister.

We walked down hall after hall. Our footsteps echoed on the linoleum floors and empty sterile hallways, it filled my ears and rattled my thoughts.

We finally reached a nurses' station and Becky Lee asked about Wyatt. My vision blurred and I blinked, thinking my contacts were dry. I watched as she pointed to a room down a short hallway.

Becky Lee squeezed my hand. "Come on, Sabrina."

Nodding dumbly, I followed her into Wyatt's room.

An orderly was stripping the bed. He looked over at us when we walked through the doorway.

"We're looking for Wyatt Monroe," Becky Lee told him. I didn't know how she could remain so calm. My insides were trying to tear themselves apart.

"I don't even know why they brought him into this room. There was nothing to do for him," he grumbled and continued working on the bed.

I stood frozen on my little square of linoleum. Time stopped. Or if it was, it was spinning backward because the past had swallowed me up and spit me right back up into the terrible present. Tears filled my eyes, but I blinked them back. I bit my lip and clenched my fists until my fingernails dug painfully into my palms. But the steady tide of panic and grief rising inside of me would not recede no matter how hard I tried to force it away.

I spun around and tried to walk, but ended up running out of Wyatt's room instead. I passed Wyatt's father, his face full of concern, in the hall. I did not stop running until I was outside, my racing heart threatening to pound out of my chest.

I saw a taxi idling on the curb. Someone got out and I ran to the car before it could leave.

"Can you take me home?" I must have looked as desperate as I felt because he immediately nodded.

"Sure thing. Hop inside, miss."

"Thank you." I got in and slammed the door, glancing out the window in time to see Becky Lee hurrying out the door with Wyatt's father close behind.

"Go. Please go now," I said frantically.

He pulled away from the curb. "Where to?"

"Green Valley. The Logan Horse Ranch." I sank back in the seat.

I choked back a sob. My chest hurt.

"Are you okay?"

I could barely form words around the lump in my throat. "I'm fine," I squeaked out.

"You sure?"

I nodded, but he couldn't see that, he was driving. "Yes," I managed to say.

My throat hurt. I wanted to scream. I wanted to run home, not sit here. Sitting in this taxi was like sitting in a tiny box I couldn't get out of. Or maybe these thoughts swirling around my head were the box.

I let my head fall to the side against the cool window. I looked up at the moon, shining white, high up in the sky. Nothing like the brilliance of the Harvest Moon that night in the pasture with Wyatt.

He was gone, and I never told him how much I loved him because I was too afraid.

Soon, the moon was not the only white spot in my vision. I couldn't catch my breath.

Breathe.

I managed a shallow breath. I turned my head and looked at my knees.

Put your head down.

I leaned forward as much as the seat belt would allow. It helped. A bit. I should be home soon. Maryville was only thirty minutes away.

"We're here. Are you sure you're okay?"

"Fine. I—" I reached into my pocket and pulled out two twenties. "Here." I tossed the bills to the front seat, got out, and ran to the gate. I hurriedly punched in the code. As soon as the black iron parted, I ran up the gravel path toward the house not even waiting for the driver to pull away. I didn't know why I was in such a rush. I had nothing to run toward anymore. I stopped and stood there as I choked on a sob.

I stumbled to the porch swing and tried to catch my breath as I stared out at the darkness. Tears filled my eyes but I couldn't let them fall because they'd never stop.

I rocked in the porch swing and tried to get a breath. I waited for my chest to rise while I searched for air that wouldn't come.

"No, no, no," I whispered, as if the repeated denials could chase this pain away. But nothing could get rid of it. It lived inside of me now, and always would.

CHAPTER TWENTY-EIGHT

WYATT

Halloween was the worst night of the year, without fail. Even worse than New Year's Eve. Goddamn Halloween with its bunch of dumbass drunks and idiots who only cared about hitting the next party. I thought Green Valley would be better than Nashville. Nope, everybody in town was riled up like it was their last chance to have a drink or get a piece of ass. Half-naked girls dressed as sexy-something-or-others ran around every which way and anonymous dirty-minded revelry spread into the bars, the streets, parks, even the damn Piggly Wiggly. I was one of the unlucky bastards who got to clean up the messes. Fuck this. Next year I was going to be sick for Halloween.

I stalked down the hall of the hospital in Maryville with murder on my mind. Who was I going to kill? Anyone that got in my goddamn way, that's who. But I'd start with Devron Stokes and his drunk ass. I'd pulled him over for weaving all over the highway right outside of town, near The Wooden Plank. He'd obviously just tied one on. While I was in the process of arresting him a car full of asshole teenagers opened their door as they drove by. The door hit me on the side, and I went flying into the street. I was lucky they didn't run me over as they drove by. But I got their plate number and Jackson had probably already arrested their punk asses by now. I was also lucky Stokes pulled my ass out of the road and called 911. Maybe I'd take him off my murder list.

I was not hurt. I walked away from the scene and refused to let them cart my ass off on a stretcher to the ambulance like an invalid. All I needed was a few ibuprofen and I'd be just fine. But procedure dictated that I be checked out thoroughly at the hospital. Sheriff James was a stickler for procedures. I admired him, I respected him, and I even agreed with him. But I had no patience for this kind of thing. I hated hospitals. I spent a lot of time in the hospital in college after my knee blew out and I had no desire to repeat that experience. Plus, this hospital was an overcrowded clusterfuck tonight. No one could tell their asses from their elbows. I'd waited in the ambulance bay for almost an hour before a doctor saw me. Only to receive a prescription for industrial strength ibuprofen and told me to take it easy. *No fucking shit.*

"Wyatt! Oh my God. Wyatt—" My sobbing mother hurled herself into my arms when she caught sight of me turning the corner.

"Mom, what's going on? Are you okay?" I looked over her shoulder to my father.

Tears filled his eyes as he wrapped his arms around the both of us. "You're alive. You're okay."

"What the fuck is going on? And I love y'all too."

"We didn't know what happened to you," my mother cried. "I just got a call to come down here. Sabrina came with me, but she ran off when your room was empty. The orderly—he made it sound like you'd died. I just knew that couldn't be. I'd know it, I'd feel it. We've been looking around for someone who knows what the heck is going on. This place is a madhouse tonight—"

I cut her off. "Sabrina? Where is she?" I pulled my mother to the side as people rushed by us down the hall.

My father answered, "She took off runnin'. I tried to catch her, but she was too fast. She hopped into a cab outside the hospital. We've been trying to find out what happened to you, and then we were going to go and find her—"

"Shit. Fuck. Damn it," I growled. "This whole entire night has been a disaster. I've gotta go find her. She probably went home. She's probably frantic."

My mother handed me her car key. "Take my car. I met your father here, so I'll ride home with him. You find her. The poor thing was shook up something fierce."

"Wait a second, Wyatt. Please." My father stopped me with a hand on my arm.

"What is it?"

"I owe you an apology. If tonight has taught me one thing, it's that life is just too short to hold stupid grudges. I'm proud of you, and I'm sorry. Now go and get your girl."

I pulled my father into a hug. "Thanks, Dad."

I turned to dart down the hall, then whirled back to my parents. "The girls?" I asked.

"They're with Everett and Willa at the house. Ruby and Harry were with them. They were going to call Roy to pick them up. They are all fine, watching movies on the TV. I called to check not too long ago. We'll drive straight home. I'll take care of them, honey."

"Thanks, Mom."

Now, I had to find Sabrina. I tried to call her cell as I walked out to my mother's car, but it went straight to voice mail. Damn it. I had to get to her. I couldn't stand the thought of her frantic and upset. And I knew her—she was thinking the worst. My heart seized at the thought of her somewhere crying and alone.

I pulled onto the road and headed for Green Valley. Maryville was about a half-hour drive. I tapped my hand against the steering wheel when I got caught up in the Halloween traffic. *Come on, dammit.*

I entered the gate code to the Logan Ranch and drove through, pulling to a stop in front of the house. The lights were on outside, but the house was dark. I stepped onto the porch and looked around. There was Sabrina's leather jacket draped over the back of the chair next to her cell phone. I recognized the Smash-Girl case.

Just in case she was inside, I banged on the door then tried to open it; it was locked. Where would she go? I ran out to the front lawn. I stood there and spun in a circle trying to scan the dark for a sign of her.

The pasture! That was her spot. I didn't bother with my truck. I pulled my flashlight from my belt and ran, skidding down the slight slope to the pasture calling her name.

I spotted her. Lying in that same spot in the grass we'd shared during the Harvest Moon. The night when I knew for certain exactly what she would mean to me.

"Wyatt?" She sat up. Then she stood up. Then she started running toward me.

I dropped the flashlight and caught her as she flew into my arms.

"I love you. I love you. I love you," she repeated, over and over through her sobs.

"I love you, Sabrina. I'm so sorry I scared you. So, so sorry. I love you too."

She pulled back and cupped my face in her hands. The look in her eyes pierced right through my heart. Straight into my soul.

She loved me.

This was what love should look like.

A wide-open soul—bared so it could shine in the dark.

Sabrina shone brighter than the moon and I loved her more than my own life.

"I'm sorry, darlin'. Everything was a mess tonight—"

"It's okay. Everything is okay now. You're here, that's the only thing that matters." Her voice cracked as another sob escaped. She pressed her lips together to hold the rest back.

I pulled her into my chest and held her as she cried. "Shh, I'm here. I'm here and I will never leave you, I swear it. Just let it out, baby. Let it go." She trembled in my arms as her tears flowed until she was still and quiet in my arms.

I tipped her face back so I could kiss her. Once, twice, then again as we sunk into each other and the whole world disappeared around us.

CHAPTER TWENTY-NINE

WYATT

The early evening sun shone low in the sky over the pasture at the Logan Ranch. We rolled to a stop and got out of my truck. But this time I was prepared—with more than just blankets. I also had plans. Big ones.

Sabrina pulled the picnic basket from the cab and I grabbed the blanket. It was almost Thanksgiving, but I was grateful for the warm November night. We'd stopped at the Front Porch for a takeout picnic in her favorite spot.

"I miss you when you work nights," she whispered in my ear after we spread the thick, waterproof blanket on the grass and sat down. I had just come off two weeks of night shifts. It made it more complicated to spend time with her, and I hated it.

I reached for her hand and used it to pull her into my arms. "I missed you too. We're going to have to do something about that. I don't like being away from you so much. We're in the same town but I hardly ever get to see you when I'm on nights."

Her eyes got big but before she could say anything, I took her sweet mouth with mine and got lost in her. I needed her, every day, every minute. Every second I was apart from her built a thirst in my soul that only she could quench. As I drank from her lips, she replenished me.

I tasted her skin with open-mouthed kisses and listened to her moan and sigh when I added soft bites to the mix. I shouldn't have started this yet. Every time I got near her—got my hands and mouth on her gorgeous body—I wanted more. I wanted us naked and moving together until I made her come. I loved watching her fall apart in my arms.

I wrenched my mouth away from her warm skin. "Dinner will get cold. We should eat," I said, but the words came out in a groan.

"I don't care," she said and reached out for me.

"Do you want to have kids?" We'd tiptoed around the subject before and I was pretty certain she did. But I asked her directly to distract her from jumping back into my lap. I also wanted to know. It fit in with my big plans.

She froze, then sat back down across from me on the blanket. Her eyes darted to mine, she smiled. "Yes. I would love to have a baby someday. Do you want more kids?"

"Yes. I already know you're a great mother."

Her eyes dropped to the blanket as a blush rose over her cheeks. "Thank you," she breathed. "Does this mean…?"

"I've thought about it. With you it will be perfect; it will be what it should be."

We ate our dinner and talked as the sun descended behind the mountains in the distance.

"It's getting dark. Should we get back?" she asked.

"No, I have pillows, sleeping bags, and a tent that fits over the truck bed in case it starts raining. We're camping out here tonight. That's the plan," I informed her with a wink. I tried to wink at her often; it always made her blush. I stood up and moved to the back of the truck. I pulled battery powered lanterns out of the back and turned them on.

She grabbed one and helped me distribute them around our area. "I like this plan." She grinned.

"Good. Because there's more to the plan." I grabbed her waist and pushed her gently to sit on the lowered tailgate.

"There is?"

"Yep. I love you. You've made my life better. You are sweetness and light. Softness and strength. You have filled every inch of my heart with your love and I want to spend the rest of my life filling yours too. Sabrina, we should get married. I'll move into the ranch with the girls if you want me to. They want this too. I've already talked to them and they love you, Sabrina. I have their blessing to ask you to be my wife, to be their mother."

She sat there and blinked at me.

I sank to a knee in front of her and reached into my pocket.

She nodded before I could even get the words out to ask her.

I grinned as tears filled her eyes and spilled down her cheeks.

I pulled out the small red velvet box. "Sabrina Louise Logan, will you marry me?" I asked.

She smiled. "Yes," she gasped. "Yes, I will marry you, Wyatt William Monroe."

I slipped the shiny round solitaire on her finger. It fit perfectly. Just like she fit into my life—perfectly, seamlessly, like she was always meant to be a part of it. "You're mine," I marveled. I kissed her hand where my ring sat in its gold band on her finger.

She held her hand out in front of her and gazed at it. The diamond sparkled in the glow of the fiery Tennessee sunset.

"I'm yours," she agreed. Her eyes shifted to mine and burned into them. "And you're mine. Forever, Wyatt. Me, you, the girls, and Harry. We're going to be a family."

"I'll never let you go, darlin'," I promised.

"Good, see that you don't." A giddy laugh escaped her, and I smiled.

I stood and lifted her from the tailgate into my arms. I stepped back and twirled with her into the pasture. "Dance with me," I said and put her down. I held out my hand, she took it.

"I will dance with you forever," she declared.

"I'm gonna marry you." I gazed into her smiling eyes then yanked her into my arms.

There was no music—we didn't need it. We danced together in the pasture with the moon high in the sky and the soft glow of the lantern lights to illuminate us. I thought back to the night of the Harvest Moon, the night of our botched first date. I remembered her, my Sabrina. Beautiful and sweet, tempting me from the grass with her outstretched arms and newfound siren's smile. The innocence in her eyes belied the depth of her heart. I knew back then I could fall in love with her and I was right. I loved her. I would love her until the day I died—even after. In this life and into whatever came next.

We spent the rest of the night in the truck's bed wrapped up in blankets, wrapped up in each other—whispering about our future and making love under the stars. Each time I sank inside of her it felt like coming home. Sabrina was my life, my heart—she was everything I'd ever wanted and never expected to find.

EPILOGUE

SABRINA

Spring

"You are about to become Mrs. Sabrina Logan-Monroe," I said to myself in the mirror.

I pushed my hair over my shoulders to fall down my back and adjusted my simple tulle veil. Mel had wanted me to wear a tiara, but...no. I was not the tiara type, and I was okay with that. I would garner enough—too much—attention just by walking down the aisle. I didn't need a big sparkly 'look at me' announcement sitting on top of my head. I finished applying my lipstick—MAC Dance with Me—and put it back in the tray. This lipstick would stay put no matter how much kissing I did tonight.

"Aunt Sabrina, you look like an angel." Ruby smiled and dabbed at her eyes as she approached me.

I turned from the mirror to hug her. Mak had ended up choosing my dress. It was white tulle with an off the shoulder ruched bodice and softly flowing skirt that fell to my feet. It was airy, ethereal, and apparently, angelic. "Thank you, Ruby."

"I bet Wyatt will start crying when he sees you. He seems like that type of guy. Crying grooms are hot. I told the videographer to make sure to get a good shot of it, don't worry."

I laughed. "Thanks. And look at you, Ruby. You're gorgeous." Ruby was my maid of honor. Ruby, Willa, and Mak were in matching pink satin dresses. Mel was in lavender tulle. Her basket was full of pink rose petals and she was ready to rock. I could hear her in the next room asking Willa if it was time to start the wedding.

"It's time to get down there." Willa popped her head in the door and announced. "Are you ready?"

Ruby and I headed to the door.

"Riri! It's time, it's time!" Mel shrieked when she saw me. "I've been practicing throwing the petals and picking them back up. I'm going to be so good at this!"

I smiled at her. "You'll be a perfect flower girl, Mel."

Mak came up behind her and discreetly slipped a handful of the petals back inside the basket dangling from her hand. Mak looked up at me with a bemused smile.

I grinned back and held my hands out to them. "I'm going to marry your father today but I'm extra lucky because I'm not just getting him. I'm getting his girls, too. My girls."

They took my hands, and I knelt to gather them in my arms. "I love you both."

"I love you too, Riri," Mak whispered.

"And I love you both, the most." Mel threw her arms around us.

"Weston's outside with the truck," Ruby said.

"This is really going to happen," Mak said with tears in her eyes.

"Oh, honey." I pulled her close and whispered in her ear. "It's happening. And it's forever. You never have to worry."

"Come on, Mak. Daddy is waiting for us," Mel said and held out her hand.

Mak took a deep breath and followed her sister.

"I'm happy for you, Sabrina." Willa took my hand.

Ruby took the other, and we headed downstairs.

"Ready to go, Sabrina?" Weston called from the cab of the truck.

"I'm ready." And I was ready—even though I had let my father plan the guest list. I didn't even look at it; it was better that way. I'd come far, but crowds still weren't my thing. But Green Valley was my home and my home was full of good folks. And if my wedding was filled to the brim with good folks then I couldn't see a thing wrong with it. I'd just have to wait and see what was waiting for me down at the pasture. One look, then I'd pretend they weren't there—I was good at that.

We piled into the back of Wyatt's truck and Weston drove us around the garage and down the gravel path to the place where everything began.

My father was waiting at the edge. I smiled at him, then looked beyond where he stood to see the simple wooden arch set against the beautiful backdrop of the rolling Tennessee mountains and the shimmering spring sunshine.

I also saw chair after chair after chair of people turning to look as the music started. My father must have invited the whole dang town.

I watched as Ruby, Willa, and the girls followed Weston down the aisle. Mel brought up the rear, flinging rose petals left and right. She was perfect. She turned to wave at me. I blew her a kiss.

Weston took a seat. And all my girls took their places at the side of the arch.

Wyatt and his brothers waited on the other side, with Harry, my son, on the end. I waved to him and he hollered, "Riri! You're getting married!"

I let out a giggle and caught the kiss he blew to me and stuck it to my cheek.

My father took my hand. "I'm proud of you, sweet pea. Not for getting married—anyone can do that. I'm proud of you for taking charge of your life. You've opened your heart—"

"And let people in?" I interrupted with a smile.

"No—well, yes—but no. You've let the love you kept locked up in your heart out, and it is beautiful to see."

I turned and hugged my dad. "Thank you," I whispered. I took a deep breath and smiled at him. My eyes tingled but I refused to let the tears fall.

I had spent ten minutes winging my eyeliner this morning and no matter how sweet my father was, I was not going to cry before he walked me down the aisle.

The music started—Pachelbel's "Canon in D." I figured keeping with tradition would make for less of a spectacle.

As I got closer and closer, I saw Wyatt scrub his hand under his eyes to wipe away his tears. I beamed at him and laughed softly when I saw all three of his brothers reach their hands out to pass him a handkerchief.

As I walked down the aisle and looked at the smiling faces, I remembered what my father had said just moments before.

My heart was overflowing. I had so much love to give. The fear that had held it back for so long was gone.

I couldn't wait to see what the future would bring.

ABOUT THE AUTHOR

Nora Everly is a life long reader, writer, and happily ever after junkie. She is a wife and stay-at-home mom to two tiny humans and one fat cat. She lives in Oregon with her family and her overactive imagination.

Newsletter: https://www.noraeverly.com/newsletter-1
Website: https://www.noraeverly.com/
Facebook: https://www.facebook.com/authornoraeverly
Goodreads: https://www.goodreads.com/author/show/19302304.Nora_Everly
Twitter: https://twitter.com/NoraEverly
Instagram: https://www.instagram.com/nora.everly/

Find Smartypants Romance online:
Website: www.smartypantsromance.com
Facebook: www.facebook.com/smartypantsromance/
Goodreads: www.goodreads.com/smartypantsromance
Twitter: @smartypantsrom
Instagram: @smartypantsromance

CPSIA information can be obtained
at www.ICGtesting.com
Printed in the USA
LVHW031623181219
640938LV00006B/822/P